"The *Excalibur*..."

Si Cwan went on: "... has a wider mission of not only altruism but also exploration, discovery ... things that I have little to no use for. The Danteri, on the other hand, are quite focused. They don't care about seeking out new life and new civilizations ... boldly going where no one has gone before. They care about power. So do I. In that sense, our goals are mutual and beneficial to one another. It is ..." He paused, figuring the best way to say it. "... it is a better fit ... than the one that currently exists. On the *Excalibur* I am, and will continue to be—what is the phrase you use ... ?"

"A square peg in a round hole," she suggested tonelessly.

"Yes! Yes, that is it. That is it exactly," he told her. "But on Danter, I will be a square peg in a square hole." He stood and spread wide his arms, his eyes glistening with anticipation. "Don't you see, Robin? The majesty of the Thallonian Empire need not be limited to a nostalgic, hollow re-creation of the past. It can, instead, be the future...."

STAR TREK
NEW FRONTIER®

BEING HUMAN

Peter David

Based upon STAR TREK®
created by Gene Roddenberry

POCKET BOOKS

New York   London   Toronto   Sydney   Singapore

For information regarding special discounts for bulk purchases, please contact Simon & Schuster Special Sales at 1-800-456-6798 or business@simonandschuster.com

This book is a work of fiction. Names, characters, places and incidents are products of the author's imagination or are used fictitiously. Any resemblance to actual events or locales or persons, living or dead, is entirely coincidental.

An *Original* Publication of POCKET BOOKS

POCKET BOOKS, a division of Simon & Schuster, Inc.
1230 Avenue of the Americas, New York, NY 10020

A VIACOM COMPANY

STAR TREK is a Registered Trademark of Paramount Pictures.

This book is published by Pocket Books, a division of Simon & Schuster, Inc., under exclusive license from Paramount Pictures.

ISBN: 0-671-04240-8

First Pocket Books printing November 2001

10 9 8 7 6 5 4 3 2 1

POCKET and colophon are registered trademarks of Simon & Schuster, Inc.

Printed in the U.S.A.

THEN . . .

THEY WERE FOUR WORDS, four innocuous words which—considered individually—were not especially alarming. But they had become personal nightmares for George, especially when uttered together and sequentially. When he saw Sheila approaching him that afternoon, he knew before she even opened her mouth to speak that they were going to come leaping, unwanted, from her lips.

He was sitting in his favorite chair in their rather unassuming living room, reading a text about his new favorite obsession: ancient mythologies. This particular text had been produced by a twentieth-century scholar, Joseph Campbell. For a man who had lived several hundred years ago, this Campbell fellow seemed to know what he was going on about, and George considered the text far more sweeping and interesting than, say, *Bullfinch's Mythology*.

As for George, he himself was about as unassuming as his living room was. There was nothing particularly memorable about him, and he prided himself on that. He had an ordinary face, not particularly interesting sandy hair, and a nondescript face, all of which suited him just fine. He would leave for his job at the research project in the mornings, spend the day not being noticed, and come home to where his wife paid attention to him on occasion while their offspring seemed to live in his own world anyway. To a degree, George was in absentia from his own life. That suited him just fine.

Sheila, his wife, had found this irritating, once upon a time. She had known she was marrying an unambitious man, and had labored under the belief that she could change him. She had quickly learned otherwise, and had spent much of her subsequent married years in denial over her own failure. "He has potential," she would say to her mother whenever the subject was brought up. As to whether that potential would ever be met or addressed, that was another question entirely and one that seemed something of a mystery. Every day, Sheila would look into the mirror in the morning, and every day would find yet another gray hair, or a crow's-foot or a wrinkle that she was certain had not been there the previous morning. She wasn't sure whether it was George who was causing them, or the simple passage of time. If it was the former, it angered her. If the latter, then she was watching a mute condemnation of the time that she was wasting as her life passed her by.

Not that she didn't have her own work, as an anthropologist teaching at Starfleet Academy right there in San Francisco. But she felt a growing frustration over her union with George, and found herself wondering every day if she wasn't investing time in a project that was never going to come to fruition. Sheila was, if nothing else, goal-oriented, and she felt as if she was losing sight as to what the goal for George was. She tended to wear her frustration like a shroud, and she knew that he must have sensed it. Furthermore, she knew that she wasn't doing their marriage any good by feeling that way, but how could she be less than honest with him? What good would that have done?

Nevertheless, she stayed with him because they had promised one another they would do so. Also, there was the matter of Sandy.

"Sandy" was not his given name. He had acquired it somewhere around the age of three, when his grandparents had commented that he seemed to spend the day in a dreamlike haze. He would stare off into space for long periods of time, fixating on blank spots on the wall. "That child," opined his grandmother, "lives his life as if he's in a dream." This prompted his grandfather to call him "Sandman," which eventually got shortened to "Sandy." The name stuck, if for no other reason than that he seemed to answer to it as readily as he did anything else.

Although his name changed, his behavior did not. He would always sit around, apparently oblivious of the world around him, his dark eyes seeming to look at everything and nothing at the same time. He would always bring his knees up to his chin, resting it there, giving his mother looks of vague disinterest when she would tell him to go outside. On occasion, apparently to satisfy her, he would do so . . . and then sit around outside. His father would watch in fascination as flies would alight on his nose.

"You need friends, Sandy!" said Sheila, despairing, convinced that her son was developing strange and frightening antisocial attitudes.

Somewhere around the age of five, he acquired a friend. That made things worse.

Sandy had reached the ripe old age of eight on this particular afternoon, when George discovered that he was about to have his peaceful reading ruined by his clearly agitated wife. It had rained the previous day, cooling off the San Francisco humidity, and George had been briefly considering the possibility of getting out for some air. When he saw the way Sheila was approaching him, with something clearly on her mind, he regretted that he hadn't departed while it was still possible to do so.

Then came the four words, the words he'd been dreading.

"Talk to your son," said Sheila, pointing upstairs. Red shag carpeting lined the stairs that led to the upstairs bedrooms, similar to the carpeting throughout the rest of the house. George hated it. It was like living on the surface of Mars, only fuzzier.

George sighed and put down his reader, folding his hands on his lap in what he hoped was an avuncular manner. "He's your son, too," George pointed out. This was self-evident. He was just stalling for time, hoping that Sheila would become so annoyed with him that she would go off and handle whatever the infraction was herself. If Sandy had misbehaved, George had no real desire to be the disciplinarian. He had too much desire to be liked. Besides, he didn't get worked up all that much. Things that Sandy did that annoyed the hell out of Sheila barely registered on George's personal radar.

"What's the problem?" George asked tentatively.

"He's doing it again," Sheila told him, sending an annoyed glance up the stairs.

"It?" He had the feeling he knew what "it" was, but he reasoned that if he delayed long enough, some sort of reprieve might present itself . . . such as, for instance, the sun going nova.

The sun, however, seemed disinclined to explode in the near future, and Sheila wasn't being put off. "It," she said with affirmation. "He's talking to her again."

George moaned softly and rubbed the bridge of his nose by pressing both his thumbs against it, looking as if he was worried that it would fall off unless he tended to it right then. "Are you sure?"

"Of course I'm sure," said Sheila, hands on her hips. Once upon a time, he'd admired the hell out of those hips. Now they were spreading. He didn't like to dwell upon what they'd look like in a few years. "I walked past his room and heard him chatting with her. On and on and on . . ." When George didn't seem properly exercised about it, she waved her hands about as if they were about to flop off her wrist and said, "He's eight years old, George! This is getting ridiculous!"

Crossing his legs delicately at the knees, George did his best to affect a reasonable, mannered tone with his wife. "As you say yourself, Sheila, he *is* eight. Imaginary friends aren't exactly out of line for—"

"They're out of line for someone as intelligent as

Sandy is," she said firmly. "You saw what his charts said."

Indeed he had. Sandy's aptitude scores had practically been off the scale. The most impressive thing had been that, after he'd taken the initial tests, the proctor had sadly informed them that he'd been watching the boy, and it seemed as if he was barely paying attention to any of the questions. He simply chose answers in what appeared to be an utterly haphazard manner. They had despaired upon hearing that . . . until the aptitude tests came back, showing that Sandy was bright enough and displayed enough potential to write his ticket . . . well, practically anywhere.

George had tried to parlay that score into the boy's mother easing up on him a bit. No go. Instead she'd wanted to step up the pressure on him to learn, feeling that he should be "maximized to his full potential." This was not an expression that George was especially fond of. In any event, Sandy hadn't seemed overly cooperative with the maximizing philosophy, and that resistance had only caused matters to deteriorate further.

"It doesn't matter how intelligent Sandy is," George told her, and when she tried to interrupt with shocked indignation, he continued right over her, "He's still only eight, for crying out loud. Let the boy be a boy, why can't we?"

"Talk. To him," she told him quite firmly, and George really didn't see any way around it. With a sigh that was as heavy as his heart, George hauled himself wistfully out of his favorite chair and walked with heavy footfall, *thump thump thump*, up the stairs. Normally the annoying shag carpet absorbed all noise, but George made a point of producing an extra racket, just so Sheila would be aware of how annoyed he was. She didn't seem to care especially, which naturally annoyed George all the more.

The door to Sandy's room was open, and George stood outside a moment, reminding himself that he was simply trying to act on behalf of the boy's own good. Imagination was fine as far as it went, but, well . . . enough was enough. (Or was that Sheila's voice in his head? George was beginning to wonder how much of the person he was was actually left in him, and how much was Sheila's personality having insinuated itself into his.)

He heard his son's voice from within. He sounded as if he was talking to someone. Well, no mystery there: He knew perfectly well with whom Sandy was conversing, just the same as he'd been for the last two years. Okay, there was something to be said for just how badly it was getting on Sheila's nerves, and he had to admit, there was a certain degree of embarrassment involved. If they had friends over, Sandy would invariably wander in, chatting with thin air and barely noticing the company standing around and staring at him. A number of them thought it was cute. But there were always those few who regarded him with suspicion or even pity, and that attitude would then be reflected in the looks they gave George and Sheila. George would force a smile and Sheila would get extremely uncomfortable, as if he wasn't being a good enough father somehow.

Perhaps enough was enough at that.

He cleared his throat to serve as warning to Sandy

that he was entering the room, and then he walked in. Sandy was seated cross-legged on the bed. The bed was neatly made, top smooth, corners folded, as per Sheila's insistence and long years of discipline. The rest of his room was likewise immaculate; Sheila would simply have it no other way. His stuffed animals sat neatly lined up on shelves, under assorted star maps that he had mounted on his wall, not being satisfied with the ones that he was able to call up on his computer screen. The carpet was that same annoying shag red. By the one window in his room, there was a telescope that he used to observe the stars for what seemed hours on end. It was the only other thing he tended to do other than look at nothing at all.

He was wearing a simple white crewneck pullover shirt, and blue shorts. His face, with a row of freckles arranged on his cheeks and his questioning eyes opened wide, was turned upward toward his father in what seemed passive curiosity. He said nothing, having halted his chat the moment he became aware of his father's presence.

George ruffled his son's hair. Sandy didn't budge as the strands settled back down onto his scalp. "How you doing, Sandy?" George asked.

Sandy tilted his head in a manner that looked vaguely like a shrug. The question didn't seem to interest him much.

Feeling as if he was uncomfortable in his own body, George sat on the edge of the bed. Sandy waited patiently, his hands resting, neatly folded, in his lap.

"We need to talk, Sandy," he said finally.

" 'Kay."

Unsure of how to start, George finally said, "When a boy reaches a certain age . . . there are some things that just, well . . . just aren't appropriate . . ."

"Is this about when I walked in on Mom in the shower? 'Cause she already yelled at me."

George stifled a laugh at that. "No. No, it's not about that at all."

"Good." Sandy seemed visibly relieved at that.

"No, it's . . ." He shifted on the bed, which seemed extremely small to him at that point. "It's about things that you do as a little boy that aren't, well . . . appropriate when you get older. You see what I'm saying?"

"Yes. You're saying the same thing you said before."

There was no hint of arrogance or snottiness in the way Sandy informed him of the fact that he was repeating himself. It was more in the nature of an "FYI." He just wanted his dad to know that he was not moving forward in the conversation. George had to admit that that much was true.

"Okay, well . . ." He slapped his thighs a couple of times and rocked slightly, as if preparing to launch himself off a high dive. "Well, here's the thing: It's about Missy."

Sandy turned his head and addressed the empty air to his immediate left. "You were right," he said, and then turned back to his father. "Missy said she thought it was going to be about her. I wasn't sure, 'cause she always thinks everything is about her. So it's kind of hard to tell."

"Well, that's Missy for you," George said, and then realized that acknowledging quirks in the imaginary friend's behavior was probably not the best way to proceed. "Look, Sandy, the thing is . . . here's the thing, it's . . . well, I don't think you should be talking to Missy anymore."

The child blinked once, very slowly. "Why not?" he asked.

"Because it's not . . . well . . . appropriate."

"Why not?"

"Well, there are certain things that are all right for small children, but not for bigger children. And you're getting to be a very big boy. You know that, right?"

Sandy nodded absently. "But . . . I like talking to Missy."

"I know that, but . . ."

"I'm not hurting anybody."

Letting out another, even heavier sigh and feeling much older than he had when he'd come into the room, George drew closer to his son and draped an arm commiseratingly around the boy's shoulders. "I know you're not hurting anybody, Sandy, but . . ."

"Missy says you're an idiot."

The words, coming out of the boy's mouth in so matter-of-fact a fashion, caught George completely off guard. "Wh-what . . . ?"

"Unh-hunh," Sandy said, his head bobbing up and down as if it were mounted on a spring. "She says you're an idiot, and a fool, and you don't understand anything."

"Now wait just one minute, young man," George said heatedly. He'd removed the arm from the boy's shoulder. Suddenly there was no sense of empathy for his son. Instead he was beginning to wonder whether Sheila hadn't been more correct than she'd known. Perhaps what they were seeing was, in fact, a hint of a deeper problem, and this imaginary friend business was only an outward manifestation of it. "You are not allowed to talk to me in that manner."

"I didn't," said Sandy. "Missy did."

"No, Missy did not!"

"Well, you can't hear her, Dad," Sandy said, sounding remarkably reasonable given the circumstances. "So how would you know?"

Now George was on his feet, bristling with full parental indignation. "Stop talking back to me, young man!"

Sandy had never looked more perplexed in his life. "So . . . so I can't talk to you or Missy? Can I talk to Mom still?" Suddenly he looked again to empty air and there was genuine worry on his face. "Missy, I can't say that to him!"

"What? What can't you say?"

"Nothing, Dad . . ."

"What can't you say?"

Sandy had slid off the bed, and he was backing up, never taking his eyes off his father. "I . . . I better not tell you . . . I mean, you got mad when Missy called you a . . . you know . . . and this is much worse . . ."

"You can't keep hiding behind your imaginary friend, Sandy." George felt as if he was being overwhelmed, even suffocated by the anger he was feeling. He suddenly felt as if he was much taller, the boy much shorter. "Talk to me."

Sandy's hands were moving in vague patterns in the air, as if he was trying to snag dust motes between his fingertips. "You said I shouldn't talk back . . . if . . ."

"Talk to me!"

His father had spoken with such abruptness and force that Sandy jumped slightly. He had kept backing up, and his back bumped up against a shelf of toys. He grabbed one, a rabbit, and held it in front of him, his small arms curled around it as if it afforded him protection. The words spilled out of him. "She . . . she said you were dumb, and didn't know anything, and that you were jealous of her. And that if you did anything, or tried to make her go away, then she would do bad things to you. Really bad things."

George was trying to keep his calm, but he felt it slipping away. "Now you're threatening me? Is that it, Sandy?"

"No, Dad—!"

In two quick paces, George was in front of his son, gripping Sandy by either shoulder. Although he wasn't hurting the child, he was nevertheless scaring the hell out of him. "Now you listen to me!" he bellowed. "It's enough! Do you hear me? Enough! *You're a big boy, and you're too old to play with imaginary friends! Do you understand?"*

"She's not imaginary!" wailed Sandy. "She's not! Don't make her angry, Daddy! Please! It'll be bad!"

George shook him again harder, as if the very notion of an invisible playmate could be sent tumbling right out of him if he was just agitated with sufficient force. *"There is no Missy!"* he shouted. *"There is no invisible friend! There is no—!"*

That was when the hair on the back of George's head began to stand on end. But it wasn't from fear or some sense of foreboding. Instead there was some kind of buildup of energy, like static electricity, except . . . worse.

His mind tried to justify a reason for it, and he thought that maybe he'd been rubbing his feet on the carpet too quickly, or something equally ludicrous. But the power was building up, stronger, more intense with each passing moment. Sandy was sobbing wildly, and he looked terrified as he kept crying out repeatedly, *"I warned you! I warned you, Daddy!"*

The power was coming from all over the room. George saw blue-white energy crackling along the toys, knocking them off the shelves, like plush-filled cannonballs. The threads of the shag carpet were standing straight up and down. Over on the desk, the computer station was trembling, first a little, and then a lot. The screen pitched backward off the desk, crashing to the floor. The racket prompted Sheila to shout from downstairs, *"What the hell is going on up there?!"*

"Stay away! Stay down there!" bellowed George. He had backed away from Sandy, and now he spun on his heel and bolted for the door. It slammed shut in his face. He'd been moving so fast that he crashed into it, rebounding and staggering from the impact.

"Missy! Stop it! Don't hurt him! He's my daddy!" Sandy begged, but his pleas did no good. The power buildup continued. George let out a scream of unbridled terror, and then energy blasts erupted all around him. He jumped to the right, to the left, barely staying out of the way . . . or was it that whatever-it-was was playing with him, toying with him? He ducked and a blast tore through the air just over his head. He hit the ground, smelled something burning, thought it was he himself and then realized it was the carpet. There were no flames, but it was smoldering, and the air was thick with the smell of ozone. Over the cacophony of unleashed power all around him, he heard Sandy's voice crying out, begging Missy to stop what she was doing. Toys were flying everywhere, as if being knocked aside by an invisible baseball bat.

The computer screen shattered, fragments scattering through the air like a grenade. George, lying flat on the floor, buried his head beneath his arms and cried out for it to stop, to stop already, just stop . . .

"Daddy!" screamed Sandy, and suddenly George snapped out of his paralysis. He was on his hands and knees, scrambling for the door again, cutting himself on broken shards of the computer and not caring. His knee crushed the stomach of a teddy bear, which let out a squeak of protest. This time, when he got to the door, it opened. He didn't question his luck, and when Sandy cried out for him again and again, he didn't so much as cast a glance back over his shoulder. He started for the door, and suddenly he was lifted into the air, propelled, as if a giant hand had picked him up and tossed him across the rest of the room, his weight meaning nothing.

George tumbled through the door, hit the outside corridor still rolling, and came incredibly close to rolling headfirst down the stairs. He snagged the banister at the last moment, preventing a painful and even a possibly fatal fall, had he fallen in such a way that his neck had been snapped. As it was, he managed to right himself at the last moment, but just barely.

He sucked air into his lungs. They were burning, the smell of ozone still seared into them, and then as if abruptly realizing where he was—galvanized by the chaos being unleashed in his son's room—he scrambled to his feet and tore down the stairs.

A terrified Sheila was waiting at the bottom of the stairs for him, crying out to him, demanding to know what was going on. He didn't bother to tell her. He couldn't find the words, couldn't push past the terror that was pounding through him. Instead he sprinted for the front door, and then he was out, out into the open air. There were a few puddles left over from the previous night's rain, and he splashed through them, running as fast as he could.

It was only later, when he had a chance to catch his breath and assess the panic that had seized him, that he would realize that he had left his son behind. That a braver man, a better father, would have picked the child up bodily and carried him out of the room, away from that . . . that thing. That creature that apparently inhabited the room and had tried its level best to kill him. But even as the thought occurred to him, he dismissed it. Whatever the thing was that had unleashed its wrath upon him, there was no reason to assume that it was going to stay localized in Sandy's room. He might very well have picked up the child and carted him out, only to have the whatever-it-was follow along right behind him.

His fleeing was an act of cowardice. He knew that beyond question as well. He should have remained, should have done something . . . but he had given in to utter terror, and he could think of absolutely no way that he could face his wife and child again. Of course, it might have been a harder decision for him to make had he actually *wanted* to face them again.

But he didn't.

It might very well have been that Missy had done him a favor. She had, in the final analysis, given him a concrete reason to do what he'd always considered doing, but never had the nerve to accomplish. He felt free and alive, and he would have Missy to thank, were he actually capable of dwelling upon what had happened without breaking out into cold sweats.

He hopped a freighter off Earth that night. It never occurred to Sheila, until too late, that he might pursue that route, because he'd always had a phobia about space travel. He'd never trusted that the relatively fragile hull of a ship could withstand the rigors of space travel, and had been more than content in his being utterly and blissfully Earthbound. By the time she did try to track him, he had effectively disappeared, leaving Sheila with Sandy . . . and her.

Sheila, not knowing that she was seeing her husband for the last time as he dashed out the door, looked up the stairs to the source of the commotion. Her maternal instinct kicked in and she called "Sandy?" with considerable worry.

There was no answer. The only response she got was the sounds of crackling energy subsiding. Slowly, apprehensively, she made her way up the stairs. She had only the vaguest of notions as to what had just happened, but she knew one thing beyond question: She was terrified of what might happen next. She got to the top of the stairs, peered in through the door.

Sandy was seated in the middle of the floor of his room. Toys were scattered all over, and he was bleeding from some minor cuts on his forehead, caused by shards from the computer that had exploded. His hair was standing on end as if he'd been hit with a lightning bolt, and his eyebrows were now a lighter shade of red than they'd been before. There was a dazed look in his eyes, and as was his custom, his knees were drawn to his chin. He was rocking himself gently, and it took him some moments to focus on his mother calling to him. When he did, he seemed to be staring at her from another quadrant of space, as if he was looking right through her even as he focused on her.

"Missy shouldn't have done that," said Sandy. "She shouldn't have done that. And now everybody's going to be mad at me."

Sheila stood there, transfixed, her body trembling as if someone had run a spear through her chest. She licked her dried lips, tried to say something. Nothing emerged. Sandy looked up at her, seeming to notice her for the first time, and asked, "Are you mad at me, Mommy?"

She tried to respond. Nothing came out.

With a hint of admonition, he said, "Missy wants to know."

"No," Sheila said instantly. She gripped the doorframe, steadying herself. "No. I'm not mad. At you. At all. Not at all."

Sandy let out a breath of relief. "That's good. I love you, Mommy. And Missy loves you."

"I love you both, too," said Sheila, which was what she had to say. Everything else she needed to say could wait for later. For when Sandy was grown . . . and Missy was gone . . .

. . . if she ever would be, that was.

And as she stared into her son's pleasant, soulful face, she couldn't help but feel that, more than ever, she had looked upon the face of her future.

It terrified her.

NOW . . .

EXCALIBUR

i.

BURGOYNE 172, seated in hir command chair on the bridge, watched the *Trident* with fascination as the other starship floated within range of the *Excalibur.* Even though s/he had nothing to do with that ship, Burgoyne still felt a measure of pride whenever s/he was nearby another starship. S/he decided that perhaps it was because it was the way hir own people, the Hermats, had made hir feel unaccepted, even excluded, from the rest of hir race simply because s/he wasn't as stodgy as the rest of—

"Is he here?"

The unexpected interruption jolted Burgoyne from hir reverie, and s/he turned to see that hir mate—in life if not in any sort of formalized ceremony—Dr. Selar, was standing just behind hir. Selar's face was as impassive as always, and yet Burgoyne couldn't help but feel that there was a slightly unusual sense of urgency to hir tone. Burgoyne couldn't help but marvel over the fact that it seemed as if Selar had literally materialized on the bridge. S/he hadn't even noticed the hiss of the turbolift doors. Perhaps Selar had come up the emergency access ladder. But . . . why would she take the time to do that?

"He? You mean the captain?" asked Burgoyne. "He's in conference with Captain Shelby at the mo—"

"No. Not the captain. Him."

"Him?"

"Him," said Selar with greater urgency. Her gaze was darting around at the others on the bridge, who were starting to turn and look at her with open curiosity.

"Him *whom?* Whom is—?" And then, suddenly, Burgoyne got it. "Oh! *Him!"*

"Yes," said Selar, with obvious relief, and a touch of equally obvious annoyance that it had taken so long for Burgoyne to comprehend what was being discussed . . . or not being discussed, as the case may be. "Have you seen him? I thought he might have come up here."

"No. No, he hasn't. How long has he—?"

"Dreyfuss is not certain." Dreyfuss was the individual who ran the children's recreation center on the *Excalibur.*

Burgoyne shook hir head, drumming hir fingers for a moment on the armrest of hir chair. "Do you want me to—?"

"No," Selar said immediately.

"But I didn't tell you what I was going to do."

"Since I do not wish you to do anything about it, the response of 'no' is relatively all-purpose," Selar replied. "I will attend to it."

"If you're sure . . ."

"I," said Selar, "am always sure." With that, she turned on her heel, squared her shoulders, and strode toward the turbolift. At the last moment, however, she seemed to think better of it and instead clambered down the auxiliary exit ladder. That was, Burgoyne realized, indeed the way she'd come up to the bridge in the first place. Furthermore, he understood why: It was because the object of her search enjoyed climbing, and the auxiliary ladders of the *Excalibur* provided a much more likely arena in which to find him than the turbolift.

She'd said she wanted to handle it. Nevertheless, Burgoyne certainly had a stake in the matter as well, and s/he decided that s/he wasn't going to allow hirself to be dismissed from consideration in such an offhand fashion. After a moment's thought more, s/he said, "Mr. Kebron."

Zak Kebron, the immense, rock-hard Brikar who was the ship's chief of security, rose from his position at tactical. He moved toward Burgoyne; it never seemed as if Kebron was walking so much as that he was a sentient avalanche, moving with one singular purpose. When Zak Kebron was going at high speed, there was no place one wanted to be less than directly in his path. He stopped a couple of feet away from Burgoyne and waited.

"Lieutenant," said Burgoyne, and waggled one finger to indicate that Kebron should lean over so s/he could speak in a softer, more confidential tone. Kebron, typically, remained standing exactly where he was, without so much as the slightest bend at the waist. He was going to do nothing to make this easier on Burgoyne. Burgoyne sighed in annoyance. *Very well. Be that way,* s/he thought. "Lieutenant," Burgoyne started again, "we . . . which is to say, I . . . have a slight problem."

Kebron said nothing. He simply stood there, waiting, displaying the scintillating emotional range of a statue.

"The problem," said Burgoyne, "is with . . . *him.*"

"Your son."

Burgoyne blinked in surprise. "How did you know?"

Kebron might have shrugged, although if he did, he did so inwardly. "Who else?"

There were many answers that Burgoyne could have given to that, but realized that there probably wouldn't be much point to it. Instead s/he rose from hir chair so that s/he was facing Kebron, although s/he was still at least a head shorter. "It appears he's out and about on the ship. His mother's looking for him. Could you ask your security people to keep an eye out for him? Track him down, perhaps?"

"It's not a security matter."

"All right, but . . . if you did it . . . you'd be doing me a personal favor."

"Why do that?"

Burgoyne felt a faint pounding in the back of hir head, and couldn't help but wonder if this was how Elizabeth Shelby had felt from time to time, back when she held the position of first officer. "You realize that I could, of course, order you to do it."

"Yes."

Kebron waited, and finally Burgoyne threw hir arms up in aggravation. "Forget it. I'll attend to it myself. Don't worry about a—"

"My people are already on it."

Burgoyne stared at Kebron uncomprehendingly. "Wh-what?"

Gesturing slightly with his shoulder in the direction that Selar had gone—since indicating things with a nod of his head was not really possible for him—Kebron said, "I overheard Selar. By the time she'd left, I'd alerted security."

"Oh. Well . . . thank you."

Kebron grunted and turned to head back to his post. Then Burgoyne said, with a little irritation, "You could have simply said so immediately, you know."

"Yes."

That was all he said in reply. Just "yes." Then he returned to his station, leaving Burgoyne to sink back into hir chair and have, yet again, more sympathy for Elizabeth Shelby than s/he'd ever thought possible.

ii.

"I'm not happy about this."

Shelby had been lying in bed next to Calhoun, idly running her fingers across his bare chest. The lighting in his cabin was quite dim, and she was curled up next to him, basking in the afterglow of their activities. There was still a film of sweat on her, and she wondered—not for the first time—how it was that he was able to keep so cool and dry at such times. Perhaps, she reasoned, it had something to do with his Xenexian physiology. As for Shelby, her strawberry blond hair was hanging wet and sweaty around her face as she relaxed against him.

She twisted her body against his, bringing her bare left leg up and against his left thigh. "If you're trying to make me feel inadequate as a wife and lover, Calhoun, that's certainly just the right thing to say to me."

His deep-set purple eyes looked at her blankly for a moment. Clearly he wasn't connecting what he'd just said with the situation they were in. Then he laughed softly, causing the arm she had draped across his chest to rise and fall with the motion. "This isn't the 'this' I was referring to. This 'this' was fine."

"Just fine?"

"Better than fine. Great. Fantastic."

"Spectacular?"

He gave it a moment's thought. "I think that'd be pushing it."

With a gasp of mock annoyance, she slapped his belly with sufficient force that it got him to sit up. In retaliation, he yanked at the covers. She tried to pull back, but he was too strong for her, and a moment later he was completely cocooned in the sheets, leaving Shelby lying completely uncovered on the bed.

"Okay, be that way," she said archly. She rolled off the bed, padded across the room, and threw on Calhoun's bathrobe. She was positively swimming in it even as she belted it and folded her arms—hands invisible inside the sleeves.

"Seriously, Eppy," he said. "It's this assignment. You going to Danter . . ."

She strode toward him and sat on the edge of the bed. She pulled the sheet up a bit so that his feet were exposed, and started massaging his soles. This prompted

Calhoun to let out a contented noise, one that Shelby was reasonably certain she was the only living being who'd ever heard. "I guess the honeymoon's officially over, Mac, if all we can muster for postcoital pillow talk is a discussion of various assignments."

"This is not . . . mmmm . . ." Calhoun made a contented noise, and then with determination pulled his feet away from her ministrations. Curling them underneath the blanket, he propped his head up on one hand and looked at her, clearly deciding that he had to keep matters all-business. "This is not just one of our 'various assignments,' Eppy. I know the Danteri. You don't."

"You know them, Mac, because they enslaved your homeworld of Xenex and you fought to drive them off. And you did so. But that was a long time ago."

"Meaning I should simply let it go, is that it?" Now he was sitting upright in the bed, and any hint of the lover he'd been merely moments before was gone. "I would let it go, Eppy, if I could comprehend Starfleet's thinking on this. But let's review." He ticked off each item on his fingers. "The Danteri inform Starfleet that they want a starship to be dispatched to Danter. They state that they want that ship to carry Si Cwan, since he's the one to whom they actually want to talk. They don't give a reason for either of these requests. Instead they state that it's a matter of 'utmost urgency' without giving any more detail than that. The entire thing smells of a trap . . . and Starfleet decides to send your ship instead of mine."

"Is your male ego wounded by the choice, Mac?" she asked, only half-teasingly.

"It has nothing to do with male ego, Eppy. It has to do with who's the more qualified."

"That may very well be the problem, Mac. It may be that Starfleet feels a fresh perspective on the situation is in order. There's too much bad blood between you and the Danteri. They might well feel that you wouldn't be able to handle the situation in a dispassionate manner." She leaned forward, bringing her face that much closer to his. "Admit it: Isn't there just a chance that they're right?"

He gazed at her for a long moment.

"No," he said.

She growled and flopped facedown on the bed. Her face smothered in the sheet, she said, "You are the single most aggravating man I have ever met."

"Of course. That's why you married me."

"Don't be ridiculous. I married you for the sex."

He raised an eyebrow. "But we only see each other from time to time. We don't get to have sex all that often."

"Right. I married you for the infrequency of it, so I wouldn't have to endure it all that often."

Calhoun let out a moan and threw himself back onto the bed. "Command has made you bitter and cynical, do you know that, Captain?"

"I learned from the master." She curled herself around so that she was next to him again, and she kissed him on the cheek. Then, her teasing voice aside, she said, "Mac, I know you don't approve. But we don't take those orders that we only approve of. The fact is that our two ships have their own respective areas of the sector for which we're responsible, and Danter is in my section."

"It's borderline. It could be either, depending upon orbit."

"Well, right now, it's mine. What, are you saying that you think I can't handle it?"

"Of course not, Eppy," he said wistfully. "I know you can handle it. There's nothing out there I can handle that you can't. But you shouldn't *have* to handle it. It's the Danteri. They're not to be trusted."

"And I know what their track record is like, Mac. I know what to expect. And Si Cwan will know as well. Besides, you should be grateful."

He cocked an eyebrow. "How do you figure that?"

"Well, if we hadn't had to have this unscheduled rendezvous between our ships, in order to transfer Si Cwan from one vessel to the other, then you and I couldn't have had this little rendezvous as well."

"Gee, Eppy, you're absolutely right. I'll be sure to send the Danteri a nice fruit basket as a token of appreciation."

Suddenly the door chime sounded. Calhoun and Shelby exchanged puzzled looks. "Were you expecting anyone?" she asked.

"I told Burgoyne we were going to be in conference."

"Oh, right," said Shelby with a snort. "I'm sure that fooled hir completely. Because of course, there was a new directive that conferences should be held in the captain's private quarters rather than in the conference lounge."

"What, you didn't get that memo? I know I did." Even as he spoke jokingly, Calhoun was already out of bed. Since Shelby was wearing his bathrobe and seemed disinclined to give it up, Calhoun pulled on his uniform trousers even as he called out, "Who's there?"

"Ensign Janos, sir."

Once again a look of befuddlement passed between the two captains. "Were you expecting him?" asked Calhoun.

"Yes, I told him to show up about this time, because I figured I'd be through with you and ready for an escort home."

"Planning ahead. Good thinking," Calhoun said approvingly and—ignoring Shelby as she stuck her tongue out at him—said, "Enter."

The door slid open and Janos walked in with the usual rolling gait that the white-furred, anthropoid security officer utilized. He looked from the barefoot and barechested Calhoun to the robed Shelby, who managed to expose her hand from the oversized sleeve and manage a little wave. He looked back to Calhoun. "I'm sorry, sir, I thought you were in conference."

"It was an informal conference," said Calhoun. "What can I do for you?"

Janos was busy staring at Shelby, who had by that point sat in a chair in a far corner of the room, neatly arranging the bathrobe around her knees. He forced his attention back to the matter at hand. "Yes, uhm . . . right. I was looking for Xyon. Not your late son," he added quickly when he saw Calhoun's momentarily puzzled expression. "His namesake."

"Oh. Right. Selar and Burgoyne's offspring. But . . . he's not here."

Janos's nose wrinkled slightly and he sniffed the air. "Yes. He is."

"Janos, I really have to—"

The door chimed.

"I don't believe this," muttered Shelby.

"Come in," Calhoun called.

The door hissed open and Si Cwan's large frame filled the doorway. He paused, his eyes adjusting to the light. Since he remained in the doorway, the sliding door remained open. "Yes, Captain, I . . . oh," he said. "Is . . . this a bad time?"

"No, not at all," Shelby chimed in before Calhoun could get a word out. "We were actually planning to have a party. You saved us having to send out invitations."

"If you'd wanted to speak to me, Ambassador, you could have just paged me on my com unit, which," and he closed his eyes in pain, "I ordered the computer to shut down so I wouldn't be disturbed. All right, Cwan, go ahead, what is it?"

"Yes, well," and he cleared his throat loudly, "I had wanted to inform you that I was ready to head over to the *Trident,* and I wanted to ask whether you had arranged for—"

"For Robin Lefler to go with you? Yes, that's been attended to," said Calhoun.

"Excellent. She's proven invaluable as my aide, and I appreciate your loaning her to . . . Captain, perhaps this is not a good time."

"Why do you say that?"

"Because Ensign Janos is crawling around on your floor."

Which happened to be the case. Janos, his nostrils sniffing the ground, was on his hands and knees, looking carefully around the quarters like an oversized bloodhound. Captain Shelby, her feet tucked up under her so they'd be out of Janos's way, had her eyes closed as if she was imagining herself being somewhere else altogether.

"Ah" was all Calhoun could think of to say.

Janos tapped his com badge, his face near the underside of Calhoun's bed. "Janos to Kebron. Please inform the first officer that I've found hir son."

That brought Shelby back to full attention, as she sat straight up and stopped thumping her head. "You've *what?* Where?"

"Si Cwan!" came a female voice from down the hall. "Is the captain in there? I need to talk to him!"

"Oh, my lord," said Shelby. Calhoun was just shaking his head incredulously.

Robin Lefler appeared at the door, said "Captain!," and immediately spun on her heel, putting her back to the room, covering her face. "God, oh God, I'm so sorry, I'll come back later . . ."

"What is it, Lieutenant?" sighed Calhoun.

"No, really, I think I should come back—"

"Out with it, Lieutenant. I doubt I'll be in the mood later."

"I doubt I'll be in the mood ever again," Shelby muttered, referring to something else entirely.

Lefler's hands moved as if she were priming herself to get the words out, and finally she found them. "You're having my *mother* take over my station at ops while I'm on the *Trident?*" she asked finally.

"Yes, that's right."

"Her mother?" said a puzzled Si Cwan. "Morgan Primus? That seems an odd choice."

"And the moment you join Starfleet, Ambassador, and this becomes a democracy, then your opinion will hold some weight."

"Can we go back a moment," inquired Shelby, pointing at Janos, "to where he said that Burgoyne and Selar's son was in here . . . ? I never quite got an answer to—"

"Oh, he's—" Janos began.

But Lefler cut him off, her attention focused on Calhoun. "Why my mother, Captain?"

"She took a Starfleet equivalency test, Lieutenant, at her own request. She said she wanted to provide help wherever she could around the ship. She tested off the charts. Plus the *Excalibur* has some systems that were cobbled in from older vessels. She was assembled when there was still a parts shortage after our last major tussle with the Borg. Her knowledge of some more antiquated aspects of the ship is extremely impressive. Not only that, but she has been working closely with Burgoyne to develop some extremely novel adjustments to the battle bridge which she herself conceived. She's earned this opportunity, Lieutenant." By this point Calhoun had gone to his closet and pulled on his uniform shirt. Shelby hadn't moved from where she was. She seemed glued to the seat. "It was my call to make. If you have trouble living with it, then as luck would have it, you won't be here to have to worry about it."

"Yes, but—"

Suddenly Dr. Selar was there, pushing past the totally discomfited Lefler. "Where is he?" she demanded.

"He's under there," said Janos, pointing to the bed.

Shelby's eyes widened. "You mean you were serious?" She jerked forward to the edge of the seat. "Oh no . . . no, you can't be seri—"

"Xyon!" called Selar sharply, her arms folded, tapping her foot in as close to annoyance as a Vulcan would allow to be shown. "Come out here this instant."

There was a silence then, and some shuffling from underneath the bed, and what sounded like a long, drawn-out yawn. Then a small child, about the size of an Earth two-year-old but considerably younger chronologically, with pointed ears and quizzical expression, crawled out from beneath. But his face had definitely taken on the distinctive angularity of his father . . . or second mother, thought Calhoun, or whatever it was that one would term Burgoyne to be.

As Calhoun stood there, staring in astonishment, Shelby looked as if she wanted to curl up into a ball and die. Janos was all business, helping to dust the child off, and Si Cwan was doing everything he could not to snicker.

"Thank you, Ensign," said Selar primly as she reached down and hauled the runaway to his feet. He looked around in quiet contemplation of his surroundings, clearly uncertain as to why everyone was looking at him the way they were. Selar noticed Shelby's barely contained consternation, and said, "Count your blessings, Captain. At least he hasn't learned to talk yet."

Selar pulled him out of the captain's quarters quickly. Everyone else remained rooted to his or her spots, until Calhoun finally said, "I think we're done here."

With mumbled responses of "Yes," "Definitely," and

"I think so," everyone else cleared out. The door shut behind them, and Calhoun turned to Shelby. There was a touch of wry amusement in his eyes, but he said nothing. Shelby was sitting there, almost bent in half on the chair, her head tucked down, her arms up and covering it so that only a few tufts of her hair were visible.

"I think I'm ready to return to my ship," she said finally.

"All right," said Calhoun, maintaining an even tone. "I'll arrange for the transporter . . ."

"Oh, that won't be necessary."

"It won't?"

"No," she said, and peered up at him. "Just load me into a torpedo tube and shoot me back to the *Trident*."

Slowly he walked across the room and knelt down to bring himself to eye level. "You know . . . Eppy . . . someday—"

"So help me, Calhoun, if you say someday we'll look back on this and laugh, I will kill you where you stand."

He opened his mouth, closed it again, and then said, "Look at the bright side."

"There's a bright side?"

"Sure," he said cheerily. "Just think: If we served aboard the same ship, we'd probably be subjected to this sort of humiliation all the time."

iii.

The Ten Forward—or "Team Room," as many on the ship preferred to call it, carrying over a popular term applied to a lounge in the previous *Excalibur*—was unusually quiet that evening. That was precisely the way that Zak Kebron liked it. Then again, it was fairly widely known that Kebron liked it quiet, and as a result, the noise ratio tended to drop precipitously whenever he set his massive feet into the crew lounge.

Kebron was staring into his drink, looking with bland interest at his reflection. He frowned slightly then, noticing something around his eyes that hadn't been there before. He brought one of his thick fingers to the corner and pulled, ever so slightly.

A small piece of his skin, wafer thin, came away.

He looked at it with unabashed curiosity . . . not that anyone would have been able to discern that just by looking at him. He placed it carefully on the tabletop, then reached up again and found that another small piece of his hide came away with only the slightest of tugs. This piece he tapped on the table. It made a satisfyingly loud clicking sound, still nicely retaining its durability and strength. Nevertheless, the fact that pieces were coming off him was not something that overly thrilled him.

He held up his glass to eye level and tried to make out exactly where the pieces had peeled from. He thought it might be his imagination, but he could swear that the skin was a lighter color in the places where his nearly impenetrable hide had fallen away.

Kebron was no stranger to Brikar physiology. He knew precisely the reason that his skin might be peeling. And if that was the case, then it wasn't going to stop with this, oh no. It would start slow, but there would be more and more, an almost embarrassing amount. There would be questions asked of him throughout the ship, questions that he was not remotely prepared to answer, or interested in answering. But they would come just the same, and the contemplation alone was sufficient to make him very, very uncomfortable.

A shadow was cast over the table. "You all right, Zak?"

He recognized the voice instantly. He half rose, and bowed slightly at the waist since, as always, nodding was problematic. "Fine."

"Oh, good. Good," said Mark McHenry. As always, the ship's reddish-haired conn officer had a ready smile and an air of being perpetually distracted that he wore as comfortably as an old pair of shoes.

Kebron rose to get up, and then McHenry's hand was on his shoulder. "Stay for drinks?" suggested McHenry in a tone of voice that indicated he was not simply suggesting.

McHenry was no match when it came to strength, of course. But he was perfectly capable of pushing with a slight bit of force on Zak's shoulder, making it quite clear that he far preferred Kebron to stay where he was. If Kebron had chosen to ignore the hint, to shove McHenry out of the way, he could very likely have done so. Instead, Kebron chose to simply ease himself back into his seat. No reason he shouldn't, really. No reason he couldn't. The only thing he would have needed to be worried over was McHenry himself, and Kebron would sooner be enveloped by an avalanche and pounded into a pebble than admit that the slight conn officer provided him with so much as a moment's concern.

When Kebron was reseated, McHenry dropped into the chair opposite him. He had that familiar, distracted smile on his face. "Lovely day we're having," he said cheerily as he signaled the waitress. Kebron said nothing, not bothering to point out that there was no weather in space, and even less weather inside of a starship. It wasn't as if a summertime squall was going to break out on decks three to seven. Kebron just stared at him.

"So," McHenry continued, once a drink had been brought over to him, "the *Trident* is on its way to Danter, with Si Cwan, his sister Kalinda, and Robin Lefler aboard. Interesting the way that worked out, didn't it." When Kebron said nothing, McHenry continued, "And we've set our course to check out some sort of odd energy emissions, being generated in empty space about three days' travel from here. So I suppose there's plenty of interesting things to go around, here in beautiful Sector 221-G, right?"

Kebron tossed back his drink and placed it on the table with a delicacy that seemed at odds with his massive hands. "Are we done?" he inquired.

"Zak, Zak, Zak," sighed McHenry, shaking his head so tragically that one would have thought he was at a funeral. "You've seemed so distant lately. I'm a bit hurt by it, I have to tell you. We've known each other since our Academy days."

"Have we?"

It must have seemed an odd question to McHenry . . . or perhaps, Kebron reasoned, it didn't seem so odd at that, and McHenry knew exactly why Kebron was posing it. That didn't stop McHenry's lopsided grin from becoming even wider. "What are you saying there, Zak?

Are you suggesting that we haven't known each other? That you don't know me? You know me, Zak."

"Do I?" He kept his answers short, vague, and minimal. It would have been sufficient to drive an ordinary person mad with annoyance.

Mark McHenry, however, was no ordinary person. That much was becoming quite evident to Kebron. It was also obvious to Kebron that much of McHenry's customary dreamy attitude had dissipated. Instead of speaking with a distracted, barely-there air, McHenry seemed totally focused on Kebron. That alone was enough to convince Kebron that something was dreadfully, dreadfully wrong.

"Well," McHenry said after a time, "it appears that you believe you don't know me. That explains something, though."

"Does it?"

"Heh," McHenry laughed softly. "You're certainly not one for showing his hand, are you, Zak? And yes, it does explain something, Zak." Then, very slowly, McHenry's smile evaporated. "It explains the activities you've been engaged in lately, all of them with the single purpose of trying to find out more about me. You've logged one hell of a lot of computer time lately, Zak. Much more so than usual. Now, one might have thought you'd been engaging in something truly worthwhile, such as trying to find cures for diseases, or researching our new vessel's capabilities, or even trying to determine who, unh, who wrote the Book of Love. But apparently, none of these uniquely human—which you are not, of course—lines of inquiry had been of the slightest interest to you. Instead you've been spending an inordi-

nate amount of time and energy investigating . . .
well . . . the only person at this table who's a human
being."

"Are you?"

The question hung there, unanswered, as McHenry's
eyes narrowed. Then, with a smile that was not reflected
in the rest of his face, McHenry said very quietly, "Are
you questioning my humanity now?"

"I am questioning," said Kebron, "how you knew I'd
been researching you."

"It wasn't hard to figure out, Zak. You've been keeping your distance from me lately. Looking at me oddly. I
began to wonder. So I ran some diagnostic checks
through engineering, investigating whether or not my
files had been subject to scrutiny lately. Computer always leaves a record of such things. Always. Imagine
my surprise when I discovered they had been, and imagine my further surprise when I learned that it was being
done by my old friend Zak Kebron."

"What do you want?" asked Kebron in that same,
calm monotone he always affected.

McHenry signaled for a second drink to be brought
over. It arrived promptly, replacing the empty glass that
had been in front of him moments before. "I want answers, Zak."

"As do I."

"You know what I mean."

"As do you." Kebron leaned forward, elbows fully on
the table, causing it to tilt. McHenry grabbed at his
glass, just managing to prevent it from tumbling off the
edge of the table. In a low, gravelly, rumbling tone, he

said, "You daunted Q. No mortal does that. He intended to transform you into some other life-form, but was unable. Impossible. Are you of his continuum?"

"I don't think so," said McHenry, apparently trying to sound reasonable about it.

"Then what are you?"

"Lieutenant first class McHenry, Mark, serial number 348—"

Kebron started to get up from the table. This time McHenry didn't try to stop him. Instead he was on his feet as well, circling the table quickly so that he was standing directly between Kebron and the exit. This, mused Kebron, was a potentially dangerous place for McHenry to be, should Kebron choose to leave. "Look, what am I supposed to say?" asked McHenry plaintively, trying to sound reasonable. "You ask me things like 'what are you'? You know who, what I am. I'm just a human . . ."

"A human so attuned to the galactic axis that he can determine our location instantly. A human so 'merged' with the ship that he can sense it when the vessel goes off course by so much as a meter. That, McHenry, is not just any human."

"Well, I never said I was just any human," McHenry said, obviously trying to sound modest.

But Kebron was shaking his head, via swiveling his torso at the waist. "Your spatial abilities . . . they are supernormal. Because of the many oddities of your nature, these skills are lumped in with them and given no thought. But only I have seen a Q prove powerless against you."

"Well, then," McHenry said slowly, "if I'm all that—supernormal, and more than human, and all those other things—then I guess you should be relieved I'm on your side."

"Are you?" rumbled Kebron.

Mark McHenry actually looked taken aback by the comment. "My God, Zak . . . with everything we've been through . . . you'd ask that now? Now?"

Kebron didn't flinch. "You are an unknown. Unknowns present security risks."

"And have you reported this potential threat I pose to the captain?" McHenry asked him.

"Not yet."

"You're waiting until you find some sort of definitive answer about me."

"Yes." He paused. "Are you volunteering?"

McHenry took a step back from him, his shoulders sagging. He seemed both tired and rather sad. "Zak . . . I cannot believe we're having this conversation. I'm human. My Starfleet medical records will attest to that."

"I know."

McHenry flinched slightly at that comment, since it reminded him of just how much research Kebron had been doing about him. "Except for my father and mother, my family's been in Starfleet for well over a century. I'm part of a family tradition of serving proudly. No one's ever questioned my loyalty . . ."

"Nor do I."

"That's a relief.

"I question you yourself."

Shaking his head, his eyes closed in what looked like pain, McHenry said, "Do what you want, Zak. Believe what you want. I know you have nothing to fear from me . . ."

"I know that."

"You do?"

"Yes," Kebron said, studying McHenry's face, as if he was capable of peeling the skin away and leaving the grinning skull. "No fear. You see . . . if it develops that you present a risk . . . I will simply squash you. Like a bug. No offense."

"None taken," McHenry said hollowly.

And Kebron, feeling that everything that needed to be said had in fact been said, walked around McHenry and out the door. He strode down the corridor, and was abruptly interrupted by the sound of running feet. He turned to see McHenry standing there, his skin reddening, looking angrier than he'd ever seen him. McHenry stabbed a finger at him, thumping it against the Brikar's chest.

"I changed my mind," McHenry told him with as much force as he apparently could muster. "I . . ." He tapped Kebron's chest for emphasis. ". . . am going . . . to take it . . . personally."

Kebron stared down at him. "You do that," he said.

Then he headed off down the hallway, with McHenry's shouts of "I *will* do that!" ringing in the air behind him.

TRIDENT

i.

LIEUTENANT COMMANDER GLEAU stared at his captain as if she'd grown a second head. Shelby did not lower her eyes or look away, but literally had to keep reminding herself that there was no reason for her to do so. She sat behind her desk, her fingers interlaced, her back straight, and her full attention on Gleau. *God, he is beautiful* was what she couldn't help but think, and then she mentally withdrew from that thought and forced herself back to the issue at hand.

The Selelvian seemed to glow with such splendor, both inner and outer, that it was everything Shelby could do not to ask him to ratchet it down a few notches. She wondered if he was doing it deliberately, or if he could indeed "take it down" even if he tried to do so. "I want you to understand, Lieutenant Commander, this is nothing personal . . ." she started to say.

"Nothing personal?" As irritated as he was, his voice

still sounded musical. "Captain . . . you're asking me to take an Oath of Chastity, and you're saying that's nothing personal?" He was walking the length of Shelby's ready room, back and forth, with such grace that he barely seemed humanoid, but rather more like a caged tiger.

"If it's good enough for Deltans, Gleau . . ."

He waggled a finger at her, although he wasn't actually looking in her direction. His focus instead seemed inward, as if he were talking to himself. "No. No, the Deltans take an Oath of Celibacy, not chastity. For all their legendary sexual techniques, Deltans are still a fairly conservative race. They only engage in such congress with those who are to be lifemates. The problem is that if they become involved with a non-Deltan, then sex with his partner becomes the only thing that the non-Deltan can live for. It consumes the non-Deltan's life. So they take their Oath of Celibacy, promising not to enter in the bond of lifemating with any non-Deltan Starfleet personnel. And since they won't become sexually involved with a nonlifemate, chastity is simply an extension of that. But the oath doesn't apply to other Deltans . . ."

"Very well. You're free to become involved with other Selelvians . . ."

He stopped and turned to face her. "There are no other Selelvians in Starfleet."

"Yes, I know that," said Shelby dourly. "Just as I also know the difference between chastity and celibacy. The problem, Gleau, is that Selelvians don't believe in marriage contracts of any kind. Which is fine. But that's why an Oath of Celibacy would be utterly useless in your case, and why I must ask for more than that."

Gleau finally sat, looking like a balloon with the air released. "Captain, I cannot believe you are serious on this. It is an utterly unwarranted and unreasonable infringement on my private life . . ." Then his face folded into a frown. On a face of such beauty, a frown looked positively grotesque. "This is about M'Ress, isn't it. She complained."

"That is correct," Shelby said levelly. "She lodged a formal complaint with me."

"Captain," said Gleau, and he had never sounded more wheedling than at that moment. It was enough to get Shelby's defenses up in a hurry. "This is all just . . . just a huge misunderstanding, that's all. M'Ress, why . . . she just didn't comprehend about . . ."

"The Knack?"

"You know," laughed Gleau, as if they were sharing a chuckle over an old joke. "There are so many misunderstandings and rumors about the Knack, it's really quite funny . . ."

Shelby leaned forward, her fingers still tightly interlaced. The longer the meeting went on, the more wary she became, and the more convinced that she was on to something. "Well, let's focus on my understanding of it, and you can then clarify it for me. As it relates to this particular instance, Lieutenant M'Ress claims that a fundamental attraction she felt for you was exploited via the technique popularly known as the Knack . . ."

"Captain, that is a gross oversimplification of—"

"A sort of mental manipulation," she pressed on

forcefully, "in which already existing tendencies and desires, as they relate to a Selelvian, are 'pushed'—consciously or unconsciously on your part—so that the subject in essence loses her free will."

"See, that is where the misunderstanding comes in," Gleau said quickly, leaning so far forward on his chair that he would have tumbled off it had it not been affixed to the floor. "The 'subject,' to use your own term, does absolutely nothing that she doesn't want to do. It just makes her ... well ... a little bit less self-conscious about it. And it's not something that we Elves—to use your popular nickname for us Selelvians—do deliberately. It's just, well ... part of our natural charm."

"I see," said Shelby, her lips thinning, looking very much as if she didn't see at all. "So you can't control it."

"Not as such. I mean, some of us can, more than others. But ultimately, it's simply part of the overall package that is a Selelvian. We never hurt anyone, though, Captain, you have to understand that. Hurting someone, taking advantage of them, trying to force them to do something that they would not ordinarily do ..." He looked utterly appalled at the notion, as if he could barely form the words since they were so distasteful to him. "Why, that would be anathema to us, Captain. Total anathema."

"I see." Shelby drummed her thumbnails on the desk, appearing to consider what he was saying. When she spoke it was with the air and attitude of someone who was thoroughly on Gleau's side, hoping perhaps to somehow settle a delicate situation before it spiraled completely out of control. "And yet ... M'Ress feels as if she was taken advantage of."

"Well . . . Captain," and Gleau visibly relaxed. He leaned forward, elbows on the desk, blinking his golden eyes, adopting a "strictly between us" attitude. "Let us remember . . . our dear Caitian scientist is just a bit out of her time, since she fell through the gateway that brought her to us. We're seeing mores and attitudes that were appropriate to over a hundred years ago."

"Really. I had no idea that people were such prudes a century ago."

"Oh, yes! It was *scandalous,* how conservative they were," he told her, dragging out the first syllable of "scandalous" so that it sounded like three.

"I see. M'Ress served under Captain Kirk, you know. Are you saying James T. Kirk was a prude? That doesn't exactly jibe with anecdotal evidence."

"Well, whatever you heard, trust me. The man was a notorious conservative."

"Kirk slept with my great-great-great-grandmother."

Gleau blinked. "Oh."

"And her sister."

"Oh. Oh dear. Well, I—"

"And, years later, her daughter."

"Ah. I see. Well, uhm . . . that's . . ." Gleau suddenly looked as if he'd much rather be anywhere else. ". . . that's very interesting, and I—"

"Gleau," Shelby said in as no-nonsense a tone as she could muster. "Bottom line, I turned a blind eye toward what I had heard about Selelvian tendencies, because you're correct: That is getting involved in the personal life of my crew. It's a realm that I feel rather shaky entering. Unfortunately, this situation has pushed me through the door. Now, maybe you're right," she said a bit more loudly, speaking over Gleau, who looked as if he was about to interrupt. "Maybe what we're seeing in this situation with Lieutenant M'Ress is a bit of provincialism on her part. On the other hand, perhaps she's bringing into stark relief something that we in Starfleet should have noticed and attended to earlier."

And Gleau's golden face, seemingly incapable of any sort of anger, clouded over like a thunderhead draping itself across the sun. "Need I remind you, Captain Shelby, that you are simply one individual, and not Starfleet. You are not entitled to make fleet policy."

Shelby immediately sensed the change in the atmosphere of the proceedings. "Yes," she said carefully. "You are right about that, Lieutenant Commander. But I am entitled to make policy decisions regarding personnel of this ship. You are of course entitled to ask for a review through channels, and I'm sure it will be granted. Average review time is between nine months to a year, Earth Standard Time. In the meantime, I'm afraid that I must insist on your taking an Oath of Chastity."

"This is grotesquely unfair, Captain!"

"On some level, Gleau, I agree. On another level, however . . ." And she leaned forward and her voice dropped to a place that indicated extreme warning. "You may have taken advantage of a fellow officer who didn't know the truth of your nature. I am willing at the moment to believe that you did not do so intentionally. On that basis, I will not be bringing you up on charges of rape . . ."

"Rape!" As opposed to Terrans, who became decidedly pale when shocked, Gleau became an even shinier gold. "You can't be serious, Captain—!"

"Do I look at all like someone who isn't serious?" she demanded. When he didn't respond, she continued, "As I was saying, at the moment I am willing not to bring you up on charges. Nor is M'Ress asking me to do so. She has, however, made her displeasure known. Now I am making my displeasure known to you. I've adapted the intended oath based upon the Deltan Oath of Celibacy. I suggest you take it and then stick to it."

"Or . . . ?"

And there it was. The single word, hanging challengingly in the air between them. Her eyes narrowed and Shelby said, "Or I will consider your intentions toward Lieutenant M'Ress to be hostile and act accordingly. It's your choice."

"This is blackmail!"

" 'Blackmail' is such an ugly word," Shelby said. "I prefer 'coercion.' "

"And as such, Starfleet will not consider it binding."

She shrugged. "Perhaps. But that's a matter for the appeals process . . . by which time we will have, at some point, put in at a space station or dry dock for repairs, and you may decide you want to transfer to somewhere you find more welcoming. In the meantime, make your decision, Gleau. And make it now."

She swiveled the computer screen around so that the vow of chastity was displayed upon the screen. She watched his face carefully, saw his gaze flicker to the screen, saw him recoil slightly like a vampire faced with garlic or holy water. Then, somewhat to her surprise, his irreverent and annoyingly attractive smile reappeared upon his face. "Anything," he said with as much suavity as he could muster under the circumstances, "to maintain harmony in the family."

Gleau leaned forward and said, "Computer . . . identify via voiceprint and retinal scan."

"Identifying, Lieutenant Commander Gleau," the computer said promptly. "Science officer, *U.S.S. Trident.* Serial Number S152–520 SP."

"Computer . . . note and log that I have read the Oath of Chastity presented to me by Captain Elizabeth Shelby, at this time, on this date, and that I agree to abide by its stipulations and decrees."

"Noted and logged."

He nodded once as if in satisfaction of a job well done, and then rose from his chair. "There. That's attended to. Now, if there's nothing else, Captain . . ."

"One other thing, actually." He waited, and she said, "There are to be no recriminations against Lieutenant M'Ress for this action. Is that understood?"

"Perfectly, Captain," said Gleau without hesitation . . . so little hesitation, in fact, that it left Shelby nervous and silently contemplative long after Gleau had left her office.

ii.

The ground was flat and barren, and Si Cwan braced himself, balancing on the balls of his feet, keeping one hand outstretched to ward off blows while the other arm, back and cocked, had a sword leveled and ready.

He was faced with three opponents, all clad entirely in black from head to toe. When they moved across the rocky terrain, coming in from three sides, they made no sound whatsoever. He might as well have found himself facing ghosts. They disdained to walk like normal beings, instead vaulting from one spot to the next as they converged upon him.

"Care to join me?" he called. "There's a sword right nearby you."

Seated sedately on a rocky outcropping, Robin Lefler watched the proceedings with mild amusement. She knew that others swore by holodeck scenarios, but the truth was that she had never been much for such imaginings-given-air-of-reality. Robin considered herself somewhat more down-to-earth than that . . . which, she supposed, was a bit ironic considering the environment in which she chose to make her life. Nevertheless, she always watched holodeck sessions with bemusement, not quite able to fathom for herself what the big attraction was. It was all so . . . so damned fake. The warm breeze blowing in wasn't really there; the aridity of the atmosphere was meticulously manufactured, and could just have easily have been humid or filled with snow, all at the slightest request of the person playing out the scenario. It was all just smoke and mirrors, and Robin fancied herself just a little bit above all of it. It was nothing more than playtime, really, and she was an adult. An adult who had no time for such foolishness.

"I really don't think so, Cwan," she told him.

"It will be good training for you," he said as he made

a jump to the left. His attackers, drawing closer, followed suit. He took a step to the right. They matched it.

"Of course it will, Cwan. The very next time I'm attacked by sword-wielding ninjas, which I should mention happens absolutely all the time in the vacuum of space."

"Tragic to see one so young become so cynical at such an early age." Even as he spoke, he never took his eye off any of the individuals slowly approaching him.

Suddenly two of them moved in quickly, leaving the third one behind, presumably to mop up.

Their swords flashed in, and Cwan deftly stepped between them, his robes whirling out so he looked like a black-clad pinwheel. His red face was set in grim mirth as he drove an elbow into the face of one of the ninjas while slashing forward with his sword at the other. The ninja deflected the blow, and they exchanged rapid-fire parries and thrust so quickly that Lefler was unable to follow it.

Abruptly there was a tearing of cloth, a sudden intake of breath from Cwan, and Lefler saw that blood was welling from a ribbon cut on Cwan's left forearm. "Si Cwan!" she called out in alarm. "That's enough! Shut down the simulation!"

"Why? It's just getting interesting!" he called out. The ninja was coming in fast, his sword whipping around, and Si Cwan bent backward, the blade slicing just above his face, missing him by a scant inch. Then he lashed out with one foot, striking the ninja's sword from his hand, and before the ninja could recover, Si Cwan had run him through.

Even as the one ninja went down, the other two charged.

Lefler had seen enough. "End program!" she called.

The ninjas were still coming. Si Cwan forward-rolled past them, just managing to dodge their thrusts, and when he came up he was holding the fallen blade of the first ninja in his other hand. They came at him, and wielding both blades with equal dexterity—one in either hand—he managed to keep them back even as a roar of satisfied laughter erupted from his throat.

"End program!" an exasperated Lefler cried out, but the holodeck scenario continued to play out. "Si Cwan, did you key this to your voice only?"

"Of course!" he said cheerfully as he drove both ninjas back.

"Si Cwan, you idiot—!"

Before he could reply, one of the ninjas had suddenly somersaulted through the air. Si Cwan had no time to move before the ninja landed on his shoulders, wrapping his legs around Si Cwan's throat. Si Cwan staggered, and tried to bring the swords up and around to stab at the ninja. But the ninja had a better vantage point, enabling him to deflect deftly each of Si Cwan's thrusts.

"Si Cwan! You didn't disengage the safety protocols, did you?" demanded Lefler.

Si Cwan didn't answer. Instead he just struggled mightily as his eyes began to roll up into the top of his head.

"Oh, hell!" Lefler shouted. She hit her com badge. "Lefler to—"

Suddenly there was a blur of movement through the air, and then the ninja was gone. Instead of being atop Si Cwan, the ninja was sprawled on the ground, looking exceedingly confused.

Robin's eyes widened as she saw that a woman had shown up, practically out of nowhere. She was wearing uniform slacks and boots, but she had removed her uniform jacket so that she was left in the red mock-turtleneck. She had blond hair, an attitude that could have been chipped from a block of ice, and a vicious scar down one cheek.

Robin recognized her instantly as Kat Mueller. Formerly Mueller had been the nightside executive officer of the *Excalibur,* and as such had had almost no interaction with Robin. Nightside people in terms of their involvement with dayside were, well, like night and day. Now she was first officer aboard the *Trident.*

Mueller had picked up the sword that Si Cwan had suggested to Robin. She whipped it briskly through the air a couple of times to test its heft, then nodded approvingly. "This will do," she said, and then glanced challengingly at Si Cwan. "I hope you have no problem with even odds."

"None," said Cwan.

The two remaining ninjas came at them, and briefly Cwan and Mueller were on the defensive. But in a short time they had turned it around, fighting the ninjas hard, driving them back, and further back. As fast and as deft with a blade as Si Cwan was, Mueller was faster still. The ninja she was facing didn't come close to scoring with a thrust, while Mueller continued to advance. The clatter of metal upon metal was nearly deafening to Robin, and try as she might, she couldn't visually track what was happening.

Then, with a final drive forward, Si Cwan and Mueller moving in perfect synchronization with one another, their respective sword blades darting through the air, they sent the weapons of their opponents clattering to the ground. The ninjas exchanged glances and then, as one, turned and bolted. Si Cwan laughed as the ninjas dashed away, leaving their fallen comrade behind. Mueller did not allow herself to make a sound, but she did smile in grim satisfaction, and she tossed off a mocking salute with her blade as her erstwhile opponents fled.

Si Cwan turned to her. "Well met, Commander," he said approvingly. "Of course, I could have handled them on my own."

"Of course," said Mueller with a neutral smile. "And you are cordially welcome to continue telling yourself that."

The Thallonian noble laughed at that with such gusto, and so much more loudly than he needed to, that Robin felt a sudden surge of annoyance with him. It was as if he was going out of his way to enjoy the woman's company. "I have to admit, I did enjoy the element of danger since, as Lieutenant Lefler surmised," and he pointed to Robin, "I did in fact disengage the safety protocols."

"You did, in fact, do no such thing," Mueller informed him. She seemed to enjoy the look of surprise on his face. "You may have thought you did, but the captain has installed absolute fail-safe overrides. You're allowed to think that you have the safeties off, but the only one on the ship authorized to disconnect them is the captain, and she's not about to."

"Hardly seems sporting," grumbled Si Cwan.

"Perhaps. But on her previous command, she wound

up with her chief of security dead by unfortunate happenstance. So she swore there'd be no repeats during her watch here. My apologies that we went to extra effort to prevent you from being killed."

"I shall have to learn to live with it." Robin saw that his red skin was still glistening from the exertion of the battle, but he was breathing steadily . . . and he hadn't taken his eyes off Mueller. "You are quite the swordswoman," he allowed. "Is that where you got the scar . . . if you don't mind my asking."

"If I did mind your asking, it would be a bit late," she said, as she touched the scar with one finger. "In answer to your question, yes. It's a Heidelberg fencing scar. Don't worry: I acquired it far too long ago to be self-conscious about it now."

"Well, it gives your face character. Don't you think it gives her face character, Robin?" he asked.

For no reason that she could determine, Robin felt her jaw tightening. "Absolutely. If she had any more character, she'd be someone else completely," she said with exaggerated overpoliteness.

Mueller seemed to pick up on it. It was hard to tell. There was a slight flash of annoyed amusement on her face, and then it passed and Kat was once again her imperturbable self. "You did not join the ambassador in his . . . exercise," she observed.

"Don't have much skill with large cutting implements," said Robin.

"I would be more than happy to give you some lessons, if you were interested."

Again for no reason, Robin had a mental image of

lunging forward and driving the sword directly through Mueller's heart. *My God, get a grip, Lefler,* she scolded herself, and forced a smile. "That's . . . quite all right. Maybe some other time."

"As you wish," said Mueller, tapping the sword to her forehead in a salute. Robin was unable to determine whether it was meant to be a mocking gesture or not, but as if she'd already forgotten that Lefler was there, Mueller turned her attention back to Si Cwan. "I came in person to inform you that the captain is extending an invitation for you and your sister to join her for dinner tonight. You as well, Lieutenant," she added, without looking in Robin's direction.

"I would be honored," Si Cwan said. "I've certainly served enough time with Elizabeth Shelby aboard the *Excalibur,* but in this regard, it is as if I am making her acquaintance all over again. I am certain that I speak for Kalinda as well . . . and Robin . . . ?"

"Oh . . . wouldn't miss it," said Lefler with a cheery smile.

"Excellent. Nineteen hundred hours, if that will be suitable for you."

She bowed slightly and formally to Si Cwan, and then, with a sideways twist of her arm, tossed the sword to Lefler. Robin took a step back, nervous and startled, and made a stab at catching it. It bounced off her knuckles and clattered to the floor. Mueller gave one of those annoying little smirk/smiles and let herself out of the holodeck.

"End program," said Si Cwan, and the rough terrain was replaced with the familiar black walls and yellow grid. He took a few steps toward Robin, his hands draped behind his back, and said cheerfully, "Interesting woman, wouldn't you say, Robin?"

"Fascinating."

"Didn't have much social intercourse with her back on the *Excalibur.*"

"Yes, well," said Robin dryly, "I could tell just by the way she was looking at you that she's probably interested in changing that situation."

"Do you think so?"

"Oh, I'd bet on it."

iii.

"Ohhhh, honey," Morgan Primus said, "if I could reach right through this screen and give you a big hug, I would do that. You know that, don't you?"

"I know, I know," sighed Robin. She was stretched out flat on her bed, looking at her mother's image over the com screen in her quarters. Morgan, of course, was back on the *Excalibur.* She had already gone to bed when her daughter's hail came through, but Morgan had promptly shaken off the last vestiges of sleep and pulled her full attention on Robin's needs . . . although she did yawn a bit as she endeavored to keep her attention focused on the conversation at hand. "I appreciate that, Mother."

"So the dinner didn't go well, then?"

"Ohhh, the dinner went fine," Robin said. She curled her legs up and pulled off her boots one by one. "It was pleasant enough catching up with everyone, I guess. Command—I'm sorry, *Captain* Shelby, had some interesting stories to tell, especially about everything that happened with her and Captain Calhoun during the whole gateways thing. Some of it is so crazy that it almost makes me wonder if they hallucinated the whole thing in some frostbitten haze. And their honeymoon on Xenex . . . now *that* was something else . . ."

"But none of that mattered all that much, did it," asked her mother.

Robin tossed her second boot loudly to the floor. "No. Not much. God, Mother, you should have seen the way she was looking at him . . ."

"Her being . . . ?"

"Mueller."

"Ah. And she was looking at . . ."

"Si Cwan."

"Ah."

Robin pulled a pillow over her head and screamed into it in frustration. When she yanked it off her head and looked back to the screen, her mother was watching with one curious eyebrow arched. "Are you done?"

Lefler considered the question a long moment. Then she pulled the pillow over her face once more, let out one more scream, and removed it. "I am now."

"So let's see if I understand this," said Morgan. "You had a lovely dinner catching up on old times with Captain Shelby."

"Right."

"And Commander Mueller appeared, as near as you could tell, to be chatting up Si Cwan."

"Also right."

"And he seemed to find her attractive, and as near as you could tell, it was reciprocal."

"Oh, I don't know, Mother," she said, sitting up and swinging her feet over the edge of the bed so that they were dangling just short of the floor. She pulled her uniform jacket over her head, not even bothering to unfasten the front, and tossed it in a heap on the floor. "Maybe I was reading into it. Maybe I was imagining it. Maybe," and she pulled fistfuls of her hair in opposite directions, "I'm just losing my mind."

"Robin, I'm just a bit confused about something," said Morgan, raising a finger in the air as if she were testing wind direction. "I thought . . . and correct me if I'm wrong on this . . . that you had lost interest in Si Cwan."

She nodded.

"Because," Morgan continued, "you'd been appalled by the merciless brutality you saw him display during the business on Risa. As I recall, you considered his actions to be so repellent that you wanted nothing more to do with him. For that matter, you had trouble believing that you were ever attracted to him in the first place. Is any of this ringing a bell?"

"Yes, Mother, it's all ringing a bell. I haven't forgotten any of that."

"Oh, good. And if all that is the case, then it prompts the question . . ."

"Why do I give a damn whether Mueller is interested in him, and him in her?"

"Exactly, yes."

Lefler drew her legs up so that her knees were under

her chin. "I've given that very question a great deal of consideration."

"And the answer you've come up with is . . . ?"

"Not a clue."

"Ah."

"Mother," Lefler said in annoyance, "if you say 'ah' one more time, I'm going to slap you silly with a tongue depressor."

"From light-years away? I'd like to see that," said her mother with a smile so infectious that Robin couldn't help but smile in response. "See, there's my girl. There's my Robin's happy face."

"Your Robin isn't feeling all that happy."

"Because you feel conflicted about Si Cwan."

"Yes, exactly." She felt her voice was very thick, as if she were speaking through a heavy fog. "I was so certain that I'd put all those feelings I'd had for him to rest, back on Risa. I'd been so certain that he wasn't the man for me. That we were too different, too far apart philosophically, to ever have a chance together . . . but when I'm with him, he has a charisma that just . . ."

"Robin . . ."

"Yes, Mother?"

Morgan smiled at her indulgently. "You know I love you."

"Yeah, Mom, I know."

"So I can say this to you . . ."

"Yeah, Mom?"

Taking a deep breath, Morgan told her, "Shut the hell up."

Robin sat in her bed, staring at the screen. The fact

that her feet were not touching the ground made her feel like a small child. The fact that her mother had spoken to her in that manner completed the sensation. All she could think to say in response to that was "Ah."

"Robin," sighed Morgan, shaking her head, looking discouraged. "Honey, I don't think you realize it, but ever since we reunited, you and I, you've been going on and on and round and round in regards to Si Cwan. It's getting old, darling. Actually, it got old a while ago. At this point it's reached the point of being superannuated."

"I . . . don't know what that means," admitted Robin.

"It means that enough is enough, dear. Either you care about Si Cwan, you tell him how you feel, and you take what comes. Or you decide once and for all that it's never going to happen and you just move on."

"I tried moving on," Robin reminded her. "I wound up getting involved with a clone of a murderer."

"No one ever said the course of love was smooth."

"Mother, for God's sake!" exclaimed Robin. She bounced off the bed, landed on her feet, and nearly twisted her ankle when she did it. She leaned on a chair for support. "I know it doesn't have to be smooth, but for most people, at least it doesn't involve felons!"

"Robin, it's time—as my long-departed mother used to say—to fish or cut bait."

"Mother, you're nearly invulnerable. You probably *will* be around forever, or close to it, remember?"

She waved her hands impatiently. "Whatever you say, Robin. Just get your life in order, all right? You're a Starfleet officer, for heaven's sake. Make a damned decision and stick to it. This endless vacillation . . . it's unseemly. All right?"

"All right, Mother. Whatever you say," said Robin, trying not to be upset. She knew her mother meant well.

"Good," Morgan said. "Mark my words, Robin: You go through life thinking that you have all the time in the world, and then you suddenly find that it's used up. Tomorrow becomes yesterday before you know it, and if you don't plan for those tomorrows, you wind up mourning a hell of a lot of yesterdays."

"I'll remember that."

"Good."

Robin smiled. "Good night, Mother,"

"Good night, Robin," said Morgan, and the screen blinked off.

EXCALIBUR

i.

SOLETA, THE VULCAN SCIENCE OFFICER of the *Excalibur,* walked briskly into the conference lounge, slowed, and then stopped. She looked around, as if concerned that she'd walked into the wrong room. The only individual sitting there was Zak Kebron. He was as immobile as the statues he resembled, his hands resting one atop the other on the table, sitting perfectly upright in the chair that had been specially designed to accommodate his size.

"Am I early?" she inquired. "My understanding is that there was to be a meeting here . . ."

"Yes."

She pointed at herself and then at Kebron. "You and I . . . and who else? You informed me that I was needed up here . . ."

"Yes."

"Kebron, I was off duty. My assumption was that this was a matter of some urgency."

"Yes."

She folded her arms and sat in a chair near him, crossing her legs at the knees and adopting one of the more severe looks in her repertoire. She was not the least bit pleased at this current state of affairs, nor was she at all amused over Kebron's one-word answers. She had certainly grown used to them, but that didn't necessarily make them any easier to take. And they were certainly ill timed. "Is anyone else coming to this little get-together?"

"No."

"So you, unilaterally, decided to call a conference here in the conference lounge, the subject of which is apparently known only to you, and the only other individual to be part of this conference is me. Does that about sum it up?"

He pondered it a moment. "Yes," he decided.

She uncrossed her legs and stood. Since she had come quickly at his summons, she had not taken the time to put her hair up in its usual chignon, held in place by the IDIC pin she'd had since her youth. Instead her long hair was down around her shoulders, and some of it was getting in her face. She pushed it back, covering her irritation with her customary ease, and announced, "I am going to bed now. That is not an invitation. That is simply a statement of fact. Good night, Kebron."

"Aren't you curious?"

"No," she said flatly. "Curiosity is for when I am on duty. When I am off duty, I don't give a damn. I said good ni—"

"Sit."

Although he had not measurably raised his voice,

there was something in his tone that brought her up short.

It was at that moment that Soleta came as close to panicking as she had ever had in her life. For she was suddenly certain that Zak Kebron, security chief of the *Excalibur,* knew the truth about her. Knew that she was actually half-Romulan, and had hidden that fact from Starfleet. Knew that she was inadvertently involved with an act of sabotage upon the Romulan homeworld that had left them in disarray. This was probably going to be an initial interrogation, conducted by Kebron in the line of duty. Even though she had known Zak Kebron her entire adult life, suddenly she was looking at him as if he were a total stranger. He represented everything that she was afraid of, every secret she kept hidden away that would probably put an end to life as she knew it and her career as she had built it. He was the enemy. He was the end of everything for her, all incarnated in one inscrutable, daunting Brikar package.

She sat. There really wasn't much choice; she suddenly had no strength in her knees. It was everything she could do, it took every ounce of willpower she could muster, to keep her attention focused on Kebron.

"We've known each other since the Academy, Soleta. You, McHenry, and I . . . we came up together."

Her lips were absolutely dry. She felt as if there were no moisture in her body at all. She nodded. For once, it was Kebron who was speaking, and Soleta who was the taciturn one.

He leaned forward. She dreaded the next words from his mouth.

"Have you ever wondered about McHenry?" he asked. She kept her demeanor utter calm. "McHenry."

"Yes."

"Mark McHenry?"

He looked at her curiously. "Are you . . . all right?"

"Yes. Why do you ask?"

"Well," he said uncertainly, "you look as if you want to . . . laugh."

"Do not be ridiculous," replied Soleta archly. "Why are you asking about McHenry?"

"Doesn't he seem," and Kebron tapped one large finger on the table, "odd?"

Soleta stared at him. "Is this," she asked at last, "part of a bet to see if you can actually get me to laugh."

"No. Not at all."

"Then you could have fooled me," she said. "Asking me if I've noticed that McHenry is odd is like asking if I've noticed that it's cold outside."

"That isn't what I mean. Soleta . . . there are many things about McHenry that we simply . . . accept."

"What would you suggest we do, Kebron? Reject them?"

Undaunted, Kebron continued, "His location abilities. His navigational abilities."

"They're above the norm," she admitted.

"No. They are abnormal. They are impossible. No one can do the things McHenry can do. These . . . skills . . . have only become more pronounced over the years. Would you not say that is correct?"

"I . . . I suppose . . ."

"You are a scientist, Soleta. You have an inquisitive

mind. All these years you have known McHenry, known him to do such impossible things," and he lowered his voice even more than it already was, "and you have never . . . ever . . . questioned him? Is that not, in and of itself . . . extremely strange?"

Her mouth moved but no words came out. She was having trouble processing the switch in her priorities. Soleta had been so worried that she was the subject of inquiry that she had to fight past her surging relief and bring her focus onto McHenry. Once she reached that point, she had to bring herself to acknowledge that Kebron might have a point. She just . . . wasn't sure what it was

"What is your point, Kebron?" she asked impatiently.

"I looked up McHenry's psych profile. His charts. His psi scores. Nothing tested out of the ordinary."

"It . . . didn't?"

"No."

"That . . . " Now the part of her personality dedicated to scientific curiosity began to stir as she rubbed her chin thoughtfully. "That . . . should not be the case. I mean . . . when one considers the things of which McHenry is capable . . . one would think certainly there is *some* degree of psionic ability present. Psychic or parapsychic tendencies, at the least."

"Yes," agreed Kebron.

"But there was . . . nothing, you say?"

"And you have never questioned McHenry's abilities."

"No. Never."

Kebron leaned forward. "Soleta . . . *you should have. And I say that not to condemn you. I say that to indicate that something is wrong because you did not.*"

There was a long silence then. Soleta looked around as if she was suddenly concerned that there was some invisible presence in the room, watching, considering her next words. "Are you . . . suggesting," she said slowly, "that McHenry, somehow, on some level . . . *prevented* me from wondering? 'Prevented' anyone in Starfleet from looking too closely? That he . . . suppressed any desire that anyone would have to look too closely at what he was able to do?"

"Yes," Kebron said.

"Kebron," Soleta told him, "you're implying that McHenry is somehow . . . I don't know . . . more than human. That he's capable of shaping reality somehow, like a Q or similar being. That . . . that . . ."

"That what we are seeing when we see Mark McHenry . . . has never been what we thought it was," said Kebron. "And to realize that . . . is to do so . . . with the air of one waking from a dream."

She felt a chill working its way down her spine as she looked back on a lifetime of service, side by side with someone whom she suddenly wasn't sure she knew at all.

"I . . . don't know what to say at this moment, Kebron. I truly don't."

He leaned back in his chair, now drumming all his fingers on the table. "Neither do I," he admitted. "It is as if we must . . . reorient our thinking."

"Have you brought this to the captain?"

"No."

"Will you?"

"There is nothing yet to bring. Vague suspicions that I cannot prove. Once I know what to say . . . I will say something. I was actually hoping that you might come up with some way to approach it . . ."

He waited.

She said nothing.

"Soleta?" he asked finally. "Are you . . . ?"

"I am fine," she assured him, snapping herself back to the matter at hand. "I was just . . . considering options. To be honest, Kebron . . . I think we may not have to do anything."

"Why?" He seemed rather surprised, perhaps even a bit suspicious, at her assessment.

"Because," she said, "the fact that you're inquiring at all . . . the fact that you're wondering about him . . . may indicate that whatever it is that's happening . . . is starting to fall apart. That we're seeing a sort of . . . natural entropy unfolding in regards to McHenry's personal situation. It may all be unraveling on its own. If that is the case . . . then all you have to do is stand back and be prepared to pick up the pieces when it does."

"The question is," he said with concern, "if and when it does all fall apart . . . is it going to take all of us with it?"

She had absolutely no answer for that, except to look at Kebron askance and suddenly ask, "Is your skin peeling?"

"No," he said quickly, and discussed it no further.

ii.

By the time Burgoyne arrived at the scene of the problem, there was already a small crowd gathered at the bottom of the Jefferies tube. An apologetic-looking Lieutenant Beth was standing there, glancing up the tube and back at Burgoyne as s/he approached.

"Could we move aside, people?" asked Burgoyne with obvious irritation. "You must all have somewhere else you could be. And if not, I can certainly find places." The crowd melted before him. "Thank you," s/he said. S/he stood next to Beth, peering up the Jefferies tube. "Care to tell me how this happened?"

"I have no idea, Commander."

"Well, good," said Burgoyne, making no attempt to hide hir sarcasm. "It's nice to know that the engineering department remains on top of things."

Beth lowered her voice, glancing around at the others standing near with obvious self-consciousness. "Commander, that isn't exactly fair. Do you know how many Jefferies tubes there are on this ship?"

"Forty-two," Burgoyne said promptly.

Beth rolled her eyes. Her curly brown hair was tied back tightly, and he saw that there were smudges of dirt on her face and under her fingernails. Clearly she'd been climbing around in the tube. "Okay, fine, you would know. But that being the case," she quickly rallied, "you'd have to admit that we couldn't conceivably watch every tube in the ship."

The thing was, Burgoyne knew she was correct. But s/he was in no mood to back down, and disliked hirself for saying it even as s/he snapped, "I'm not concerned with every tube, Lieutenant. Right now I'm just concerned with this one." S/he leaned in and called up the tube, "Xyon! Xyon, can you hear me?" No reply came.

S/he withdrew and looked back at Beth. "Are we sure he's still up there?"

Beth produced a tricorder and aimed it up the tube. After a moment, she nodded. "Definitely. Got his life readings."

"Lock on to him. Let's beam him out of there."

"That could be problematic," Beth told hir. "He's in a high energy flux area. He's not in any danger," she added quickly when she saw Burgoyne's face. "But it would interfere with a transport lock. And I would hate for anything to go wrong. I mean, we could try to beam him out, but under the circumstances we could wind up getting him one piece at a time. I don't think that would sit well with his mother."

"I tend to agree," came a familiar, clipped voice from behind them. Burgoyne winced, knowing perfectly well who was going to be standing behind hir when s/he turned. And sure enough, there she was: Selar, her arms folded and her expression one of barely contained annoyance. And to make matters worse, Captain Calhoun was standing right behind her.

"Captain, what are you doing here?" asked Burgoyne.

Calhoun chucked a thumb down the hallway. "My quarters are right down there. I couldn't help but overhear the turmoil. Someone want to fill me in?"

Several people began talking at once, and Calhoun put up his hands to shush them. It was Lieutenant Beth who spoke: "Xyon crawled up this Jefferies tube. One of our tech people spotted him going up, tried to crawl in after him. But he's managed to wedge himself up in the crawlways, up near the sixth intersect, we think."

"We think. We don't know?"

"We think we know," said an uncomfortable Beth. "The problem is that the space is much too narrow for any of us to fit up there."

"Are you saying he's stuck?" asked Selar. As always, she maintained her Vulcan demeanor of stoicism, but it was plain to anyone that she was concerned.

"No, not at all. We don't think he's stuck. He's just . . ." She sighed deeply. "Apparently he thinks it's all a game."

*"Won*derful," grunted Selar.

"I'm very sorry about this, Captain," said Burgoyne.

But Calhoun simply shrugged. "Apologies aren't necessary, Commander. These things happen. And figuring out who's to blame is just a waste of time and energy." This helped Burgoyne feel some measure of relief, but even so, hir child was still stuck up there. Just because the captain wasn't condemning anyone didn't change that fact.

Calhoun scratched his beard thoughtfully for a moment. Then he tapped his com badge. "Calhoun to Dreyfuss."

"Dreyfuss here," came a worried voice from the children's recreation center. "Uhm, Captain, if this is about Xyon going missing again . . . I'm sorry, I turned away for just a minute . . ."

"That is what this is about, but there's no harm done . . . hopefully," he said with a cautious glance up the Jefferies tube. "Mr. Dreyfuss, I'm on deck five, section 23-A. Would you be so kind as to send Moke down here?"

"Of course, Captain."

Within minutes, Moke came running up to Calhoun. Starship life had agreed with the boy. He had grown an inch taller, and his dark hair was neatly trimmed as opposed to the unruly mess it had been when he'd first arrived. He had filled out nicely, gotten far more substantial, while retaining that lean and athletic look from his homeworld of Yakaba. "You needed me, Dad?"

Burgoyne couldn't help but smile at that. The child wasn't truly Calhoun's son. Calhoun had adopted the boy after his mother had died on Yakaba. And most of the time, Moke addressed the captain as "Mac." But Burgoyne had noticed that, when there were a few people around and a situation seemed more formal, or at least more serious, Moke always called him "Dad" or "Daddy." Burgoyne wasn't sure whether it was out of respect, or out of desire to prove to anyone nearby that he, Moke, had a right and reason for being there.

"You remember Xyon? Burgoyne's and Selar's son?" asked Calhoun, indicating each of them respectively with a nod of his head. "Well, he's up there, and he doesn't seem to show any interest in coming down. I was hoping you might attend to it. You see, you can fit up there and we can't."

"Okay," Moke said without hesitation.

"Captain," Selar said with clear uneasiness. "Are you quite certain this is the right thing to—"

But by the time she had gotten halfway through the sentence, Moke had already gone up the Jefferies tube. He scampered up the interior, disappearing from sight in no time. They heard a bit of clattering from within, and then the sound of something breaking. A moment later a data disk fell out. "Sorry," Moke's voice floated down.

"Don't concern yourself," said Calhoun, picking up the disk and glancing at it. "All you did was take every lavatory facility from here to deck ten off line. Other than that, no problem."

"I did?" His voice was raised in alarm.

"The captain is kidding you, Moke," Burgoyne assured him.

"The captain has a rather unfortunate sense of humor which tends to exhibit itself at unfortunate times," Selar said reprovingly. Calhoun did not deign to glance in her direction.

There was some more sounds of movement, a short cough, more movement that was farther away . . .

. . . and then nothing.

They waited.

More nothing followed the nothing that they had amassed up until that time.

When more time had passed, and there was still no sound, and no movement, Burgoyne turned to Calhoun. Calhoun was standing there with remarkable sangfroid, looking not the least bit concerned with the condition or situation of either boy. "Captain," Burgoyne started to say, "request permission to . . ."

Calhoun put a finger to his lips. He was listening very attentively. "Do you—?"

"I hear it," Selar said instantly. There was a hint of excitement in her voice, which was about as out-of-control as she let herself become. "Yes . . . definitely, I hear it."

"Hear what—?" asked the confused Lieutenant Beth.

At that moment there was the sound of feet coming down the service ladder that ran the length of the Jefferies tube. They were moving quickly, briskly. It didn't sound to Burgoyne exactly like Moke, however. Instead it sounded slower . . . heavier . . .

Then he realized, of course, just before Moke dropped down out of the Jefferies tube, with a grinning Xyon hanging on to his back like a small monkey.

A ragged cheer went up from the onlookers. "Well done, Moke," Calhoun said approvingly, and Moke bowed his head in acknowledgment of the compliment.

Selar went straight for Xyon and said, with as much impatience as she allowed to show, "Come here, Xyon. You've caused enough trouble for one—"

Xyon let out a yelp, never taking his large eyes off Selar, as he gripped more tightly around Moke's throat, making it painfully obvious (painfully to Moke, in any event) that he had no desire to let go. "Xyon, stop that!" Burgoyne said.

"Just back away a moment, Doctor . . . Burgy . . ." Calhoun cautioned them, and they did indeed step back. Moke, whose air had been cut off, looked gratefully at Calhoun, since his ordering the others to step back had prompted Xyon to ease up. "Moke . . ." he prompted the boy, and then waited.

"Xyon . . . get down," Moke managed to gasp out. Instantly, albeit with a reluctant little murmur, Xyon released his choke hold and dropped off Moke's back. The moment he alighted on the ground, however, he took Moke's hand and held it firmly.

"Looks like you've got a little friend, Moke," observed Ensign Beth.

"Yes, well, enough is enough. You have taken up far too much of everyone's time already, Xyon. Come here," and she held out her hand commandingly. When Xyon didn't budge from Moke's side, she said even more firmly, "Come *here!*"

"Burgoyne, Selar . . . a moment of your time," said Calhoun, gesturing for them to step away from the scene."

"Captain," Selar said, "perhaps this is not the best opportunity for—"

"I'm sorry, were you under the impression that was a request?"

With a small grunt that indicated she did not suffer fools gladly, Selar walked over to Calhoun, Burgoyne at her side. Xyon, left to hold Moke's hand, cooed happily.

"It seems to me," said Calhoun in a low voice, once they had withdrawn sufficiently from the others in the hallway to acquire a modicum of privacy, "that Xyon seems rather attached to Moke. And I know that Moke is feeling somewhat at loose ends aboard the ship."

"Are you suggesting that Moke be 'assigned' to tend to Xyon?" asked Selar.

"Captain!" said Burgoyne, filled with relief and gratitude. "That's—"

"A terrible idea," Selar said firmly.

"Yes, Captain, with all respect, what were you thinking?" Burgoyne said, doing a quick one-eighty.

But s/he had a feeling by the fleeting smile on Calhoun's face that the captain knew perfectly well where s/he stood on the matter. That was verified by the fact that Calhoun addressed his comments almost solely to Selar. "It doesn't seem like such a terrible idea to me," he said easily.

"Moke is far too young to deal with such responsibility," Selar told him.

"Why? What's the worst that can happen? Xyon finds himself up a Jefferies tube? Under someone's bed? Last week they found him trying to climb into an empty casing for a photo torpedo. You've got a very active son there, Doctor, and frankly, I think he needs full-time attention. More to the point, he needs someone who can keep up with him. As far as I'm concerned, Moke would be the leading candidate on that score."

"I . . . I do not know . . ." Selar said uncertainly. She looked to Burgoyne, which was something of a first, since she rarely sought out anyone else's opinion when it came to Xyon. "What do you think, Burgoyne?"

Burgoyne wanted to jump up and down, pound the air with hir fist, and cry out, "Yes! Gods, thank you, yes!" But s/he wisely refrained from such an overly demonstrative display. Instead, choosing hir words carefully, s/he said, "Well . . . let's consider our alternatives. When we can't attend to him, we lock him in our cabin . . . which will not be pleasant for him. Besides, knowing our son, he'd probably find a way to pass right through the walls. Or he could stay with you in sickbay all the time . . ."

"No," she said immediately.

Well, he'd been expecting that. "And the bridge is certainly no place for a child, much less an active one. He seems to sneak out of the children's facility with ease. We could permanently assign a holodeck to him and let him spend time with simulacrums of ourselves . . ."

"I find that disturbing on so many levels I do not even know where to begin," she said.

"In that case," said Burgoyne, "this seems to be the most reasonable solution."

Selar considered it for a short time that seemed an eternity to Burgoyne. Calhoun remained calm and detached. She glanced once more in Moke's direction, saw the cheerful smile on Xyon's face as he looked adoringly up at Moke, and finally said, "Very well. If Moke is willing, I will agree to the arrangement on a trial basis."

"You won't be sorry," said Calhoun.

She gave him a look that said, *I'm sorry already.*

Calhoun strode over to Moke and went to one knee. Xyon, eyes wide with suspicion, stepped behind Moke, using the boy as a barrier between himself and the captain, never taking his eyes off the Starfleet officer. "Moke . . . would you be interested in a permanent assignment . . . ?"

"Watch Xyon?"

"You're way ahead of me. We—that is to say, Xyon's parents and I," and he glanced in their direction, "felt that you were capable of handling the responsibility of—"

"What's my rank?"

Calhoun tried not to laugh. "Your rank?"

"Everyone on the ship who has a 'sponsibility has a rank. What's my rank?"

With a small smile, Calhoun said, "Ensign, junior grade. Take it or leave it."

"Okay."

Selar quickly approached, but she did not kneel. Instead she stood tall and straight, and Moke and Xyon had to crane their necks to be able to see her face. "If there are any problems, Moke, any difficulties or questions . . . do not hesitate to come to me."

"Okay, Doctor," said Moke carelessly. Obviously he did not think there was going to be much in the way of difficulties, problems, or questions. "C'mon, Xyon. Let's go find something to do that's not dangerous."

"Okay!" Xyon said cheerfully.

DANTER

TRANSCRIPT OF WELCOMING ADDRESS *made at the Danteri Senate, to the representatives of the Starship Trident upon their arrival at the Danteri Senate Building. Representing the Trident were: vessel's captain, Elizabeth Shelby of Earth; Ambassador Si Cwan and Princess Kalinda, both late of the Thallonian Empire; Security Chief Arex Na Eth of Triex; and science officer Gleau of Selelvia. In attendance for the Senate was the entirety of the eighty-seven representatives from the thirty-nine provinces of Danter. The text of the Welcoming Address was voted upon and carried by a vote of eighty-four to none in favor, with three abstaining. It was delivered by Speaker of the Senate Lodec, formerly of the house of Falkar, in the Danter year 5724, on the fourth day of the Week of the Triumphs.*

My fellow senators . . . distinguished guests . . . greetings to you all. I apologize for the rather dreary weather outside. But don't worry; we'll find a way to blame it on one of the colony worlds. We always do. (Laughter.)

We are particularly grateful that Lord Si Cwan has taken the time, and the leap of faith, to come to us this day. (Applause). And a leap of faith it is . . . for let us be honest. Yes, my friends, at long last in the history of Danter, let us be honest with each other. The relationship that Danter had with the Thallonians has always been something of a fractious one. We shed no tears when the Thallonian Empire fell. We saw that shift in power as an opportunity for our own people, our own interests, to expand. To benefit. To step over the corpse of the Thallonian Empire and take as much advantage as possible of the opportunities its demise presented us.

And what did we gain in return? What, ultimately, did we gain? You all know the answer . . . but I will spell it out for our visitors. The answer is: nothing.

We endeavored to spread our influence among those planets that had once been under Thallonian rule. It was our belief that, with the passing of the Thallonians, we would simply be able to step in and take over from where they fell. We thought we would appear on those worlds no longer subjugated to the Thallonians and pick up the pieces. We thought . . . it would be easy.

We were wrong.

It could not, in fact, have been more aggravating. Granted, a handful of worlds welcomed us. But these were the most backward, the most underdeveloped worlds. The worlds that presented the most minimal opportunity for Danteri benefit and profit. The worlds that, in short, had the most to gain and the least to lose.

The other worlds, however . . . the worlds that could have benefited the Danteri Empire . . . the worlds upon which we could have expanded our base of strength, ah, those worlds were far more problematic. Some were caught up in internal struggles. Civil wars that had been smothered during Thallonian rule but—once that rule was removed—flared anew. Some sought to manipulate us against other worlds. Some fought us outright. What we had thought would be a simple plucking of the fruits left behind by the Thallonians, instead became a very dangerous orchard with hazards perched in the branches of every tree. We found ourselves fighting a multi-front war that we were wholly unprepared for. And when we pulled back to reconsider our efforts, to redistribute our forces, then in some cases those worlds which we had sought to approach and dominate took that to be weakness on our part. They became even more aggressive, attacking our colony worlds and outposts. Naturally we were able to beat back those incursions . . . but it was not without cost.

Matters have calmed somewhat . . . mostly due to the presence of two starships on permanent assignment to the sector now designated 221-G. We of Danter are not "officially" within that sector; we are on the border. But we are close enough to make our presence felt . . . and to feel the presence of others.

It has been a difficult, even humbling experience for all of us. Indeed, it has taken us many, many months to make that admission, to come to that consensus. But once we did, my fellow senators . . . we were able to come to an inevitable, albeit difficult, conclusion.

And that conclusion, my esteemed visitors, is why

you are here. That is why we asked that Ambassador Si Cwan be brought to us. We wish to make . . . a proposition. A proposition uniquely suited for our noble Thallonian lord, and all that he brings with him.

We propose . . . the establishing of a new Thallonian Empire. (Long pause for thunderous applause to die down.)

I will deviate from my prepared text for a moment to note, for the record, the stunned expression on Lord Cwan's face. (Laughter.) You were not expecting this, were you, Lord Cwan. (Lord Si Cwan shakes his head.) To be truthful, had you suggested to us some months ago that we would be making this proposal, you very likely would have been met with derisive laughter and scorn. But time and misuse of resources can be wearing, Lord Cwan, as I am sure you will acknowledge.

The simple truth, Lord Cwan, is that our neighboring sector of space . . . your former homeland . . . was better off when the Thallonians were in charge. That is not an easy admission for us to make, but it is true. The proof of that simply cannot be ignored. Even those who, once upon a time, wished for the demise of the Thallonian Empire have come to see the error of their ways. Many are nostalgic for your rule. What was once perceived as the heavy hand of tyranny is now seen, instead, as a firm but fair hand of discipline and tolerance that kept peace among dozens and dozens of worlds for uncounted years. Although, as always, there are a few dissenters, it is our belief that there are many who ardently desire a return to a simpler time. A happier time.

Furthermore, it is not as if the entirety of the Thallonian race simply evaporated and disappeared overnight. There are many, many Thallonian expatriates who do not hold that status by choice. They recall fondly their late, lamented homeworld. They remember all too well what it was like to be part of a star-spanning nation under the rule of your family, Lord Si Cwan. They remember better days, and hunger for those days to come again. And they believe that you, Lord Cwan, hold the key to those days. Some of them, granted, were hostile to you. They blamed you and your family for the loss of Thallonian power. But time, and experience, changes the mind of even the most intransigent of individuals.

We of Danter wish to help rebuild the Thallonian Empire.

We know that seems a preposterous notion. The obvious question is: How do we profit from such an endeavor? What is there for us to gain? Believe it or not, Lord Cwan—and we fully admit, you may not believe it at first—the main benefit we have to gain is peace of mind. The neighboring region has been destabilized thanks to the fall of the Thallonian Empire, and that is no good to us at all. If the Thallonian Empire is rebuilt, the restabilization of the region alone will do us good. It will enable us to reset our priorities and focus our energies back on where they belong: the well-being of the Danteri people. (Applause.)

Naturally, however, it would be ludicrous to think that we Danteri would be able to announce to all and sundry that we are endeavoring to re-create the Thallonian Empire. None would believe us. Resistance to the notion would be overwhelming. It would cause far more problems than it would solve. We need individuals who have credibility. Who will serve as not simply figureheads, but instead true leaders around whom the downtrodden of Thallonian space can rally. And, again, to be honest, Lord Cwan . . . there is not a lengthy list of names from which we can choose. You and your sister are the last of your royal family. You are the last, best reminder of what the Thallonian Empire once aspired to. To you and you alone can your people turn in their hour of need. Only you will they trust. Only you can guide them.

The Danteri Senate stands ready to put its full weight, influence, and means behind you, Lord Cwan, in an attempt to set up a new Thallonian Empire. We look to you to throw your considerable charisma, organizational skills, and reputation behind the endeavor. Thallonian space was stronger with you than without you, and with you can become great once more. It is our proposal that we reinstitute a royal family, comprised naturally of yourself and your sister, plus any paramours or consorts you wish to include. We would form a core alliance of worlds, overseen by yourself, which would be able to enforce the will of Thallonian teachings and guidance upon the rest of Thallonian space. Expatriate Thallonians will learn of this, there is no doubt. They will come to this world. They will join you if you lead them. Things can be . . . the way they were.

And once that happens—once the Thallonian Empire has been rebuilt—then, Lord Cwan, your people and ours will be able to move forward as allies, nurturing strength from strength rather than trying to benefit from perceived weakness. We can create a new golden age for the Thallonian Empire, and achieve greatness for ourselves as a result. (Applause)

There are no tricks to this offer, Lord Si Cwan. No bargains, no demands. Simply an offer of an opportunity that will benefit all and harm none.

We await your decision.

EXCALIBUR

i.

"YOU'RE KIDDING. I mean, you can't be serious."

Calhoun sat in his ready room, staring in astonishment at the image of Shelby on the communications screen. He'd been polishing the short sword he customarily kept hanging on the wall, but he had now forgotten about it completely upon hearing what his wife had just told him.

"Do I sound like I'm kidding, Mac?"

He sat back, feeling as if he'd been physically struck in the face. "A new Thallonian Empire?"

"That's what they said." She was shaking her head in slow amazement. "That place was massive, Mac, that senate building. I've been to the UFP chambers, and this place dwarfed that. Actually, the whole capital city is like that. Big. Everything big. Big buildings, big people . . . even their pets are big . . ."

"Yes, yes, I know. It's a cultural tendency among them. Goes to their tendency to be big and boastful about everything, but that's not the point right now, Eppy." Remembering that he was still holding the sword, he laid it down flat on the desk. To some degree, he couldn't understand why Shelby looked so completely calm. On the other hand, he had to admit that he admired that about her. Here she was, faced with an insane and potentially explosive offer, and she seemed to be taking it utterly in stride. Either she was not thrown at all by what fate had tossed her way, or else she simply had no real clue of what she was being faced with. "The point is: What's going to happen? What did Si Cwan say?"

"Nothing."

He stared at her, not sure he heard her properly. "Nothing. You mean . . . nothing to them?"

"Nothing to anyone. The Senate made its offer, Si Cwan listened to it, made no reply, returned to the *Trident,* and put himself into seclusion. That was seven hours ago. We haven't heard a thing since."

"And Kalinda?"

"Same thing."

He rose and began to pace, fury and suspicion at war within him. "That is unacceptable. Simply unacceptable."

"To whom, Mac? To you?" She was looking at him skeptically with one eyebrow cocked. "Need I remind you, it's not your call to make. It's my ship. I'm on station here. And if Si Cwan wants to keep everyone guessing for a time, I don't have a problem with that. Better to take one's time in order to say the right thing, rather than rush into saying the wrong thing."

"But Eppy . . ."

"Come on, Mac, be realistic," she said, speaking right over him. "They dumped one hell of an offer on Si Cwan. It's a lot for him to digest, and if he tries to do it too fast, he could choke on it. There's just no point in rushing things. We'll stay in orbit around Danter until this matter is decided . . ."

"I don't see how it can be decided in any way but one," said Calhoun, resting his knuckles on his desk and leaning forward on them. "The Danteri are not to be trusted under the best of circumstances, and these are not they. This Senate Speaker . . . what was his name . . . ?"

She appeared to glance down, apparently consulting notes on another screen. "Lodec," she said.

Calhoun felt as if his mind was freezing. He simply stood there, staring at Shelby, and it took him a little time to realize that her mouth was moving and words were coming out. "Mac," she was saying, "are you all right?"

"Lodec? Are you sure? Of the house of Falkar?"

Shelby frowned. "Actually they said, 'Formerly of the house of Falkar.' Why? Do you know him?"

The *Excalibur* captain laughed very softly at that. "In a sense, yes. The last time I saw him was in the depths of space, after the business with Gerrid Thul and the Double Helix. I wanted to blow him to bits at the time. I didn't. Before that, you'd have to go back, oh, about thirty years or so . . . when I stood there helplessly and watched him murder my father."

She paled when he said that. He could see it, even on the small view screen. "Oh, Mac. Oh, honey, I didn't know . . . I'm so sorry . . ."

"There's no way you could have known," and he drew

a deep breath, "and no way it should be relevant. But it is. These are bad people, Eppy. Bad people. Si Cwan has to understand that. You can't let him—"

Suddenly the screen became thick with static, Shelby's picture blurring out. Not only that, but the lights overhead flickered. "Elizabeth!" he called.

"Mac, I can't hear you!" she said, but her voice was no longer synching up with her mouth. Moments later, her image vanished completely.

"Grozit!" snarled Calhoun, and he tapped his com badge. "Calhoun to bridge. What the hell happened to our com channel?"

"Just about to summon you, Captain," Burgoyne's voice came back. "We're approaching Zone 18 Alpha. The energy emissions that we were supposed to explore here appear to be interfering with some of our systems."

"On my way." He glanced sadly at the screen. "Sorry, Eppy. We'll have to pick it up later."

ii.

Soleta couldn't help herself. She felt as if she were looking at Mark McHenry differently than she had been before.

As she stood there at her science station, she kept casting glances in his direction and just . . . wondering. He didn't seem any different than usual . . . well, yes. Yes, actually, he did, slightly. Much of the time, McHenry would be at his post and looking for all the world as if he were dozing. It had been one of his most disconcerting traits. Officers from Calhoun to Shelby and even William Riker had had to make the adjustment in realizing that looks could be deceiving, and that McHenry was in fact extremely alert to everything that was going on at all times.

But McHenry was a little different this time, ever since they had begun the approach to Zone 18 Alpha. Soleta knew she wasn't imagining it, because Morgan Primus, seated at ops, had noticed it herself, even though she was relatively new to regular bridge assignment.

"Are you all right, Mark?" she inquired.

McHenry turned and glanced at Morgan. "Yes. Why?"

"Well . . . you're awake," she said.

McHenry smiled wanly. "That's not the strangest thing in the world, is it?"

"For you, yes, it is a little odd."

As Calhoun walked out onto the bridge, Soleta looked over to Kebron. Ever since their conversation earlier, he had not broached the subject of his suspicions about McHenry. He seemed, in fact, utterly focused on his job . . . which was, Soleta supposed, as it should be. She found it disconcerting, though, that she was now regarding Mark McHenry—whom she had known for years—as if he were a total stranger. On one level, it seemed absurd. After all, how could anyone reasonably be suspicious of somebody simply because they were *awake?* At their post? It was patently ridiculous.

And yet . . . *look at him,* thought Soleta. He seemed fidgety, uncomfortable. If there was any individual whom she had ever met who never appeared nervous about anything, it was Mark McHenry. Or was it that she was applying her own concerns and misgivings to him, and her perceptions were being filtered through those? It was impossible for her to tell, and she found that singularly frustrating. She was supposed to be a scientist, the science officer of the *Excalibur.* What kind of scientist—hell, what kind of Vulcan—was she if she could not be trusted to provide dispassionate observation of a subject?

Well, that was what the problem was, wasn't it. She was thinking of McHenry as a "subject." Something to be considered, studied, probed, instead of a longtime friend and crewmate. It was ridiculous. At the same time, she couldn't help herself. She was totally suspicious of him.

Calhoun was standing beside his chair, staring at the empty space presented on the screen. Burgoyne had just brought him up to speed on their present situation. "Do we have any other problems besides long-range communications?" he asked.

Burgoyne, addressing the broad question to the rest of the bridge crew, said, "Status reports?"

"All ships systems operating normally," Morgan Primus said promptly, checking her instrumentation.

McHenry didn't even bother to look. "Helm and navigation holding steady."

Soleta turned her mind back to the business at hand, pulling it away from pointless speculation about McHenry. "We're experiencing difficulties with long-range sensor sweeps. Although I'm getting energy readings, I'm unable to determine the point of origin or precisely what types of energies they might be."

"Short-range scanners?" asked Burgoyne.

"Operational norm."

Burgoyne turned to Kebron. "Weapons? Tactical?"

"Normal."

Nodding in approval, he called out, "Bridge to engine room."

"Engine room. Mitchell here."

"Status report on the engines, Mr. Mitchell?"

There was a pause, and then Mitchell's shocked voice came back, "Oh my God! They're gone!"

Soleta saw Morgan twist around in her seat, looking utterly perplexed. Several other bridge crew members were likewise startled by the outburst. But Calhoun simply rolled his eyes while the unflappable Burgoyne said mildly, "Mr. Mitchell . . ."

"They were right here, I swear! The moment I turned my back, though . . ."

"Craig—" Burgoyne said in a warning tone.

"Engines are fine, Lieutenant Commander. All readouts are normal."

"Good. You might have said that in the first pla—"

"They ask about you all the time, though. They have trouble sleeping at night."

"Thank you for sharing that. Bridge out."

Calhoun stared at Burgoyne. "He was the best we could do for chief engineer, was he?"

Burgoyne shrugged. "A number of people said that in regards to your choosing me for first officer, Captain."

"I know I did," McHenry volunteered.

Leaning against his chair thoughtfully for a moment, Calhoun then turned to Soleta and said, "Thoughts, Lieutenant?"

Soleta pulled her mind back to the matter at hand. "In

regards to the scrambling of our long-range sensors?" He nodded. She gave it some thought and said, "I see two possibilities, Captain. Either the interference is an unavoidable result, caused by the fundamental and as-yet-unknown nature of the phenomenon that we have been sent to explore . . ."

"Or?"

She took a breath. "Or that there is something out there deliberately blocking our long-distance sensors in order to force us to come in closer."

"Agreed," said Calhoun. "Recommendations?"

"I don't see how we can go in unless we have more information," Burgoyne said, pacing the upper ramp of the bridge.

"Our assignment is to explore it," said Soleta. "I, for one, do not see how we can reasonably remain where we are and do our job. There is concern from Starfleet that an unknown energy source might be, at the very least, a previously unknown gateway."

"Lord, I hope not," said Calhoun. He started to tug thoughtfully on his beard, and then caught himself and lowered his hand. "I'm getting a feeling that we are indeed heading into something that is not simply 'natural.' On the other hand, people: We knew the job was dangerous when we took it. Mr. McHenry, ahead full impulse. Soleta, keep sensor scans on maximum. If you find anything out there that even looks at us funny, we'll . . ." He stopped and looked in the direction of the conn. "Mr. McHenry . . . was my order unclear?"

"No, sir," said McHenry. He sat there with his hands

resting on the conn board, but he was making no move to drive the ship forward.

Soleta exchanged silent looks with Kebron. The look in the Brikar's eyes seemed to speak volumes: *See?* But Soleta quickly pushed that away. So McHenry was acting strangely. So what? It wasn't as if it was the first time, and he'd always come through in the past.

Calhoun stepped forward, leaning over and looking into McHenry's face. The captain didn't seem angry so much as he did concerned. "Mark?" he said softly. "Is there a problem? Something you wish to discuss?"

Whatever was bothering McHenry, he shook it off. "No, sir," he said, forcing himself to sound brisk and businesslike. "Just a bit distracted. No problem at all. Half impulse—"

"*Full* . . . impulse, Mr. McHenry," Calhoun corrected.

"Full impulse, aye," said McHenry, and a moment later the starship was heading toward the area in question.

There was silence on the bridge for a time. Everyone was going about his or her business, and there was no one thing that made Soleta think that anything was wrong. But McHenry's hesitation had struck everyone there as odd, and it was as if it was feeding into a pensive atmosphere. She almost wished that Calhoun would take McHenry aside and ask him what was going on, but Calhoun did not do so. Instead he would glance in McHenry's direction, and once as he passed by he rested his hand on the conn officer's shoulder as if to silently assure him that all was well. But Kebron was not taking his eyes off McHenry, as if he expected the helmsman to have some sort of sudden breakdown, or perhaps launch an assault on another crewman.

This is ridiculous, she thought. *Kebron's got me watching Mark as if I've never seen him before in my life. This is* Mark McHenry. *He's as loyal as a basset hound, and about as dangerous as a carrot. There can't be any problems with him. Kebron is just imagining it, that's all.*

The thing was, she knew that Zak Kebron might have been many things, but he was not given to flights of fancy. If he thought something was up with McHenry, then something was most likely up. The fact that McHenry didn't seem to have his head in the game during this latest assignment didn't help matters at all.

While all this was going through her head, Soleta deftly managed to multitask, keeping an eye on readings and making sure that the odd energies of Zone 18 Alpha were not wreaking further havoc with any instrumentation.

The long-range sensors were still providing her with nothing. Using the long-range sensors to track down the energy emissions was like trying to pick up liquid mercury with chopsticks. Every so often she thought she could extract some sort of reading on these very odd, very unusual energy waves, radiating in patterns that were unlike any she'd ever seen. She would get tantalizingly close and then . . . nothing. Gone again. "Chimera," she muttered.

"What?" asked Burgoyne, overhearing. "It's shimmering?"

"Not shimmering. Chimera," said Soleta.

"Isn't that a beast from Greek myth?" asked Morgan,

turning to look at Soleta. "With a lion's head and a goat's body?"

"And a serpent's tail, yes."

"We're chasing a mythological beast?" asked a confused Burgoyne.

McHenry looked uneasily at the screen. "I certainly hope not."

It was Calhoun who stepped in. "A chimera also refers to any creature or being that's an agglomeration of unrelated parts. But I suspect that what our lieutenant is referring to is the concept of a goal that is unattainable; an illusion of the mind. You seek it out but, just when you think you're within reach . . . it's gone."

" 'A fancy, a chimera in my brain, troubles me in my prayer,' " said McHenry.

"Very good, Lieutenant," Calhoun said approvingly. "You're familiar with the works of John Donne?"

"Some. I've just always taken that quote to heart, that's all," McHenry told him.

Soleta was beginning to get genuinely concerned. McHenry wasn't sounding like himself at all. And even from where she was, she could sense Kebron's gaze boring into the back of McHenry's neck. "In any event, you are correct, Captain," she said, trying to bring attention away from McHenry. "My sensor scans appear to pick up something, but then become vague and unspecific. I am having great difficulty locking down the source of the energy emissions. It's there . . . but it's not."

" 'I thought I saw upon the stair, a little man who wasn't there,' " quoted Morgan. " 'He wasn't there again today. Oh, how I wish he'd go away.' " She stopped, pleased with herself, and then added, "Ogden Nash."

"Yes, I know," said Calhoun, and although his calm demeanor remained, he also displayed a flash of impatience. "And if we happened to be a literature-appreciation circle, I would be extremely pleased with the direction in which things are going. However, what with this being a starship and all, I'd be far more pleased if we could actually accomplish our mission. Soleta, a probe perhaps . . . ?"

"I was just going to recommend that, Captain. The problem is that the interference from the energy emission's source . . . whatever that may be . . . could impede our ability to stay in contact with the probe."

"Granted, but it may still be worth a try," said Calhoun, easing himself into his chair. "At this rate, we still have no idea what's giving off these emissions. A ship, an uncharted sun, a wormhole, a spatial rip of some sort . . . it could be anything. The probe might enable us to . . ."

"Captain!" Soleta said abruptly, looking at her instrumentation. "I'm getting something on the short-range scanners. It just . . . it just appeared there, sir."

"You mean it came into range?"

"No, I mean one moment it wasn't there, and the next, it was." She hated not being able to give a more coherent answer than that, but she was befuddled by what was presenting itself to her.

"Can you get me anything on screen?" Calhoun was leaning forward in his chair, his full attention on the main viewer.

The screen wavered for a moment as Soleta fed her sensors through it, but what appeared there didn't seem to be especially satisfying. It floated, nebulous, its shape shifting, stars visible through it. "It seems similar to an ion cloud," she said thoughtfully, "but there are significant differences between—"

But Calhoun suddenly wasn't listening. Instead his head snapped around, and Soleta saw that he was looking at McHenry. "Lieutenant, what are you doing?"

Soleta saw it a moment after Calhoun had. McHenry, with no warning and with no explanation, was changing the course of the ship. He didn't even seem to be aware that he was doing it. His eyes were wide, his body stiffened as if someone had jammed a rod down his spine. He was muttering under his breath, and at first Soleta couldn't make out what he was saying. But then she heard it. "Got to go . . . got to go," he kept saying, more to himself than anyone else around.

"McHenry!" said Calhoun sharply. "Belay that! Reset heading for previous course and speed and maintain it!"

McHenry simply shook his head, like a man trying to shake off a dream. The *Excalibur,* under his deft handling, was already well on its way to doing a one-eighty and heading away from its previous destination.

"McHenry!" Calhoun was out of his seat, and Burgoyne was moving toward him as well. Even as the captain and first officer converged on McHenry, a hail came in from the engineering room.

"Engineering to bridge!" came Mitchell's voice. "We just got a signal from conn for warp nine! That speed is usually authorized directly from command. Do you want—"

"Ignore it!" snapped Calhoun, and he was almost to

McHenry, as was Burgoyne. "Mr. McHenry, you are relieved of duty! Ensign Pfizer," he called to one of the duty officers, "take over for—"

That was as close to McHenry as Calhoun and Burgoyne got. A sudden discharge of energy rent the air. Calhoun was knocked flat on his back. Burgoyne was hit even harder, perhaps because s/he had been moving faster. S/he was sent flying over the back railing, and only Kebron's quick intercession prevented hir from crashing into the rear tactical array.

"You'll just make it worse," McHenry said, and there was something in his voice that was a bit singsong . . . that sounded almost childlike to Soleta.

Then she spotted something via her instruments that snagged her full attention. "Captain!" she called out.

"I'm a little busy at the moment, Lieutenant!" he growled, scrambling to his feet. "Kebron! Place Mr. McHenry under arrest!"

"Yes, sir!" said Kebron, easing the dazed Burgoyne into his chair as he strode with distance-eating strides toward McHenry. "Out of the chair, McHenry. Now."

"Zak, you don't understand," McHenry said, pleading, but the Brikar paid him no mind and reached for him. Instantly the same energy that had knocked Calhoun and Burgoyne for a loop enveloped Kebron. Kebron staggered and let out an uncharacteristic roar of fury, tried to push his way through it, and was rebuffed as the energy surge doubled. *"Stop it! Stop it!"* shouted McHenry, and still Kebron tried to push through. The crackling energy went from blue to blue white and suddenly Kebron, as incredible as it seemed, was hurtling through the air. Nobody tried to break his fall; they were too busy getting the hell out of the way. Kebron crashed into the guardrail in front of the tactical station, and there was a shuddering, creaking noise as the rail bent from the impact. Kebron sagged against it, almost losing his footing and trying to shake off the aftereffects. His uniform was scorched in places, and Soleta could have sworn that more of his skin was peeling at the base of his head. "Kebron, are you all right?" Burgoyne called. Kebron grunted, more in annoyance than anything, looking as if he was endeavoring to get his second wind.

Energy was still crackling through the bridge, although it had taken on a more defensive posture. Everyone hung back as bolts danced between them, keeping them off balance. Morgan, the closest to McHenry, was in the most danger, but she clung stubbornly to the ops station and when a bolt came so close that it crisped her hair, she snarled, *"Go to hell!"*

"McHenry!" shouted Calhoun. "You're only making this worse for yourself!"

"I'm not doing it, Captain! Don't you understand that?" McHenry said desperately. "It's not me! I'm the one who's trying to get us out of here!" and he manipulated the controls with his customary deftness.

The mighty starship, even moving at the relatively piglike crawl of sublight, had still reversed itself, and was now heading away from Zone 18 Alpha. But Calhoun was having none of it. "Engineering, full stop! All engines full stop! Do you hear? Full st—"

Soleta, meantime, had not taken her eyes off her scanners, and then she saw something that practically caused her heart to leap into her throat. *"Captain!"* she called, louder than she had before.

Calhoun started to turn to her in irritation, clearly not knowing where to look first. But Soleta had already changed the view on the main screen to angle behind the ship and she pointed mutely. Calhoun turned to see what it was that had struck her dumb, and his eyes widened. Suddenly everyone on the bridge had something to think about besides McHenry's apparently incredible assault on them.

On the screen, the nebulous cloud of energy that they had been approaching and which was now behind them had coalesced into something very discernible. It was a gigantic hand. The fingers were slim and elegant, clearly female. It was, nevertheless, gargantuan; from wrist to fingertip, it was half again as large as the *Excalibur.*

"Holy God," muttered Morgan.

McHenry looked at her in a way that Soleta could only think was supposed to be commiserating. "You don't know the half of it," he said.

"What . . . *is* that thing?" asked a perplexed Calhoun, staring at the screen.

"It's a giant hand, sir," said Soleta.

"I *know* that!"

She looked back at her scanners. "It's giving off identical wave readings as the energy emissions we were supposed to chart. It's energy *as* matter, converted without any means of artificial devices that I can detect."

"It . . . looks like it's getting closer. Are we . . . heading toward it?" asked Burgoyne.

"No," said McHenry, looking utterly depressed.

"Oh, hell," Morgan said, "it's getting closer."

At that moment, Mitchell's voice sounded from down in engineering. "Engineering to bridge. Sorry we weren't able to stop on a dime for you, Captain, but we've brought engines to full stop. Thought you'd want to—"

"Get us out of here," Calhoun said quickly, moving toward his chair.

Mitchell sounded incredulous. *"What?* But we just—"

"Best possible speed. Do it! McHenry, punch it. Now."

"Captain!" Kebron, who had just managed to disentangle himself from the rail, looked almost irate. "He was under arrest—!"

"Not now, Kebron! McHenry, go! *Go!"*

"Won't do any good. It's too late," said McHenry, but he dutifully piloted the ship forward as fast as he could.

Like a dinosaur ripping deliriously free from a tar pit, the *Excalibur* vaulted into warp space.

For long moments it was extremely uneasy on the bridge. No one knew quite where to look, including Soleta: At the viewscreen, where the enormous hand seemed to be receding? Or at her old classmate, McHenry, who had somehow repelled any attempts to take them out of the area . . . except out of the area was where they were now heading, which made McHenry seem prescient. But then how, Soleta wondered, could he possibly have known? And how did he start producing incredible displays of energy that kept everyone back, including the usually unstoppable Kebron? Questions, piling up, one upon the next, with no answer in sight . . .

Soleta's scanners gave her barely enough notice to shout warning, even as the pursuing hand finally disappeared into the distance. *"Conn! Dead ahead!"* she shouted a warning to McHenry.

The screen changed views to chart space directly in front of them, and there was the hand, looming and huge, so close that they could see fingerprints that looked like valleys. The lines on the palm bore a striking resemblance to the fabled canals of Mars.

"Evasive action!" Calhoun called, and McHenry was already doing it. The ship lurched a sharp 45 degrees, away from the hand, and then there it was again, closer still.

"Leave them alone, dammit! This doesn't involve them!" McHenry shouted, even as he sent the ship straight down, relative to the mammoth hand that was moving to intercept them. The ship took a relative nose-dive, and for a heartbeat they were in the clear. And then the hand was in front of them, so close that the fingers couldn't be seen.

The hand started to close and Soleta realized that they were too close. Calhoun must have known it, too, for he hit the intercom and bellowed, *"All hands! Brace for impact!"*

It was about two seconds' worth of warning, and Soleta hoped that that was enough time, for the ship suddenly jolted. Morgan's head slammed against the console, causing blood to start flowing from a cut just above her eye. Burgoyne smashed into the immobile Kebron and came close to sustaining a concussion. Calhoun fell backward, but luckily fell into his command chair. Everyone else hit the floor except for McHenry, who maintained his position but looked utterly miserable doing it.

For a moment all power went out on the bridge, and then the backups kicked in. The light was dim but everything was still visible. Soleta, using her station for support, pulled herself to her feet even as she wondered, for the umpteenth time, what the hell Starfleet had against seat restraints.

"All stations, report in," ordered Calhoun, and immediately status reports flooded in to Morgan at ops. Calhoun moved to help Burgoyne up. "You okay, Burgy?" he asked solicitously.

"I will be," Burgoyne said, "as soon as my transfer to Captain Shelby's ship comes through."

"Your transfer request is noted, logged, and lost," said Calhoun. "Everyone else?" There were ragged choruses of affirmatives from all around. Calhoun then turned and looked at the screen. It was impossible to see much of anything since the immediately exterior view was blocked. "Soleta, give me a different angle on this thing, will you? All I'm seeing is a giant palm."

The screen switched over to a different view.

"Much better," said Calhoun. "Now all I'm seeing is a giant fingernail."

He considered the situation a moment. "Something tells me shooting it isn't going to accomplish much. Kebron . . . open a channel."

"To what?" asked Kebron.

"That." He pointed at the screen.

"Captain . . . you're going to talk to the hand?" asked Burgoyne.

"No alternatives come to mind . . ." He walked toward the conn station, pausing a moment to see if more energy surges reared up to drive him back. None did, and he stood next to McHenry, looking down at him. "Unless the lieutenant here wishes to offer some up." McHenry just stared resolutely down, not lifting his gaze to look up at his captain. "Mr. McHenry," Calhoun continued with forced patience, "I am getting the distinct impression that you have at least *some* idea of what's going on here. True?" McHenry managed a nod. "Would you care to enlighten the rest of us?"

McHenry let out a long, tremulous sigh. "I don't think I'll have to, Captain."

"You don't?"

"No, sir. I expect you'll be finding out any moment without my—"

Suddenly the ship began to tremble. Soleta saw that it wasn't from the hand; it was staying rock steady. It was as if energy was building and the ship was shaking at some sort of molecular level, in sympathy with it. Energy leaped through the air as before, except this time more focused, and then from all different points in the bridge came together right in the middle. There was an earsplitting hum, as if something was materializing via the world's noisiest transporter. Soleta, whose eyes were genetically resistant to extremely bright light, squinted slightly but stayed focused on the center of the burst, while everyone else shielded his or her eyes against it. The intensity of the sound almost overwhelmed her, however, and then there was sudden, blessed relief as the noise ceased along with the light.

And when it did, it left behind it a woman.

Her face was triangular, coming to a chin so pointed that it seemed as if she could cut someone with it. Her nose was aquiline, her jade eyes gleamed with vigor. She had curly red hair piled high on her head, little ringlets framing her face. Her lips were round and set in what seemed a permanent pout, the edges twitching as if she was totally secure in her superiority to all she surveyed. Her face . . . her face was so absolutely perfect that it appeared unreal, and Soleta couldn't figure out why.

Her neck was extraordinary, giving her an almost swanlike grace as she surveyed her new surroundings. Her body was slim and muscular, and it was easy to make judgments in that regard, for she was quite scantily attired. She wore only a short toga, made from a material that appeared to be a light pink chiffon, and an off-the-shoulder cape that hung to just below her thighs. Her right shoulder was bare, and it—along with her long legs—was very tanned. She also wore Greek sandals with laces that ran up to just under her knees. A quiver of arrows was slung over her left shoulder, and she held an elegantly curved bow in her right hand.

Soleta was reasonably sure she was imagining it, but she could have sworn that she heard a fanfare of trumpets in the back of her head.

The woman looked at each one of them, one at a time, her gaze lingering longest on Calhoun as if silently acknowledging that he, of all those on the bridge, was most likely to give her problems. Calhoun's brow furrowed, and he seemed about to say something, but didn't. Then she turned and looked straight at McHenry, her chin tilted upward so that she was gazing down at him with a look that spoke of arrogance and superiority.

He said nothing; just returned the stare.

Then she walked over to him, placed a hand at the back of his neck, hauled him to his feet and—without a word—kissed him passionately. Her hands ran down his back, drawing him more closely to her.

Everyone stared, jaws dropping collectively . . . all except Kebron, who merely appeared annoyed, and Calhoun, who watched the display with cold calculation and a hint of grim amusement.

"Friend of yours, Mr. McHenry?" he deadpanned.

TRIDENT

i.

Lieutenant Commander Gleau contentedly manipulated the star charts that played across the cavernous walls of stellar cartography. Star study and mapping remained his first love, his greatest passion, and it was rare that he had the time to indulge himself in it. So caught up in his activities was he that he barely noticed when the doors hissed open behind him. He was, however, startled from his findings when an angry female voice called out his name.

"Hello, Lieutenant M'Ress," he said without bothering to turn and look at her. "What can I do for you?"

The Caitian strode toward him, her tail twitching in what could only be considered irritation, her muzzle drawn back to reveal the points of her teeth. He couldn't help but notice, despite all that had happened, how exotic and intriguing her cat's eyes remained, even clouded as they were now in irritation.

"I think you know damned well what you can 'do for me,' " she snapped at him.

"Well, some things come to mind," he said, "but I've taken specific oaths that forbid them. So I would think they don't enter into the mix."

Since he'd been seated, he easily kept his back to her, but she stepped around him so that she was facing him. She looked none too pleased. "The duties you've assigned me lately have been nothing short of menial," she said. "They could have been done by ensigns or science techs."

"My, my, M'Ress, you're quite the snob, aren't you," said Gleau with amusement. "I don't know how they did things in *your* time, but in ours, we don't focus on whether particular duties are beneath our respective stations. We all pitch in to get the job done without complaining. *Especially* those of us who are still on the learning curve and trying to get caught up with scientific advancements of the past century."

"Soil samples, lab cleanups," she fumed. "These were things I was doing when *I* was an ensign. You're not utilizing my capabilities in an appropriate manner . . ."

"Oddly enough, M'Ress, what with my being science officer," said Gleau, "I believe it's up to me to decide what is and is not appropriate . . . in science matters, if not personal ones." He gestured for her to step aside. "If you wouldn't mind . . . you're in my way."

"And you're in mine," shot back M'Ress. "The fact is, Gleau, that you've downgraded my duties ever since I filed the complaint with Captain Shelby."

"The fact is, M'Ress, that I am doing nothing that is outside my bounds as science officer." The pleasant tone that he'd been maintaining was starting to fracture slightly. "You have taken it upon yourself to draw boundaries for me in other aspects of my life. I will thank you not to challenge me on those that are proscribed by Starfleet command. As long as you are under my command, you will do what you're told, when you're told. If you do not like the duties assigned you, you are always welcome to request a transfer to another department . . . or better yet, another vessel . . . providing you can find one that will have you."

She stepped in close to him. He was irritated to discover that her mere presence was alluring to him. "Everyone in the science department," she said, her body trembling with anger, "looks at me as if I'm carrying a disease. You told them all about the situation, didn't you."

"It's a small ship. Word gets around."

"And you told it in such a way as to make me look like a shrew, correct? Like a whining, complaining, provincial complainer."

He met her with leveled gaze. "The truth hurts, Lieutenant."

M'Ress drew herself up and looked at him imperiously. "Gleau . . . we have been lovers, however briefly. But do not presume for a moment to know me. Don't presume to know what makes me tick. Don't think to know what I am and am not capable of. Certainly don't think to know what I find acceptable and what I do not from a sexual point of view."

"And I will thank you," he replied, "to extend me the same courtesy."

They glared at each other for a long moment, and then he sighed heavily. "M'Ress . . . look at this," he said, indicating the stars around them with a sweeping gesture. All around them the star maps, projected against the wall, shined invitingly, not twinkling since they were not distorted by any atmosphere. "Look at the enormity of the galaxy . . . of the universe. Look at these stars, alive for millions upon millions of years. All of them there long before any of us came upon the scene, and all of them guaranteed to be there long after we are gone. This, M'Ress . . . this is what we're all about. This is the type of thing that should be concerning us: the exploration of the greatness that is the universe around us. In the face of such boundlessness, why are we wasting time with petty, individual concerns? We need to have our priorities in place."

"Our priorities."

"Yes.

"In place."

"Yes."

She smiled. Unpleasantly. "Gleau . . . where do you think it all came from?"

Gleau tilted his head questioningly. "Pardon?"

"All this," and she gestured in the same way that he had. "The stars, the planets, the boundlessness. Where did it all come from?"

"Are you asking me about the origins of the universe, M'Ress? I don't pretend to have all the answers, but certainly there are schools of scientific thought that were present even when you were first studying," he said sardonically.

"Yes. Yes, there were." She circled him, and with one finger she played with a lock of his hair. It was a surprisingly intimate gesture, considering. "But you know what the oldest one is, I assume."

"Presumably," said Gleau, "you are referring to the school of thought that says that some sort of cosmic being was responsible for it all. It's a quaint fairy tale."

"There are some who say that. Then again," she pointed out, still moving around him, "there are those who say elves are quaint fairy tales. Or that Earth stories of elves were based upon early visits by your own people to that world."

"A valid enough point, I suppose," admitted Gleau, "but I don't—"

"Believe it or not, Lieutenant Commander . . . to some degree, I embrace the notion that there was indeed some sort of guiding intelligence forming the universe."

Gleau laughed, leaning back in the observation chair. "Do you. How very intriguing. And how very unscientific."

"We haven't *disproved* the notion, Lieutenant Commander, which makes it to my mind a possibility. After all, have we not encountered our share of near-omnipotent beings in our travels? With so many creatures who are godlike, one can only wonder if there in fact might not be a god for them to *be* like. I consider it to be . . . an interesting matter for speculation."

He laughed again. "Very well, Lieutenant. Obviously I have not given the matter as much thought as you, and therefore I will defer to you. Perhaps there is indeed some sort of presence. Should there be, I can but hope that He will choose to make himself available for scientific observation and discourse at some point, because I certainly have a variety of questions I would like to pose."

"As would I. Because if He exists, there are quite a few things He's done that make no sense to me. However, He did do one thing that makes perfect sense: He gave us free will. And you," and then she leaned in very close to Gleau, and he felt her warm breath, and heard the low growl in her voice like a predator about to leap upon its prey. "You . . . usurped mine. Whether you admit to it or not, whether you believe it or not . . . that is what you did. You flew against the intention of the being who had a hand in creating all this."

"Should I fear His wrath?" he asked quietly.

"No. Fear mine."

He paused, and then, maintaining his ready smile, he asked, "Is that a threat? Because threatening a superior officer . . . is a court-martial offense."

She drew back at that point, said nothing at first. Then she told him, "I know that you're endeavoring to 'teach me a lesson' because I made a stand for my rights. Perhaps others don't understand that . . . but you know it's true, and I know it's true. And this is not over." She turned on her heel and walked away.

"I hope not," Gleau called after her. "Considering I am now laboring under an Oath of Chastity, I have to find my amusements where I can."

ii.

Si Cwan walked through the empty halls of the palace on his homeworld of Thallon. He remembered how, in his youth, he would tear around the place, much to his father's consternation. The palace, while large under even the best of circumstances, was positively cavernous to Si Cwan at that age. It just seemed to go on and on. The corridors seemed to stretch to the horizon; the curved ceilings appeared high enough to touch the sky. Sometimes—and this was the thing that would most drive his father to distraction—Si Cwan would throw back his head and let out a yell at the top of his lungs that would reverberate for what seemed hours. The paintings, the murals, the busts of famous Thallonians . . . the palace was rich with the heritage and greatness of the Thallonian Empire.

The funny thing about the happiest times of one's life, Si Cwan mused, was that one didn't know that's what they were while one was experiencing them.

The solitude that he was experiencing now brought back that feeling of vastness he experienced as a child. The place was simply too big for one person. But one person was all that was filling it now. When Si Cwan was inclined to do so, he could move with utter silence. He did not choose to do so now. Instead he allowed his heels to *click-clack* up and down the hallways, listening to the echo and pulling from his heart all his recollections of the times when the palace had been filled with life. So filled with life, in fact, that it seemed less a dwelling than a force of nature, as teeming with vitality and power as the mightiest waves rolling into the surf.

He heard footsteps behind him.

There was a ceremonial spear in a stand to his right. Without hesitation, he snagged the spear out of its place, whipped it around and stood, poised, and prepared to take on any unexpected opponent.

Robin Lefler let out a gasp, stumbled backward, and grabbed on to a bust for support. Unfortunately the bust was not affixed to the pedestal upon which it was standing. It came away in her arms as Robin tumbled to the floor and, a moment later, the bust crashed to the ground beside her, shattering into a hundred zigzag fragments.

Si Cwan surveyed the damage in silence. Then he said, "You may be interested to know that my great-uncle, Jarek Cwan, never once fell in battle . . . until now."

"I'm so sorry," said Robin, clambering to her feet. She made a halfhearted attempt to reassemble the pieces before she acknowledged to herself the hopelessness of the endeavor.

"Don't concern yourself with it," he said. "Had it been real . . . had any of this been real . . . I would be upset. As it is . . ." His voice trailed off. Then he smiled slightly as he looked at Robin with pieces of the statue gathered in her lap. He extended a hand to her. "Come, come. No point in sitting around clutching a pathetic excuse for a bust."

She stood up and dusted herself off, allowing the pieces to fall to the ground. "Kalinda told me you'd be here. I'm starting to worry about you a little."

"Are you?" His red brow furrowed. "Why?"

"Because you're spending an inordinate amount of time in holodecks. It's making me wonder whether you just find everyone and everything else so deathly dull that we're not worth your time anymore."

"Hardly," he said. He continued to wander, and Robin fell into step beside him. "However, I find myself facing moments in my life where I have to determine in what direction it will go. It helps, in such instances, to remind myself via the firsthand aid of the holodeck, where it's been. The glory and majesty that was once Thallon lives only in my memory . . . and in the capabilities of this instrumentation to reproduce it." He stopped and stared at her curiously. "Are you quite all right, Robin?"

"Yes. Why?"

"Well, you're . . . you're looking at me . . . rather oddly. Not in a negative way, but still . . ."

"I just . . ." She cleared her throat and grinned. "I just . . . like to listen to you talk sometimes. You have a very musical voice. Even when you're speaking normally, it seems like you're singing sometimes, accompanied by an orchestra that only you can hear."

"Why, thank you, Robin." He reached over and squeezed her hand. It was so small in comparison that it seemed to disappear into his. Her smile widened. He took her other hand in his as well. "I so wish you could have seen this palace when it was real, rather than this . . . this construct. The pure majesty of our empire and heritage could only stir pride in the heart of any observer, no matter who they were."

"Unless they happened to be locked in a dungeon," Robin said, and then instantly looked as if she'd regretted saying it.

But Si Cwan took the comment in stride. "You mean as Soleta was, for a time. I will not deny, Robin, that there were darker aspects to our society. No matter how brightly any sun may shine, that upon which it sheds its light will always cast a shadow. Nevertheless, I regret that our empire did not have the time to learn and grow more than it did. It was my goal to eliminate such unfortunate sides of our world. To aspire only to greatness." He shrugged. "But we shall never know what I might have accomplished in that earlier circumstance. Still . . . that does not preclude performing great deeds in the future."

Robin was smiling when she heard that, and continued to do so until she fully digested just what it was that Si Cwan was saying. Then the smile began to fade. "Wait, you're . . ." She seemed at a loss for words.

"I'm what?" he prompted.

"You're not . . . *seriously* considering taking up the Danteri on their offer." She sounded thunderstruck, as if Si Cwan had suddenly announced that he was, in fact, a Hermat.

"I am very seriously considering it, yes."

"But . . . but you can't!" she stammered.

"Why ever not?"

Once more words did not appear to ally themselves with her. Then she found her voice. "First of all, you can't trust the Danteri . . ."

"Oh, I don't," Si Cwan said matter-of-factly. "I don't trust them at all. However, there are different degrees of lack of trust."

"I'm not following."

Except she was following: She was following Si Cwan into the main hall. He looked to the far end, to the great chair of judgment in which his father routinely sat when hearing matters of dispute between various races. Si Cwan had always wondered what it would be like for him to assume that mantle, to be the sole ruler of the sprawling Thallonian Empire. In some ways, he felt as if he had let down the memories of those who had come before him. Granted, he knew he shouldn't have taken that failure personally. It wasn't as if, due to lack of attention on his part, planets had risen up in rebellion and he'd lost control. Instead he'd stood there and watched his planet be rent asunder by a gigantic flaming bird, effectively sounding the death knell of the Thallonian Empire. How could anyone, short of a god, prepare for an eventuality such as that?

He brought his attention away from his free-floating thoughts, from the proud columns that lined the majestic hall, from the memories of what were, and focused instead on not only his conversation with Robin, but on the possibilities of what were to come. "I believe that the Danteri are motivated entirely by self-interest," he said. "On the one hand, they have admitted as much. On the other hand, it is entirely possible they are withholding other elements of the current circumstances that will play even more to their favor . . . elements that I have not even begun to consider. I do not trust that they have been entirely forthcoming. Nor do I trust that they will not endeavor to toss Kalinda and I aside, once we have served our purpose to them."

"Well, then—?"

Slowly Si Cwan walked up the steps to the chair of his father, turned, and sat carefully in it. He wondered if doing so would instantly cause all his faculties of judgment to snap into the crystal clarity that his father always seemed to possess. It didn't happen. He had known that it wouldn't. That was, after all, the province of the child: to believe that adulthood would bring with it instant comprehension of the world and the ability to make the right choice in any given situation. Instead adulthood brought with it only the crushing realization that one spent one's childhood utterly misinformed, shattering forever the childlike aspect of one's psyche. The rest of one's life more or less amounted to damage control.

"On the other hand . . . Kalinda and I are not stupid," he told Robin. "Nor are we novices when it comes to playing political games. We have been in situations that entail and require the acquisition and maintaining of power. I believe that the Danteri are sincere in their desire to see the Thallonian Empire rise again. It suits their purposes. I have verified their accounts of their recent difficulties with ship's records and historical documents. All of it is true. The region around Danteri has become a hotbed of unrest, and in those areas into which they attempted to expand their influence, they succeeded instead in destroying what little stability there already was. They need help. To be specific," and he chuckled at the thought, "they need *my* help. Our help, mine and Kalinda's."

"And you're actually thinking of giving it to them." She stared at him in amazement. "Si Cwan, in all the time I've known you, I've thought you to be many things. But never, for one moment, have I thought that you were . . . were . . ."

"Stupid?" He arched a shaved brow.

"I was going to say 'naïve,' but 'stupid' works just as well."

"And would be an acceptable term if I chose to pass up this offer."

"But . . ." She approached him. He wondered if she was going to genuflect, as was the custom for those approaching the great seat of judgment, but she remained standing. He supposed that was all right; even if she had known the custom, chances were she wouldn't have attended to it. "But . . . why? Why would you be stupid? Why . . . ?"

He reached forward and this time took both her hands into one of his, placing his other hand atop hers. Si Cwan smiled indulgently, and he might have been imagining it, but it almost seemed as if she was melting at his touch. *How charming,* he thought. *Despite the emptiness of this place, she still feels a bit caught up in the grandeur that was the Thallonian Empire. I suppose it would be enough to make any woman weak-kneed.*

"Robin," he said patiently, patting the top of her hands as he did so, "you seem to be forgetting how it is that I first came aboard the *Excalibur.* How it is that our paths first crossed."

When she spoke, it was with an obvious effort to keep her voice steady. "I . . . haven't forgotten anything. You stowed away."

"Yes. I stowed away, aboard the *Excalibur.* You have no idea," and he looked down, "no idea at all how difficult that was for me."

"I'd imagine so. Climbing into the cargo container, managing to remain that way for—"

He shook his head. "I'm not speaking logistically, or of the physical demands. I mean emotionally. Robin . . . I was a prince of Thallon. I had servants, courtiers . . . people who responded to my every desire. To lower myself to a thief of services, to hide like the lowliest beggar . . . my actions revolted me even as I undertook them. But I did so, willingly, for two reasons, to accomplish two goals. The first was to find Kalinda, my sister. The second was to use the resources of the *Excalibur* to try and pull together the shattered remnants of my once-great empire. As a noble—even a noble with no homeworld—I could do no less."

Robin pulled away from him, then, her face clouding. "So what are you saying? That the *Excalibur* has served its purpose? That you don't need us anymore?"

He sighed heavily. "It has less to do with need, Robin, than it does with proper distribution of resources. Robin, don't you understand? When I'm aboard the *Excalibur* . . ." He ran his hand across the top of his bald pate, as if trying to stimulate the correct ideas to present themselves. "On the *Excalibur,* I am surrounded by people who go about their jobs, do their duties, in order to benefit the galaxy around them, and their vessel, and their fleet. While I . . . I have been selfish . . ."

Robin appeared surprised, as if he'd slapped her across the face. "No . . . you're being too hard on yourself . . ."

"No, I am being honest. The *Excalibur* began as a means to an end for me. And although I have grown to respect and admire its crew and its mission—although I've never exactly warmed to Zak Kebron," he observed ruefully, "I have never really, truly moved beyond that essential self-interest. I am, at core, a selfish bastard."

"Si Cwan—"

"If one does not know oneself, Robin, then one knows nothing at all." He leaned back in his chair, steepling his fingers in a manner that was evocative of his father. "I have never, and would never, act in a manner contrary to the interests of the *Excalibur*. But my priority remains, first and foremost, myself. And when I see you, and most everyone else on the vessel, acting so unselfishly . . . caring about how and where you can provide aid purely in the interest of helping others . . . it drives home for me my own shortcomings."

"I think, Si Cwan . . . that you are being much too hard on yourself."

He shrugged slightly. "I do appreciate your vote of confidence. I do not necessarily share in the opinion . . . but that is neither here nor there. The point is that the *Excalibur* has a wider mission of not only altruism but also exploration, discovery . . . things that I have little to no use for. The Danteri, on the other hand, are quite focused. They don't care about seeking out new life and new civilizations . . . boldly going where no one has gone before. They care about power. So do I. In that sense, our goals are mutual and beneficial to one another. It is . . ." He paused, figuring the best way to say it. ". . . it is a better fit . . . than the one that currently exists. On the *Excalibur* I am, and will continue to be— what is the phrase you use . . . ?"

"A square peg in a round hole," she suggested tonelessly.

"Yes! Yes, that is it. That is it exactly," he told her. "But on Danter, I will be a square peg in a square hole."

He stood and spread wide his arms, his eyes glistening with anticipation. "Don't you see, Robin? The majesty of the Thallonian Empire need not be limited to a nostalgic, hollow re-creation of the past. It can, instead, be the future. My future."

"By making it your future, you're essentially living in your past," pointed out Robin. Her arms were folded tightly across her chest. She looked extremely defensive, which Si Cwan found rather sad. If only she could be made to understand. "Doesn't that bother you at all?"

"No," he said promptly. "Because I cannot escape my past, Robin. When I walk out of this holodeck, all this will still remain with me, in here," and he tapped his chest. "The impetus to build up the Thallonian Empire, to be great . . . it is a part of me, embedded within me by generations of those who have proceeded me."

"You don't need an empire to be great, Si Cwan," said Robin with surprising urgency. "That greatness is also in you, empire or not. And I just don't see how you can not realize that."

"I realize you believe it, Robin, and I thank you for it. And I will always consider you a great friend because of it. But I know what I have to do . . . and I strongly suspect the Danteri will enable me to do it far more efficiently than the *Excalibur.* It simply comes down to best use of resources, as I said."

Robin didn't appear to have heard the latter part of what he'd said. Instead she had a fixed smile on her face as she repeated, " 'A great friend.' Well, that's . . . that's good, Si Cwan. You have no idea how much that means to me."

"Or to me," said Si Cwan sincerely. "But the bottom line is . . . there really isn't anything to keep me on the *Excalibur.* With Kalinda found, and the Danteri offering me the opportunity to take greater steps than ever to reestablish the Thallonian Empire . . . name me one reason, just one, to remain with the *Excalibur.*"

She smiled wanly, although she didn't look especially happy. "Well, you've got me there, Cwan. If you can't think of one damned thing, then I don't think I can, either."

He stepped down from the chair, walking over to Robin, and he rested his hands on either shoulder. She looked up at him, unflinching. "Look, Robin . . . I haven't completely made up my mind yet. But I just felt that, out of deference to our long relationship, and the many times you've helped me in the past, that I owed it to you to tell you exactly what my current frame of mind is. Don't you think we owe total honesty to one another."

Something seemed to click into place behind her eyes. She suddenly seemed to be standing a little straighter, and her voice was a bit more confident. "Yes. Yes, we do. And I . . . should be honest with you. As honest as you've been with me, correct?"

"Absolutely. I'm glad we had this talk, Robin. But now, if you'll excuse me . . ."

"What?" She looked puzzled. "But—"

"End program," he said, and the long-gone palace of Thallon shimmered out of existence. He turned back to her. "I'm sorry . . . I did not mean to come across as rude. Was there something else you wanted to say?"

"Well . . . yes, I didn't think that the discussion was over, but if you're in a hurry . . ."

"I'm afraid I am," he said. "You see, I promised XO Mueller that we would spend some . . . personal time together."

"Oh." She sounded very quiet.

"Yes, she's . . . a rather intriguing woman. I never interacted with her much back on the *Excalibur*, but here . . ."

"Well, by all means," Robin said, "I wouldn't want to keep you from that. It sounds very . . . stimulating . . . intellectually."

"I think it might be." He hesitated. There seemed to be something else that should be said here, but he wasn't entirely certain what that might be. "Do you . . . wish to come along? To join our . . . discussions?"

"Oh, no, no. No, no, no," she said with a laugh that was just ever so slightly tinged with bitterness. "No, I don't think that will be necessary. I don't think I'd exactly fit in . . . in all honesty. That is what we're trying to be, right? Honest with each other?"

"Well . . . yes." He looked at her askance. "Robin . . . is there anything else you wanted to say . . . ?"

"No, not at all," she said, heading quickly for the door. "Go. Have fun with Mueller. I'm sure it'll be very entertaining for both of you. As for me, there's only so much honesty I can take in one day." And she was out the door before he could stop her.

EXCALIBUR

i.

CALHOUN COULD NOT RECALL a time when the atmosphere in the conference lounge was so uneasy. There had been any number of times that they'd been dealing with potentially hostile beings with whom they had been forced by circumstances to work with peacefully. Calhoun had faced individuals whom he had wanted to kill, or who had wanted to kill him, or both. He had sat across the table from people who possessed weaponry or vessels that were capable of blowing the *Excalibur* to scrap metal.

In all those instances, however, he had been backed up by a crew with a united purpose: to pull together and get the job done. Even when he and Shelby had been at their most fractious, he had always known she would ultimately be there for him. And even when there were occasions that she one hundred percent disagreed with him, when they were in front of the crew, she had always been consistently supportive . . . most of the time.

But the situation with which he was faced now was unique in his experience.

He was seated in his customary spot at the far end of the table, and at the opposite end was a being of such phenomenal power that she had been able to stop the ship dead in space. Yet she was attired in a manner more appropriate for more than a millennia ago. Not only that, but she was leaning on the arm of Mark McHenry. She had insisted he pull his chair over and sit right next to her, and she had then looped her arm around his in a manner that could only be described as possessive. She rested her head on his shoulder, looking charmingly girlish in a way, if she hadn't been capable of crushing the ship with a thought.

Soleta, Kebron, Burgoyne, and Selar were also present. The two Vulcans were making absolutely no attempt to hide their priorities: Soleta was taking scientific energy readings off her, while Selar was studying the readouts from a medical tricorder. The woman calling herself Artemis didn't seem to notice . . . or, if she did, she certainly didn't appear to care. She just sat there with a small smirk, as if to say that no matter what anyone else said or did, she was secure and content in her power over the situation.

Kebron sat there, rock steady . . . although Calhoun was concerned that Kebron had been hurt. There appeared to be flakes of skin falling away from around his throat (or lack of throat, as the case may be). That concerned Calhoun, since Kebron's hide had always seemed more or less impenetrable. Although Kebron had been hammered by Artemis' attack, it didn't seem so catastrophic that he would have been badly injured.

Still, the skin irritation didn't appear infected (whatever a Brikar infection might look like). And the skin beneath was the same color as Kebron's original hue. So maybe it wasn't so bad. What was more disturbing, though, was the way that Kebron was looking at McHenry. He wasn't just watching him carefully; he was glowering at him. One of Kebron's greatest strengths had always been his relative unflappability. He'd been a virtual engine of destruction when the situation had called for it, but he never allowed his passions to color his actions. For whatever reason, he was taking this McHenry situation personally. That could prove dangerous, and he realized he might have to take Kebron aside and speak to him privately.

Burgoyne seemed rather focused on McHenry as well, appearing sympathetic to his obvious discomfort. Immediately Calhoun realized why: Burgoyne and McHenry had been involved at one point. Although Burgoyne was most definitely, and happily, with Dr. Selar now, nevertheless there still might have been some old feelings left rattling about in Burgoyne's mind.

"We need to get several things sorted out," Calhoun said slowly, "before we go any further. First: The assault on my bridge crew . . ."

"You assaulted Marcus," she replied.

There were blank looks.

"That would be me," sighed McHenry.

" '*Marcus?*' "

"Don't start, Burgy."

Artemis ruffled her fingers through McHenry's hair. He flinched away slightly at it. "Now, of course, naughty Marcus was actually trying to get away from me. Trying to take this vessel and send it in the other direction. Naturally I didn't approve of his actions. But on the other hand, I disliked the way you were treating him . . . and so I stepped in." Then she looked at them, glowering, and for a moment Calhoun felt as if storm energies were gathering in the room. But just as quickly, they passed, and she simply concluded mildly, "I do not suggest," and she fired a very specific, and warning, look to Kebron, "that you try such things again."

Kebron said nothing.

"Second," Calhoun resumed speaking, "you have released my ship?"

"Of course we have, Captain," said Artemis. Her voice was deep and throaty, and also maddeningly attractive. She spoke with an airy confidence, and worse, she spoke like someone who had the power to back up that confidence. "We have no reason to continue to hold it. After all, if we are so inclined, we can recapture it at any time."

"We?" Burgoyne asked, which was exactly what was going through Calhoun's mind.

"Yes. 'We.' " She smiled ingratiatingly. "Certainly you did not think I came alone."

Soleta lowered her tricorder and, placing it on the table, interlaced her fingers. "It might not seem an unreasonable surmise," she said. "After all . . . your twin brother contended that he was alone."

Artemis was appreciatively startled by Soleta's remark. She released her hold on McHenry's arm and placed her full attention on Soleta. "You know of him? You know of Apollo?"

"It was not a difficult incident to research," Soleta said, eyebrow raised. Across from her, Selar was still studying her medical tricorder. Every so often she shook her head slightly as if she could not give credence to what she was seeing. "When one asks the computer to check all incidents of Federation vessels coming into contact with Greek gods, there is—believe it or not—a very short list. To be specific: There was exactly one instance, logged by Captain—"

"Kirk," Calhoun said immediately. "James T. Kirk."

All eyes turned to him. "That's right, Captain," said Soleta. "You also researched—?"

"No. But I remember Jellico mentioning the incident some time ago. It was his opinion," Calhoun said levelly, "that Kirk's log entries regarding his encounters with Apollo were . . . dubious. How like Kirk to wait the better part of a century in order to have the last laugh."

"Kirk would have been a safe bet in any event," said Burgoyne. "Did you ever read his entries in comparison to other vessels? I did. On any given stardate you would have Captain Smith saying, 'Mapped a new star today,' and Captain Jones writing, 'Brought an ambassador to negotiate a peace treaty,' and Captain Kirk would be saying, 'Fought a giant amoeba that was going to eat a star system.' It was insane."

"Thank you for the history lesson," Selar said sharply, lowering her tricorder long enough to glance at her mate.

"The point is," Calhoun said, "yes, we do know of your brother, thanks to the encounter on—"

"Stardate 3468.1," spoke up Soleta. "And on that occasion, Apollo stated that he was the last of a race of beings who had come to Earth millennia ago and put themselves across as gods to the inhabitants of the time. He endeavored to force the crew of the *Enterprise* to worship him in a manner similar to their ancestors."

"I assume the request did not go over well," Burgoyne said.

"You assume correctly," said Soleta.

"It was . . . a tragic situation," Artemis spoke up. A slight bit of her high-handedness seemed to be gone as she spoke of that long-ago encounter. "My brother . . . of all of us, he was the most worshipped. Even more so than Zeus. He was the god of the sun, the god of the prognostication. Humans were devoted to him. All he desired from those . . . those ingrates on the *Enterprise,* was that they attend him in the way that their ancestors had. If he had come to you—if he had requested that you bend knee to him in the manner that your ancestors had—what would *you* have said?"

"They weren't my ancestors," said Calhoun immediately.

"Not mine." "Nor mine," Soleta and Selar told her. This was promptly followed by "Count me out," from Burgoyne, and a grunt acknowledging the obvious from Kebron.

"My my." Artemis seemed amused by the revelation. "Perhaps they're making humans of less sturdy stuff nowadays."

Soleta did not appear the least bit amused. "According to log entries, Apollo claimed that he was the last of his kind. That the rest of you had 'spread yourselves upon the winds' and were carried away. Was he deluded? Lying? Or are you lying?"

Artemis fixed a glare upon Soleta, even though the edges of her mouth were upturned in what could barely be called a smile. Calhoun made a mental note that problems between this "Artemis" and Soleta could likely be considerable. "You," Artemis said to Soleta, "remind me somewhat of Pan. But Pan was a bore. I never liked him much."

"Your opinion," Soleta replied, "might be of concern to me if my job were to provide you with entertainment."

"The day is young," said Artemis, the non-smile widening. "You may yet provide some."

"All right, that's enough," Calhoun said with sufficient sharpness to snap Artemis' attention over to him. She looked him up and down, obviously trying to size him up, get a feeling for the type of man he was. Calhoun was not especially interested in giving her the time to do so. He was already viewing her as a potential opponent, and as such he considered it necessary to keep her off balance as much as he possibly could. He didn't have much choice in the matter; he was still sensing the fractured relationship between his own crew, and he certainly did not need to have things aggravated. "I will not have my people threatened, Artemis."

"Nor was I threatening them," she said mildly.

"Then I would be most obliged if you would answer Lieutenant Soleta's question."

Artemis nodded slowly. She now wasn't sitting next to McHenry at all. It was almost as if she'd forgotten that he was there. "Very well," she said, even more softly, less officiously than before. "You see, one of my provinces is truth above all . . . and in the spirit of that, I suppose I owe you the truth.

"My brother was not mad . . . not in the traditional sense, the sense that you would understand. But he was desperate . . . and despondent. As I told you, he had the most worshippers, so the loss of them as your people 'matured' hit him the hardest. He would sit there in his home on Pollux IV, brooding and frustrated. Believe it or not, Captain—all of you—my people truly did have other interests to pursue. There is a galaxy of life out there, and many ways for our people to divert ourselves."

"Your people. What precisely are 'your people'?" asked Soleta.

That seemed to perk Artemis up as she warmed to the subject. "The name we use for ourselves . . . you would not be able to pronounce it. Think of us simply as 'the Beings.' "

"And you formed the basis for Greco-Roman myths?"

"More than that, actually, my dear captain. My beloved brother was actually somewhat modest. Greek, Roman, Egyptian, Norse . . . our people, my people, were the basis for all of them. Some even 'played' multiple roles. For instance, we have one among our number: Loki. Perhaps you have heard of him."

Soleta nodded. "A giant and a shapeshifter in Norse mythology. Associated with trickery."

"Yes. Except the frozen north truly was frozen, and Loki enjoyed getting away from that territory during the height of winter. So at those times he would roam the American West. There he became known as the coyote god. He adopted other personas in other regions. Perhaps I will introduce you. I suspect you might well get along with one another . . . for I believe, Captain, that you can be a very tricky man."

"I prefer the term 'resourceful.' "

"As you wish," she said lazily. She rose from her chair and began to walk in leisurely fashion around the conference lounge. She didn't appear to walk so much as glide, each move suffused with sensuality. Calhoun found it impossible to tear his gaze away from her looks. There was something incredibly captivating about her beauty . . . and yet, although he wasn't certain why, it seemed . . . off somehow.

"In any event, my beloved brother always had an appreciation for the . . . dramatic, shall we say. He told your Captain Kirk heart-wrenching tales of how we," and she said it in a breathless manner to heighten the drama, draping her arm across her forehead like a bad actress, "how each of us, despondent over not being worshipped, spread ourselves onto the winds of nothingness and vanished."

"And that wasn't true?" asked Calhoun.

She dropped the overacting poise and smiled. "It was true as far as it went. We did depart. But it wasn't out of ennui or depression. We were just tired of Apollo. Of his endless moping about and waiting for humanity to climb into space-going vessels and come out and find us again. Earth was an entertaining dalliance, to be sure, but hardly the be-all and end-all of an immortal being's soul. Let's be realistic, after all. We moved on to our business . . . and left Apollo to his. Ultimately, he chose the way out that he had originally ascribed to us. That was his choice. I . . ." She hesitated, and for a moment her pomposity wavered. "I . . . do miss him. I wish he had not allowed himself to dissipate. But it was his choice, and I am afraid I have no option before me save to accept it."

"You are too perfect," Selar said abruptly.

Artemis turned to face her, her head cocked slightly as if in thought. "How charming for you to say that."

"I mean that literally," said Selar, snapping closed her medical tricorder. "Your face, your body, are perfectly symmetrical. That does not exist in nature. There are always some minor variances. But not in your physiognomy. The left side of your face is identical to the right; the rest of your body follows suit, as near as I can determine. It suggests that what we are seeing of you . . . is a construct of some sort. Not your real appearance."

Calhoun noticed Soleta appearing to react to that statement, as if it crystallized something she was already pondering. But Artemis, for her part, only seemed amused as she looked Selar up and down.

"My 'real appearance.' As if embellishing one's appearance is somehow limited to me. Your 'real appearance,' Dr. Selar, is obscured by carefully groomed hair . . . by makeup . . . by clothing. I do not see you volunteering to appear relatively naked and honest to your fellow crewmen. Nor do you see me carping about that decision. If you, a mortal, are to be allowed your indulgences, then please be so kind as to allow a goddess hers."

"You," Selar replied, looking unimpressed, "are not a goddess."

"Met many for comparison, have you?"

Suddenly Selar's tricorder was no longer in her hand, but instead in Artemis'. She was turning it over and over, studying it with great interest. Immediately the doctor started to get up from her chair to take it back, but Calhoun stopped her with a crisp, "Sit down, Doctor. Artemis . . . return that to Dr. Selar. Now."

McHenry stiffened, as if concerned that Artemis was going to lash out at Calhoun for the tone of his voice. Instead Artemis simply smiled . . . and then her hands flexed. There was a sharp crack, a crumbling, and just like that the tricorder was shattered shards in her palms. Bringing her hands forward carefully, she allowed the pieces to slide out from between them, collecting as a small pile of useless rubble on the table in front of Selar. "As you wish, Captain," she said, looking quite pleased with herself.

"That was unnecessary," Calhoun said.

She ignored him and continued speaking as if Selar had never interrupted her. "I will admit that Apollo's decision hit all of us quite hard. I'll never forget his pathetic, tragic 'Take me' as he allowed himself to discorporate. A number of our kind were so distraught by his decision that they followed suit. I very seriously considered it."

"Followed suit. Died, you mean."

"Captain," she laughed, "we cannot die. We are creatures of energy. So are all creatures, really, except to much lesser degrees. We can, if we are so inclined, and if we tire of our existence, discorporate ourselves as Apollo did. Spread ourselves so thin that we lose consciousness of ourselves, awareness of our very being. We become . . . one with the universe, for lack of a less pretentious phrase. Apollo chose that route. So did some others. Ultimately," and she stopped walking nearby McHenry, resting a hand on the back of his neck. "I opted to go on. As did Ra, Anubis, Thor, Loki, Baldur . . . and some . . . others . . ."

The way she hesitated immediately fired Calhoun's suspicions. She was keeping something back. He wasn't sure what, though. It might be nothing . . . or it might be something that could be tremendously useful. He decided that now was the time to press the matter. "All right," he said abruptly. "You got our attention. With those energy emissions in this sector, you drew us here. I assume that was your goal."

"All along, yes."

"Why? What do you want?"

"Why, Captain . . . isn't it obvious?" She smiled, leaned down and kissed McHenry on the cheek. "We want our beloved Marcus."

" 'Beloved'?" McHenry said, turning to look up at her. "Artemis, in case you've forgotten, our association ended previously because you tried to kill me!"

"A trifling matter," she sniffed, waving her hand domineeringly. "A misunderstanding, long forgotten."

"Not by me! You don't forget it when a goddess tries to kill you. Would you forget something like that, Captain?" asked McHenry.

"I doubt it would readily slip my mind," Calhoun admitted. "But why Marcus . . . McHenry? Why would he be of interest to you?"

Artemis didn't answer immediately. Instead she looked to McHenry, her perfect arms folded across her equally perfect breasts. "Because," she said simply, "Marcus is my lover. What woman, goddess or no, is not deserving of her lover."

"My understanding," said Soleta dryly, "is that Artemis was a virgin goddess, disdaining such things as physical love."

She flashed her perfect teeth. "That's why they call it 'myth,' dear. Don't believe *everything* you read."

"But why McHenry?" Burgoyne said. "What is there about him, of all people, that would attract a goddess to him? I mean, he's . . . he's just McHenry . . ."

"Hey!" snapped McHenry. "I never heard any complaints from *you*, Burgy."

"It's not about *that*—"

"All right, that's enough," said Calhoun. "It's a fair question. A tactless one," he acknowledged, seeing McHenry's expression, "but a fair question nonetheless. Why the interest in McHenry?"

There was a pointed silence then. "Marcus," said Artemis, nudging his shoulder, "I believe your captain asked you a question."

McHenry looked at her in a manner that was hardly loving. Then he studied the faces of all those around him. Calhoun saw that they were regarding McHenry in a manner that was more evocative of studying some sort of unusual microorganism than someone who had served faithfully at their sides.

When he did finally speak, he didn't sound remotely like the McHenry that Calhoun had known for so long. His voice was flat and sad and filled with foreboding, as if he knew that his next words would change, for all time, the way that others perceived him. "Soleta," he said slowly, "when you were researching the Kirk encounter with Apollo . . . did you happen to come across the name of Carolyn Palamas?"

Soleta nodded. "An archaeologist and anthropologist on the *Enterprise*. According to the log description, Apollo became somewhat enamored of her. Apparently . . . too enamored."

"Meaning?" asked Calhoun, although he had a funny feeling where this was going.

"The log of the *Enterprise* CMO indicates that Palamas became pregnant as a result of her encounter with Apollo."

"Pregnant?" said Selar. "From the readings I garnered before my tricorder encountered its mishap," and she gave a severe look to Artemis . . . who clearly could not have cared less . . . before continuing, "if Apollo's physical makeup was anything like his sister's, then such a thing should not have been possible."

"I am not arguing with you, Doctor. I am simply relaying a log entry from a century ago. The doctor voiced some concern, claiming that his sickbay was not designed for delivering infant gods. As it happened, he needn't have worried. Palamas transferred off the ship during her first trimester. There's no further log entry on her. I could do further research . . ."

But then McHenry began to speak. He did so very slowly and deliberately, as if he were addressing them from outside himself. "Carolyn Palamas took an assignment in an archaeological dig on Camus II. She gave birth to the child there—a little girl, named Athena, as a matter of fact. Feeling that a dig was no place to raise a child, Athena was sent to live with Carolyn's sister while Carolyn intended to finish out the dig assignment and then resign from Starfleet. Instead, there was some . . . unpleasantness on Camus II some months later, and all but two people at the dig site died. Carolyn was not one of the two survivors, unfortunately.

"Athena was subject to scrutiny from Starfleet medical for quite some time, but she displayed no . . . godly attributes, shall we say," continued McHenry. "They ultimately decided that whatever powers or abilities Apollo may have possessed, they were not transferred to his daughter."

At that, Artemis laughed. "Foolishness," she said with disdain. "As if any woman could experience the godhead and not be forever changed."

As if she hadn't spoken, McHenry went on in that same distant manner. "Athena grew up . . . had a child, another little girl . . . who grew up, had a daughter of her own, who in turn had a lovely daughter by the name of Sheila. All girls, as you may have noticed, and all only children. All of them normal . . . at least, on the surface. And then Sheila gave birth to a little boy, whom she named," and he winced, "Marcus. And Marcus, he had a Y chromosome, which was something that his mother and grandmother and great-grandmother and great-great-grandmother didn't have. And guess what was carried on that Y chromosome?"

"The godhead," said Calhoun, who suddenly felt an impulse to back out of the room very slowly, relocate the entire crew to the rear of the ship, and fire the saucer section with McHenry on it off into space. He quickly put it out of his mind, since naturally he wasn't serious about it . . . plus, for all he knew, Artemis or McHenry could read his mind, and he didn't want them to perceive him as actively plotting against them.

"The godhead," McHenry sighed.

Soleta leaned forward, and despite her Vulcan reserve, there was no hiding the incredulity on her face. Calhoun wasn't surprised; she'd come up through the Academy with McHenry. Suddenly she was discovering that her classmate was not remotely who—or even what—she had always thought. "Mark," she said, startled into informality, "are you saying that . . . that you have the powers of Apollo? Of a god?"

"No, no . . . well . . . not exactly . . . I mean, not bolts of energy and things like that . . ." He was sounding more and more uncomfortable with the whole discussion. "Keep in mind, there were four generations between myself and my . . . my great-great-great-grandfather. Things changed . . . got watered down . . . or . . . well . . ."

"We knew at an early age that he was special," said Artemis. She had now taken her seat once more, taking McHenry's hand in hers. "I took a particular interest in him. I knew he had potential. I knew that, once he was old enough, he would be mine."

"That," noted Selar, "is a somewhat incestuous relationship, you understand. According to what you are telling us, he is a direct descendant of your own sibling."

"Zeus and Hera were brother and sister, offspring of the Titans Chronus and Rhea," Artemis noted. "So what would your point be, precisely?"

McHenry stepped in before Selar could reply. "When

she first showed up, I was young . . . three, fours years old, something like that. I saw her. No one else did."

"He called me 'Missy' instead of Artemis. Wasn't that sweet?"

"Adorable," rumbled Kebron.

"There were some . . . problems when I got a bit older," McHenry said, looking even more uncomfortable than he did before, if such a thing were possible. "My father proved . . . unable to handle the situation, after one particular incident. He left when I was eight. My mother . . . she stayed, but . . . well . . . she never hugged me. Or touched me. Or came near me if she could help it."

"What happened to cause that?"

"If it's all the same to you, Captain . . . I'd rather not go into it," said McHenry. Calhoun paused a moment, then nodded. "In any event, I got older . . . and as I got older, Artemis became a greater and greater force in my life. We became . . ." He cleared his throat. ". . . friendly . . . to understate it . . ."

"A gross understatement," Artemis said. Calhoun saw Burgoyne make a face of barely repressed disgust.

"However, in later years . . . we had a falling-out. I had decided to head off to Starfleet Academy, and Artemis strongly disagreed. We had an argument. Big argument. She tried to kill me . . ."

"My loving Marcus," she said, running a finger under his chin, "if I had been trying to kill you, you would be dead. Your recollection of your youth distorts matters out of all proportion."

"All proportion!" McHenry responded. "You *blew up my house!*"

"What matter such mundane trappings to beings such as we?"

"I'm not one of you! I don't care what you say! For one thing, I'm not crazy enough and I'm not dangerous enough!"

"Don't underestimate yourself," Kebron said.

Calhoun did not need to hear comments such as that. "Save it, Lieutenant. McHenry . . . what did you have a 'falling-out' about?"

"Artemis felt as if I was not living up to my 'full potential' by dedicating my life to Starfleet."

"And what would full potential be?"

"Why," she said, as if it should have been the most self-evident thing in the world, "to act as an intermediary, of course."

There were puzzled looks from all around. "A what?" asked Calhoun.

"An intermediary," Artemis repeated, as if the world were in some sort of alien tongue. "A diplomatic go-between for ourselves and the rest of the Federation. You see, one of our number . . . one of our greatest, the mighty Zeus himself . . . has foreseen that we are going to help your Federation achieve a golden age."

"A golden age. I see."

"You sound skeptical."

Calhoun leaned back in his chair. "I am, to be candid. Some of the greatest tyrants and despots in history have announced that their intention is to make things far better than they were."

"Which makes sense," said Burgoyne. "Who is going to attract followers by announcing that they're going to subjugate everyone except a select handful, or run their resources and economies into the ground?"

"Nevertheless, Zeus has foreseen it."

"And why is Zeus not here, then?"

"Because *I* am," Artemis said easily, once again adopting a tone that indicated to Calhoun there were things she was not saying. "However, our concern was that if we simply stepped in, with all our power and presence and majesty, your reaction would not be what we desired it to be. Some of you would accept . . . yes. But others, such as the notorious Kirk did, would attempt to dismiss us out of hand. We have no desire to be dismissed. It will benefit neither you nor us. So it was our desire to have a spokesman for us . . . one who straddled both worlds. My brethren and I decided it was only fitting that Marcus, the last descendant of my beloved brother, be that spokesman."

"Why?" It was Kebron who had spoken.

She looked at him, clearly finding him to be the most curious-looking of the motley assortment before her. "Why what, large one?"

"Why do you care? About us? About this golden age? What . . . is in it for you?" he said.

Artemis appeared dismayed that he even had to ask. "Why . . . is it not evident?"

"Not readily," admitted Calhoun.

She slapped her hands on the table in dismay. "Is chivalry completely dead in your society? Is charity, loving-kindness, truly a thing of the past? We wish to help you . . . because we care about humanity. We were there, after all, for when it made its first forays into culture . . . the arts . . . theater . . . elevated thought. Those things occurred largely because we were there to facilitate it. Think what could be achieved now!"

"As others have noted," Calhoun said, "there's no one in this room who is actually a human being with the exception of Lieutenant McHenry . . ."

"Jury is still out on that," mumbled Kebron.

Calhoun ignored the comment and continued, ". . . and all of our races—Xenexians, Vulcans, Brikars, Hermats—we all managed to reach the same levels of 'civilization' as humanity achieved without the help of such elevated and lofty beings as yourselves."

And Artemis leaned forward, fixing her devastating eyes upon Calhoun, and she said very softly, "Are you *quite* certain of that? Would you be willing to bet your life on that assumption? Because you might be surprised at the outcome."

Calhoun could think of nothing to say to that. He found that lack of response disturbing.

"We wish to help," continued Artemis, "because that is what we do. We are an altruistic race. We have seen how far the Federation has come . . . but we also are able to perceive that you have all come just so far, but will be able to proceed no further. You have leveled off, as it were. Reached a sort of evolutionary plateau in your collective development as a species, as a society. We are prepared to help you now to reach the next level. I do not pretend," she laughed, "that you will be able to reach our level. The level of a race so advanced that—"

"That your most famous member committed suicide since he lacked adulation from others," Kebron said.

Calhoun felt it again . . . that same dangerous sizzling in the air, as if power were being forcibly contained, lest it lash out in all directions. Like a gathering storm, Artemis turned and looked at Kebron.

"If you say another insulting word about my brother," she said, in a voice flat and devoid of emotion, "I will hurt you. I will hurt you more than you thought possible. I will hurt you in ways you cannot imagine. And if you should ever have a loved one . . . I will hurt her. Children? I will hurt them. Their children? They will be hurt as well. Insult Apollo, and on your deathbed you will look back to this moment to consider the day that you single-handedly brought a curse down upon your house. Consider your next observation wisely, Brikar, for the well-being of those not yet born who will bear your name hinges upon it."

Kebron said nothing.

"You are wise beyond your years," Artemis informed him.

Calhoun sensed the energy buildup subsiding, but was still not pleased about what had just occurred. "I do not appreciate having my officers threatened," he said.

"Then tell them they would be well-advised to consider their words carefully when addressing the Beings," she said. She looked around the table at them with an attitude of pure smug superiority. "In some ways, Captain, we have grown closer, your species and I. Early humanity—primitive by any standards—could only frame us as gods in their minds. Since science was a barely spawned discipline, there were no scientific means to explain us. We were, to them, beings of magic: inexplicable, incomprehensible. Now, though, you have a closer understanding of who and what we are. That is acceptable as far as it goes. But there is the old saying, Captain, that a little knowledge is a dangerous thing. Do not for a moment think that, because you know us better, you know us completely. Do not allow familiarity to breed contempt, for I assure you that if you act in a manner with me and my kin that is overfamiliar, it will instead breed disaster. Considering what we are capable of offering you, that would be most unfortunate."

"Artemis," said McHenry, "this is ridiculous. How can you possibly think to bring about this 'golden age' you keep talking about? We meet about it for the first time and already you're threatening people. You're threatening my friends."

"I was your friend before any of these people knew you, Marcus," she reminded him, her eyes flashing. "They insulted me. Certainly that must count for something." Then she touched him once more on the shoulder, and he jumped slightly as if there was electricity in her fingertips. "As for how the golden age will come about, have you forgotten? That will be your job. To act as intermediary on our behalf, to set the stage for us. You will be our avatar, our standard-bearer, our herald. You will be the angel of light who will guide your people through the night to the new dawn."

"Very high-flown and impressive words," Calhoun said. "So tell me, Mr. McHenry: Are you accepting this offer? Apparently you've had some time to dwell on it:

since before Starfleet Academy, if we're to believe Artemis. Is that what you want to do with the rest of your life? Serve as spokesman for the Beings?"

All eyes were now upon McHenry. He actually seemed to be squirming in his seat, and Calhoun couldn't help but feel sorry for him. McHenry was always so laid-back, so comfortable, so uncaring about pressures that were heaped upon him. It was as if he went through life completely unfazed by anything that might be tossed at him. It was depressing to see him now, coming across as . . . as . . .

Mortal. The word came unbidden to Calhoun's thoughts. That was it, really. He seemed "merely" mortal in his concerns, in his discomfort.

Artemis seemed most interested of all in what he was going to say next. She waited expectantly, one eyebrow cocked.

"I . . . think I'll have to get back to you on that, Captain," McHenry finally said. He looked at Artemis. "To both of you."

Calhoun watched her reaction very carefully. She seemed to be wrestling with a response that would be a less than polite one . . . even a dangerous one. But then Artemis took control of herself, smiled, and said, "Very well, Marcus. I will respect your wishes. Take all the time you need . . ."

"Thank you . . ."

". . . before deciding that you will do our bidding."

And with that, Artemis turned and walked right through the bulkhead. She didn't damage it in any way; she just passed through it as if it wasn't there.

"Somehow," Burgoyne ventured, "I don't think she quite comprehended the subtlety of 'I'll get back to you.' "

ii.

McHenry had never felt more miserable in his entire life. And somehow, he had known it would be coming.

He lay stretched out on a med table, in the process of being examined by every medical scanner known to Federation science. Med techs were hovering over him like embers dancing around the top of a fire, moving with remarkable grace and coordination so as not to bang into each other going about their business.

The thing that was most upsetting to McHenry was that none of them were looking at him. At least, none of them were looking him in the eyes. Every so often he would say something that he really thought sounded at least halfway amusing. His response would be grunts or a strained smile or—if someone was feeling truly expansive—a "Really?" or "How interesting!"

But he knew. He knew what it was.

They were afraid of him.

On one level, he could understand it. These people had served with him and, all this time, had thought him one thing. Now they were having to consider him something else, and the big problem was that they didn't know what that "something else" was. The unknown had replaced the known quantity. They had no idea what he was capable of, and those aspects of his personality, which had once been looked upon as simple quirks or curiosities, were now considered to be, possibly, something deeper and more dangerous. As a result they handled him as if he was a time bomb or grenade, capable of going off at any moment and causing all manner of damage.

On another level, though . . . it hurt. He knew it shouldn't, but it did. After all, if they were just meeting him for the first time, there would be no concern on their part. He would be simply another life-form, another being, and certainly as med techs in Starfleet they had encountered all kinds in all different places. The fact that they were familiar with him should have put them more at their ease, not less. He was, in effect, being penalized for being their friend, coworker, and crewmate. No matter how much he dwelt on it, he couldn't make it feel right in his head.

He craned his neck around and saw that Captain Calhoun, Soleta, and Selar were in conference in Selar's office. He knew that either he or Artemis or both were the subject of discussion, and it irked him more than he could say. McHenry was not someone who customarily felt annoyed. His entire approach to life was always extremely relaxed. It took a lot to upset him or put him out of sorts, and since he was unaccustomed to it, he wasn't sure how to handle such roiling emotions once he reached that point.

So he went with his instinct.

McHenry abruptly sat up, startling one of the med techs who had been leaning close to him, trying to get some new damned readings or another. Dr. Maxwell, who had been overseeing the study, said patiently, "Lieutenant . . . this will go much more smoothly if you're lying down . . ."

"Get out of my way," said McHenry, swinging his legs over the edge of the table. He stared with quiet defiance into Maxwell's eyes.

All the med techs looked at one another uneasily. Maxwell appeared to be frozen to the spot. Then he forced a ready smile and said, "All right," and stepped aside.

They were afraid of him.

Damn, they *were* afraid. It was a feeling that was both depressing and liberating all at the same time, because McHenry didn't know what to do . . . but also knew that whatever he did choose to do, he could do with impunity.

He stepped down onto the floor and started across sickbay. It seemed as if the entirety of sickbay had been devoted to studying him, for everyone was looking at readings and output from the tests they'd been conducting. "Here I am, in the flesh," he said. He spread his arms to either side and turned slowly, so they could all get a good look at him. "On display for all to see. Why study readouts and reports when you can get the real thing?"

"McHenry!"

It was Calhoun, standing in the doorway of Selar's office. The two Vulcans were standing directly behind him. "McHenry . . . you said you would cooperate with the examinations," he reminded him.

"I changed my mind, Captain," he said, sounding almost giddy. "We demigods can do that, y'know. We put the 'mercury' in 'mercurial.' "

He didn't know what Calhoun was going to say. Whether the captain would shout at him or endeavor to shove him into the brig or what. But he was astounded to see that Calhoun's expression softened into something akin to understanding. "All right, son," he said, and instantly McHenry knew that he wasn't talking in the same "I'll do what you want, just don't hurt me" manner that Maxwell had been speaking with. He really seemed as if he was sympathetic to what McHenry was going through . . . which was fortunate, since McHenry's thoughts were in such turmoil that he was having trouble comprehending it all himself. "If you say it's over, it's over. Come in here. We have some things to discuss with you anyway."

McHenry sagged with visible relief, and walked into Selar's office. The clear door slid shut behind them, giving them privacy. There were only two chairs facing Selar's desk, but Calhoun gestured to McHenry that he should occupy the one that Calhoun had been sitting in. "Captain, no . . . protocol requires . . ."

"Screw protocol," Calhoun said amiably. "Something tells me you need it more than I do."

"True enough," admitted McHenry, and he sat. He could see that all the med techs out in sickbay were staring into the office . . . until Selar fired them a look that immediately sent them back to other duties.

"The first thing you have to realize, Mark . . . is that you've done nothing wrong," Calhoun said. He had folded his arms and was leaning against the wall of Selar's office. "We know now that you were not responsible for the assault on the bridge crew. The only thing you're guilty of is changing course without authorization. Considering the stress of the moment and the particular personal circumstances involved, I think we can let that one slide."

"Thank you, Captain," he said gratefully.

"What we've been discussing now is your friend, Artemis—"

" 'Friend' might be too strong a word."

"Were you her lover?" inquired Soleta. She asked the question with such deadpan detachment that it was impossible to perceive any prurient interest to the question. She could not have been more dispassionate if she'd informed McHenry that he could probably use a haircut.

McHenry drummed his hands uncomfortably on the armrest. "Only in the sense that we had sex . . ." he said.

"I see," Dr. Selar now spoke up. "So 'friend' might be too strong a word; however, 'passing acquaintance' would appear to understate the relationship."

"All right, that's enough," said Calhoun, obviously seeing McHenry's discomfort. "The thing upon which we can all agree is that McHenry has a vested interest in this. I think we owe it to him to tell him what we've found."

"Before you tell me that . . . tell me . . . about me," McHenry said slowly.

Selar leveled her gaze upon him. "You mean . . . are you human?"

"Basically, yes."

"Don't you know?" asked Soleta.

He felt as if he were shrinking into the chair. "I don't

know," he admitted. "I'm not sure I know anything anymore."

Selar was studying her computer screen, assessing what he could only assume to be the test results that had been compiled about him. "You are being ridiculous, Lieutenant," she said with the utter lack of bedside manner for which she had become so well known. "Of course you are human. Like any Starfleet officer, you have been subjected to numerous physicals. Do you think for even a moment that if you were not human, Starfleet would have somehow missed it?"

"All right. But then why the head-to-toe, inside-out study now?"

"To see if Starfleet somehow missed it," Calhoun told him.

Selar didn't look any too pleased with the captain's explanation. "To see," she said with forced patience, "if your current physical makeup is consistent with previous examinations. To see if she altered or affected you in some way. Thus far, according to these results—which would be more complete if you had been good enough to remain where you are," she added pointedly, "according to these, the answer would seem to be no. You remain, Lieutenant, a rather unremarkable specimen."

McHenry let out a sigh of relief so pronounced that he looked as if he were deflating. "That is so good to know," he said. "I . . . I don't know what I would have done if I'd found out I wasn't . . . you know . . . human."

"Yes, how *ever* would one cope with the tragic status

of not being human," Selar said in a tone of voice so lacerating that McHenry could practically feel the skin being peeled from his body. "I certainly know my life is the emptier for it."

"Sarcasm is hardly necessary, Doctor," Soleta said. "I understand what McHenry is saying. It would be as if one had thought for a time that one was Vulcan . . . and then discovered oneself to be part Romulan. Certainly such a self-discovery would be disorienting, to say the least . . . correct?"

Selar's lips thinned in response to Soleta's comment. She seemed rather irked by it, although McHenry couldn't discern why. Then she said coolly, "Point taken, Soleta. My . . . apologies if I seemed unsympathetic, Mr. McHenry."

" 'S all right," he assured her. "If you started seeming sympathetic about things, they'd probably be doing a thorough exam on you to make sure you were still you."

It was hard for McHenry to be sure, but it looked as if Calhoun was endeavoring to stifle a laugh. But it happened so fleetingly that he couldn't be sure, and then Calhoun said—all business—"What we find curious are the differences in terms of power level between Artemis and Apollo. Soleta—?" he prompted her.

"According to the *Enterprise* logs," Soleta readily continued, "Apollo's physiology was actually remarkably humanoid . . . something that should not be too surprising, I suppose, when one considers that he was able to crossbreed with a human. However, the CMO's records stated that Apollo had some sort of extra organ in his chest . . . one that enabled him to channel energy through himself and provide the illusion of godlike powers. He was able to throw bolts of energy, to grow to gargantuan size. But he required a power source . . . one that, in the case of the incident on Pollux IV, he disguised as a temple or shrine. Once the *Enterprise* destroyed the power source, Apollo became effectively helpless . . . although, curiously, he was able to still attain giant size. So he obviously possessed some sort of abilities beyond those provided him by the power source."

"And he never wandered far from his source of power," added Calhoun. "He was able to project it into space in immediate proximity to his world . . . but beyond that, he stayed put. That does not seem to be the case with Artemis."

"No, it's not," McHenry said. "As near as I can tell, she goes where she wants, whenever she wants. I've never noticed any limitations on what she can and can't do. And I'm not sure why that would be."

Soleta leaned forward, fingers interlaced. "Can you find out, Mark?"

"How am I supposed to do that?"

"Here is a thought: You could ask her," said Selar. "And this 'golden age' to which she refers: Do you know what that entails?" When he shook his head, she said, "Ask her that as well."

"This entire situation is too vague, McHenry," Calhoun said. "Our mission was to find the source of these energy emissions. We've done that . . . or rather, it found us. Obviously, however, it's not going to be left there. We need to get a firmer footing on what's happening.

You obviously have some sort of link with her, or she with you. You sensed that she was out there, after all."

"I know," said McHenry slowly. "I just . . . I knew she was there. When I was younger, and she was with me, I . . . I felt a certain way . . . I felt . . ."

"Sexually aroused?"

He gaped at Soleta, whose face remained impassive even as she had made the inquiry. "Soleta . . . is there something you want to talk about?"

"Just making scientific inquiry," she replied.

"Look, never mind how she made me feel," McHenry said, tugging at his collar slightly. "The thing is, you want me to find these things out. But it's not as if I'm in communication with her—"

"You will be," Calhoun said. "I've seen the way she looks at you, acts around you. She'll be back, Mark. And when she is, we need you to find out what you can, in order to help us. Promises of a golden age or no, the woman is a time bomb. What we have to determine is just how large a bomb she is . . . before she goes off."

TRIDENT

i.

KALINDA HAD JUST DECIDED that she liked the Ten-Forward on the *Trident* better than the Team Room of the *Excalibur* when Lieutenant Commander Gleau came hurtling through the air and crashed into her table. Fortunately she had a split second's warning when it happened, and had sufficient presence of mind to snag her drink off the tabletop so Gleau wouldn't spill it. The remains of her pastry, however, were crushed to crumbs.

Up until that point, things had been very pleasant, even convivial. Kalinda had never considered herself to be the most sociable of creatures, and yet felt herself moved to strike up conversations with people as they passed her. One of them had been Gleau himself, some minutes before he'd been transformed into a small projectile.

Radiating charm, he'd sat down at her table and she couldn't help but feel herself drawn to him. It was a most intriguing sensation for her. It made her tingle in areas where she usually did not tingle, and she could have sworn that Gleau was not only aware of the effect he was having upon her, but actually reveled in it.

"What are you eating?" he inquired, pointing at the pastry she had in front of her.

"Oh. This." She held it up. "A woman named Morgan Primus introduced me to them back on the *Excalibur.* It's called a bearclaw. Your food synthesizers can produce them."

"Do you mind if I—?" He gestured toward it.

"Not at all."

He broke off a piece of the bearclaw, chewed it with great delicacy, and licked the crumbs off his lips. There was something remarkably erotic about the way he did all that. "Not bad. Not bad at all." He smiled at her and she returned it immediately. She couldn't have helped herself. If her life had depended upon her frowning in response to his smile, she would have died at that moment.

Gleau had leaned forward and said, with extreme curiosity, "So tell me . . . is it true what I've heard about you?"

"I don't know," said the young Thallonian woman. "What have you heard?"

"That you . . . how shall I put this . . ." Even lost in thought, he was gorgeous. She just couldn't get over it. Finally he said, "Well, no way to put it but straight out, I suppose. I've heard that you've actually communed with . . . well . . ."

"The dead?"

"Yes!" he said chipperly. "Yes, that's exactly it. And I can see by your face that it's a truly absurd notion . . .

totally ridiculous . . . why, you must think me a fool for even bringing it—"

"It's true," said Kalinda.

"Really! You know, I thought it might be." He moved closer to her, waved a waiter over to get a glass of synthehol without taking his eyes off Kalinda. "How did that come about, exactly?"

"I'd . . . rather not discuss it, if it's all right with you," she said softly. "The actual event, and the things that led up to it . . . they're a bit . . ."

"Traumatic?"

She nodded.

He took her chin in his hand, and she felt her toes curling up by themselves. Suddenly she was getting fidgety in her chair and she wasn't sure why. "I fully understand," he said, and she was positive that he did. He seemed the type to whom she could say just about anything, and he would absolutely be on her side, and know exactly what was in her heart when she said it. "It must be terrifying . . . having that sort of unnatural communication . . ."

"Oh, no," she said quickly, anxious to get him to see things the way she did. "No, not at all. It's the most natural thing in the world, actually. People just don't comprehend. Death . . . they think death is the end of existence. It's not. It's simply the beginning of an entirely different *type* of existence. One with its own rules, its own way of . . . of life, I guess, although that's hardly the best way to put it."

"That is extremely fascinating," he said, and at that moment she felt as if there was nowhere in the entirety of the galaxy that she would rather be. That to be the focus of his attention . . . there was nothing better, nor could there ever be anything better. "And I suppose that by having this sort of experience, this ability to comprehend life after death . . . you probably have no fear of death yourself, then."

"Not at all. I mean, it's not something I would readily embrace for myself," she admitted. She looked down at her own drink, trying to imagine what it would be like to be on that other side. "It's an entirely new way of . . . of existing, and I'm somewhat used to the one I've presently got. But when the time comes, sooner or later," and she shrugged, "I'll be ready for it."

"Hopefully it won't come for you for a long, long time yet," he said with conviction. "You know, Kalinda . . ."

"My friends call me Kally."

He smiled a dazzling smile. "Kally, then. You know, Kally, I was thinking, perhaps we might consider—"

There was a sudden clearing of throat behind Gleau, and he turned in his seat and looked up. Standing behind him was the head of security—that oddly proportioned fellow named . . . what was it again? Oh yes . . . Arex. His head seemed higher than it did before, his neck extended, and he was scowling rather fiercely . . . although since he had a fairly low-hanging brow, it wasn't easy to be sure.

"Lieutenant Commander," he said in his warbly voice, "a moment of your time, please."

"Well, Lieutenant, now I wouldn't want to be rude . . ." said Gleau suavely, indicating Kalinda.

"Oh, this won't take long. I'm sure the young lady would be able to excuse us for a brief time."

"Of course," said Kalinda. "I wouldn't want to do anything that would get in the way of the ship running

Kris Nelscott

Walter Mosley

James Sallis

Julie Smith

SCIENCE FICTION

Steven Barnes

Octavia Butler

Samuel Delany

Ntozake Shange

Alice Walker

John Edgar Wideman

smoothly or important things." Then, in a low voice, although she wasn't sure what prompted her to say it, she added, "Don't worry, Gleau. I'll wait right here."

He smiled and cupped her chin once more, and she felt a tingle up and down her spine. "You do that," he smiled, and then got up from his chair. Arex ushered him over to a table a short distance away, and draped his three legs carefully around a chair, sitting as best he could in a seat that was not exactly built for his species. Gleau, by contrast, sat gracefully, crossed his legs at the knees, and regarded Arex with patience, mixed with mild bemusement.

Kalinda calmly sipped her drink, every so often casting a glance at Gleau and Arex's table, hoping that they would wrap up whatever they needed to discuss as briskly as possible. Even though she knew she should not, she tried to pick up bits and pieces of their conversation. She thought she heard the word "Mess" or "More Ess," whatever "ess" might be, being mentioned a number of times. And something about a knack for something, and comments about "easing up on her." At first Arex seemed to be doing most of the talking, but then Gleau started speaking, and he seemed to be getting increasingly angry at what Arex was saying.

And suddenly Gleau was on his feet, and he said, "I don't have to take that from you!" He turned and started to walk away, and one of Arex's arms snared out, fast as a whip, and snagged Gleau's right arm.

"Sit down. We're not through," said Arex, and every eye in the place was on them, but Arex didn't seem to care.

"Oh yes we are!" shouted Gleau, and he tried to shove Arex back. That was a total mistake, because thanks to his tripodial structure, Arex was the single most difficult individual on the ship to throw off balance. Instead, operating purely impulsively, Arex spun Gleau around and then shoved him as hard as he could.

It was, apparently, a little too hard, for Gleau sailed through the air. He smashed into Kalinda's table, Kalinda managing to salvage the drink. The remains of the bearclaw, however, were a total loss.

Gleau rolled off the table, landing just to Kalinda's left. He scrambled to his feet as Arex advanced on him, and other crewmen were now endeavoring to get between the two, to keep them separated and calm things down.

"You're insane, Triexian!" Gleau was shouting, and it wasn't just that he was angrier than Kalinda had ever seen him, because she knew perfectly well that she hadn't known him for all that long. But he was angrier than she would have thought possible for him, considering the utterly placid demeanor he'd been putting forward. "You're insane, and you're going to pay for this! This is not over!"

"I'm telling you to leave M'Ress alone," shot back Arex. *So that's what he'd said! Not "Mess" or "More ess" or similar idiocy! It was Muh-Ress. Probably someone's assumed name.* "If the captain telling you that wasn't sufficient, then perhaps my doing so will be." Yet he was already busy picking up after himself, righting the table that had been knocked over, dusting up the crumbs. He looked apologetically to Kalinda. "Are you all right?"

"I'm . . . I'm fine, I think . . ."

Gleau was stabbing a finger at Arex. "Not over," he

repeated. "Not over at all." Then, gathering up what was left of his battered pride, Gleau stalked out of the room.

There was an uncomfortable silence in the Ten-Forward then. Arex didn't bother looking at anyone else; he was busy cleaning up the mess that had resulted from his altercation with Gleau. Kalinda's initial reaction was to be horrified on Gleau's behalf over what she'd just seen. But as moments, and her first impulses, passed, she found herself wondering just what it was that Gleau could have said or done that would have so incensed the head of security.

She sidled over to Arex. He turned to her and said apologetically, "Again, I'm sorry for disrupting you. Where I come from, walking out the way he was trying to was extremely rude. I suppose I overreacted. Let me get you another of those—whatever that was you were eating."

"A bearclaw." She looked at him with curiosity, because he seemed most amused. "What? That's what it's called: a bearclaw. What did I say—?"

"Nothing. It's funny to me; I doubt it would seem so to you."

Then, in a very low, very quiet voice, she asked, "What did he do? Gleau, I mean."

Arex righted the nearest chair. "Do you have strong feelings for him?" he asked in that high voice of his. "Be honest."

"I . . . I think I do, yes . . . at least, I think I did."

"Well, a friend of mine developed strong feelings for him. But be careful . . . because the feelings you think you have, aren't always yours."

ii.

"I feel that I have been misused, abused, and I want to know what you're going to do about it, Captain!"

Shelby was in her office, which adjoined her private quarters. Despite the fact that she was off duty, she had complied with Gleau's request for a meeting, and had chosen to take it here rather than up in the ready room. Truth to tell, she'd been expecting him, since she'd already heard about the altercation in the Ten-Forward. However, she'd had a long day, which was getting longer by the moment, and so she wasn't especially in the mood to be bellowed at by one of her officers. So when Gleau raised his voice to her, she was on her feet in an instant, eye to eye with the angry Gleau, and she didn't feel the least bit of charm coming off him. He was purely angry, and on one level she couldn't blame him, and on another, she was rapidly reaching a crisis point of frustration. "Sit down, Lieutenant Commander. Now."

He stabbed a finger at her and remained standing. "I blame you for this, Captain."

"Me? I didn't knock you over a table."

"No," he said, his hands on his hips, looking like a defiant gold statue. "But a crew takes its lead from its commanding officer. This 'Oath of Chastity' which you forced upon me . . ."

"Mr. Gleau," she said with forced calm, "if you do not sit down, I will have security come in and force you to sit. And since we now know that our security chief can handle you with little difficulty—"

"You approve of what he did?!"

"No, I do not," Shelby told him firmly. "And Mr. Arex has been dealt with separately."

"Court-martial, I should think, for striking a superior officer."

"There will be no court-martial, and the specifics I took in Arex's case are between him, me, and Starfleet. Now sit the hell down."

He sat, but remained ramrod stiff. "Captain," said Gleau stiffly, "I have given this matter a great deal of thought, and I am seriously considering filing charges, against you, for harassment."

"Really," she said, eyebrow cocked. Shelby began to feel as if the entire thing was spinning off into the realm of the truly insane. "And I have harassed you . . . how?"

"As far as I am concerned," he told her with an air of great wounded dignity, "you have acted in direction violation to General Order Seven."

Shelby frowned. "When the hell did I visit Talos IV, and how is that remotely relevant? Unless you're trying to find a way to have me executed . . ."

She was pleased to see that that threw Gleau off his mental stride considerably. "That's not General Order Seven."

"Yes, it is."

"I'm sorry. I meant Twelve. General Order Twelve."

"You think that I didn't take adequate precautions when approaching a starship without establishing communications first?"

His face darkened. And as far as Shelby was concerned, the best thing was that he had nowhere to direct his anger except at himself. "Twenty-four, then."

She leaned back in her chair, steepling her fingers, and recited, " 'Upon receiving direct instruction from a flag officer in an emergency situation, a starship will be authorized to use deadly force upon a planetary surface unless receiving counter—' "

"Damnation!" thundered Gleau.

"Are you *sure* you graduated the Academy?"

"We Selelvians have a different numbering system. I've made the transition to Federation standard, but I get confused sometimes. The one about," he waved his hands in frustration as if he was hoping to pluck the elusive general order out of the air, "about respecting customs of crew members—"

"General Order Thirty-four? Starfleet captains will honor, respect, and display extreme tolerance for species-based customs and practices insofar as the safety of the vessel is not threatened by such practices . . . ?"

"Yes!" he clapped his hands once in an "ah-ha" manner. "Yes, thank you."

"You're welcome. Always glad to aid in my own pillorying."

"It has nothing to do with being 'pilloried,' Captain. The simple fact is that at no time have I acted in a manner that is not in keeping with customs and decorum as practiced by my people. And I have been penalized for it. I did nothing with M'Ress that she did not desire to have happen on some level. Yet now she is abrogating responsibility for it, and you are aiding and abetting her in that. You forced me to take an onerous oath of personal conduct. And now she has come complaining to you about my subsequent treatment of her, when I have done nothing to—"

"M'Ress hasn't come to me. Not since she filed her initial complaint."

Gleau was visibly startled at that. "She . . . hasn't."

"No."

Then he understood. "Ahhh . . . but she complained to Arex."

"She complained to him within the context of one friend venting frustration to another," said Shelby. "She did not, however, instruct him to have an altercation with you. Apparently he took his friend's discontent to heart, and took it upon himself to let her perceived oppressor know of his anger."

"And you're not court-martialing him for that!"

It was everything she could do not to sound smug as she said, "Well, apparently it is social custom for Triexians to step in and take actions—including physical confrontations—when they feel a friend has been ill-used. Something of a matter of honor with them, really. And I was concerned that if I penalized him too severely, that he could accuse me of violating General Order Thirty-four."

For a long moment, Gleau stared at her with his face a frozen deadpan. Then a very small smile played on the edges of his mouth. "That's very amusing, Captain. Very amusing."

Shelby then rose from her chair and came around the desk, sitting on the edge of it. "Arex also claimed that you were busy working your 'charm' on the Ambassador's sister, Kalinda . . ."

Gleau made no attempt to hide his exasperation. "I was talking to the girl! That was all! Am I now supposed to take an oath of silence as well? Hell thunder, Captain, this is going beyond the bound of ludicrousness! Our security chief takes issue with the way in which I run the science department, and you allow him to do so! I engage in civil discourse with a young woman and it's treated as if it's a high crime!"

"He said she seemed *very* taken with you. I've spoken to Kalinda as well. Her description of the conversation matches Arex's."

"Can I help it," he demanded, standing once more and throwing his arms wide, his face almost in hers, "if I am so blasted charming that people actually enjoy speaking with me? This is madness! What would you have, Captain? Shall I wear a bag over my head? Perhaps I should take to treating everyone I encounter as if they were dirt on my boots, so that no one should—heavens forbid—find my company engaging!" She watched as he reined himself in then, trying to keep a handle on the situation. "Do you see how this has spiraled out of control, Captain? In the interests of accommodating one time-displaced female, the integrity of a lieutenant commander with a blemish-free record is being challenged. It is intolerable. Intolerable!"

The door chimed. *Saved by the bell,* thought Shelby, as she called, "Come." The door slid open and Kat Mueller entered.

She glanced from Shelby to Gleau and back again before saying, "Ambassador Cwan has told me he wishes to speak with you."

Shelby let out a soft sigh. "My my. He's being rather formal about it. All right, tell him to come up."

Nodding briskly, Mueller tapped her com badge and informed Si Cwan to report to the captain's office. As he did so, Shelby turned back to her annoyed science officer. "Mr. Gleau, we're done for the moment."

"Only for the moment, Captain," said Gleau stiffly.

"Oh, and Gleau . . . ?"

He paused at the door. "Yes, Captain?"

"I certainly hope, for your sake, that you were limiting your interaction with young Kalinda to mere discussion. From myself you need merely worry about disciplinary action, and Arex seems to believe a severe tossing is the answer to things. But God help you if Ambassador Si Cwan feels you have taken . . . liberties. My guess is you simply won't be found. Ever. Si Cwan can be *very* inventive."

Gleau said nothing. He simply nodded a silent "Good day" to her and to Mueller before walking out the door.

"That man has a spectacular ass," Mueller commented when he was gone.

"He *is* a spectacular ass," replied Shelby, sitting back down behind her desk and rubbing her temples gently to offset the chance of a headache. "Unfortunately, he's a spectacular ass who also makes one or two valid points. How do you punish someone for simply doing that which is culturally and genetically inbred?"

"Firing squad?" suggested Mueller.

"You're not helping, XO." She sighed. "He accused

me of favoritism . . . of working to accommodate M'Ress's needs at the expense of other crew members, including himself."

"I said as much to you already when she first came aboard," Mueller reminded her.

"Yes, I know."

"Curse my infallibility," deadpanned Mueller.

The thudding in Shelby's temples was becoming more pronounced. She had the makings of a considerable headache coming on, she realized.

"Are you quite all right, Captain?"

"No, I'm not quite all right. I'm not even close to all right. I have a planet below that once oppressed my husband, which now wants to try and restart the empire that held an iron grip on this sector of space for hundreds upon hundreds of years. I have a science officer who may or may not be seducing women against their will, and a security officer who seems to feel that the best way to handle the situation is to use the science officer as a bowling ball. So I appreciate your concern, XO, but the truth is that I'm a rather far piece from 'all right.' I'm hoping, though, that whatever Si Cwan has to say, it will do something to alleviate the aggravation."

As if with supernatural timing—which Shelby would have been perfectly willing to credit him with—Si Cwan appeared at her door. She stood up and ushered him in, taking a moment to draw in a few deep, cleansing breaths. He looked at her with concern. "Are you all right, Captain?"

"I'm thrilled that everyone seems so concerned with

my well-being, Ambassador. Please," she gestured, "have a seat."

"I'd prefer to stand, if that is acceptable."

She turned to Mueller. "I'm going to have these chairs checked. There's something about them that just prompts people not to sit. All right, Ambassador," she said, looking up at him, crossing her arms and forcing a smile against the pain that was thumping in her head. "What's on your mind?"

"The Danteri offer."

"I suspected as much."

"I've given it a great deal of thought, and I'm very pleased to tell you—"

"Ah—!" said Shelby cheerfully.

"—that I have decided to take them up on it."

"—ha," she finished, far less cheerfully. "And . . . you are 'pleased' to tell me this . . . why?"

"Why," he said, as if it should have been the most obvious thing in the world, "because the opportunity presenting itself to me is a remarkable one, and makes me extremely happy. And since I know you are the type who is pleased to share in others' happiness, I simply concluded that you would be delighted to take pleasure in mine."

"I see." She took a deep breath, leaned back against the desk once more. Then she tapped her com badge and said, "Captain to sickbay: I'm going to be down in a few moments looking for a headache remedy. Anything short of decapitation would be greatly appreciated."

"Aye, Captain."

"Shelby out." Then Shelby returned her attention to

Si Cwan, standing before her. "Ambassador Si Cwan, I suppose that, out of consideration for the Prime Directive if nothing else, I should keep my mouth closed about this matter. But the Danteri . . . Si Cwan, their history . . ."

"History means nothing if they are truly willing to forge a new—"

"Their Senate speaker, Lodec, murdered my husband's father. Are you aware of that?"

That brought Si Cwan up short. His eyes clouded. "What?"

"Yes, that's right. The fellow who runs their senate—arguably one of the most powerful men on their world—murdered Captain Calhoun's father. These are the types of people you're going to be involving yourself with, Si Cwan. And we have an old saying back on Earth: If you lie down with pigs, you get up smelling like pigs."

"A colorful sentiment. I am quite sure I would truly appreciate the splendor and insight of this aphorism," Si Cwan informed her, "if I actually knew what a 'pig' was. As it stands, Captain Shelby . . . we all of us have darkness in our past. We've all done things that we are ashamed of, or things that we regret . . ."

"And you know that Lodec regrets it . . . how?" When she saw that Si Cwan did not respond immediately, she continued, "This was not an isolated incident, Cwan. This was not a freak happenstance. This was just another day of bloodletting and brutality perpetrated by a race with a long history of it. Is that who you want to attach your star to?"

He drew himself up, squared his shoulders. "I wish to attach my star, Captain, to a potential future for the

Thallonian Empire to which I am committed. If you wish to continue your harangue, please inform me of your intent so that I can be certain to be elsewhere. If, on the other hand, you wish to extend your congratulations, I would be most happy to receive them."

Shelby looked him up and down for a long moment. Then, stiffly, she said, "Congratulations, Ambassador. Congratulations on coming to an agreement with a race notorious for backstabbing and power-grabbing, in an endeavor to take a giant step backward in the development of this sector and quite possibly destabilizing it to the point of total chaos." She shook his hand firmly, turned, and walked out.

A speechless Si Cwan turned and stared at Mueller, who smiled sweetly at him. "She's thrilled for you," she said.

iii.

Si Cwan realized belatedly that he should not have been surprised when he discovered Robin Lefler seated in his quarters. Nevertheless, he was. That she was able to obtain entrance was likewise not surprising; since she was there as his aide, he had given her full access to his quarters so that she could obtain things whenever she needed them, even if he was not around.

What surprised him, then, was the look in her eyes. And not just the look. It was the eyes themselves. They seemed redder than usual around the rims, as if they'd been greatly irritated, and he could not figure out why that might be. Perhaps there was some sort of human virus going around, first with the captain's clear head pain, and now this odd eye redness. "Robin . . . ?" he ventured.

"Kalinda told me your decision," she said without preamble. "Have you gone to Captain Shelby with this yet?"

"Yes."

"And what did she say?"

"Well," and he walked slowly across the room toward her. She was seated in one of the chairs, looking stiff-backed and uncomfortable. He drew another chair across the room and sat opposite her. "The first time, she simply gave me a verbal tongue-lashing. Then she walked out. Then she walked right back in before I could leave to reiterate that she thought it was a mistake. Which it may be. She said that it smacked of ingratitude to people such as herself and particularly Captain Calhoun, who had gone to such efforts and extended themselves so greatly on my behalf. Which is true enough. I acknowledged that, and then told her that I had to follow my heart." She snorted disdainfully at that. "Robin—?"

"Your heart?"

"Robin . . ." His concern was starting to grow, because she was trembling with barely repressed fury.

"Your heart?" Her voice rose. "You don't have a heart."

"Robin!"

And now she was on her feet, and he had never, but never, seen her so purely furious. Her rage was towering; she seemed several heads taller than he did, even though she was a head shorter. *"You don't have any kind of heart!* Oh, ambition, yes, you've got that! And a capacity for revenge! And mercilessness and the ability to kill, yeah, you've got that. You've got tons of that! But a heart? You wouldn't know what to do with the thing!"

Si Cwan was utterly flabbergasted. "How . . . how could you say that? You, of all people. You, who knows what the Thallonian tradition means to me . . . what my sister means to me!"

"All you care about is things that are a means to your own end!" she shouted. "You care about people so long as they can be of use to you! Your sister, too! She's probably just a tool as well! You don't really care about her happiness! That's why you were so angry when she was getting involved with Captain Calhoun's son, Xyon! Her happiness wasn't half as important to you as your own selfishness! You're such an idiot! Such an—!"

"All right, that is quite enough!" Si Cwan said with such iron in his voice that it brought her up short. "Aide or no, Starfleet officer or no, friend or no . . . you still have no call to address me in that way! Gods, Lefler, once upon a time I could have had you torn apart by wild animals for daring to raise your voice to me. I do not have to suffer this abuse! I have always, always, done what I felt needed to be done! This is no different! For a time, those actions and needs intersected with the needs of Captain Calhoun and the *Excalibur,* and during that time we shared a mutually beneficial relationship. But sooner or later, all relationships end."

"And some never even start," she said bitterly. "God, I . . ." Her fists were trembling. "You are just the most infuriating . . . aggravating . . ."

"Robin," and he took her firmly by the shoulders.

Every muscle in her arm was wound-spring tense. "Robin . . . you seem to be taking this decision of mine terribly personally. As if it's a betrayal, a rejection of you and your crewmates. You have to understand: It's not personal. Not at all."

"Not personal," she repeated tonelessly.

"No. Not at all."

And to Si Cwan's immense shock, she grabbed him by either side of the head and pulled his face down to hers. She did it with such force that their teeth collided, and for a moment there was pain shooting through his skull, and then her lips were against his, hungrily, greedily. Her hands slid down his back, and her right leg wound around his left one, and Si Cwan felt as if his body was on fire. He gasped as she bit down on his lower lip and then suddenly she broke contact. She stepped away from him, and there was incredible need in her eyes, but also a hard anger that wasn't dissipating, and in a deep, husky voice she said, "You know what, Cwan? *That* was personal. Enjoy your new empire."

He tried to get words out, but couldn't find his breath, and she didn't wait for him to find it as she turned and stalked out of the room.

Stunned, he sagged onto the bed, staring into space, and uttered a word that he'd picked up from Captain Jean-Luc Picard on one occasion when Kebron had inadvertently stepped on Picard's toe.

"Merde," he said.

EXCALIBUR

i.

WHEN THE TURBOLIFT DOOR slid open, McHenry was about to step in . . . and froze. Kebron was standing there, hands draped behind his back. Soleta was next to him. There was actually momentary surprise in Soleta's eyes; Kebron, as usual, could have been carved from rock.

McHenry cleared his throat, and then said, "I'll wait for the next one—"

He took a step backward, but that was as far as he got before Kebron's massive hand reached out, snagged him by the front of his uniform, and hauled him in. The doors hissed shut behind them.

"—or I'll take this one. This one is fine," said McHenry.

"Kebron!" Soleta said with reprisal in her voice.

Kebron released him and McHenry stepped back, rubbing his chest and smoothing out the wrinkles. "So . . . how are you doing? How are your folks? I, uhm, notice that you have a kind of thing happening here," and he rubbed the base of his neck. "Are you having that looked at? Or—?"

"You should have told us," Kebron interrupted, glowering down at McHenry.

"What is this, an ambush?"

"Pure coincidence," said Soleta. "Zak, McHenry's been under a lot of pressure. This probably isn't the best time to—"

"He should have told us," repeated Kebron to her.

There was such condemnation in his voice, so much contempt, and McHenry suddenly felt very put upon, very annoyed, and very tired. "Lift, halt," he snapped, and the turbolift glided to a halt. He looked straight at Kebron and said, "Great idea there, Zak. You're absolutely right. Why, when we were first making introductions to each other back at the Academy, I should have said, 'Hi. Mark McHenry. My great-great-great-grandmother was impregnated by a god, I had a goddess for an invisible friend and lover, and maybe, just maybe, I have glimmerings of some abilities myself. How you doing?' "

"Obviously, no reasonable person could have expected you to say all that, Mark," Soleta said with what sounded like a soothing tone. "But still, in the interest of—"

"Of what? In my interest?" he said sarcastically. "When would I have brought it up? At what point could it possibly have seemed a reasonable jumping-off point in a conversation? Or maybe, just maybe, it was never anyone else's business but mine."

"But—"

"There's no 'but' here, Soleta! I wanted to be normal! Don't you get that? When I told Artemis I didn't want to see her anymore, she tried to kill me! You think those bolts she tossed around in the bridge were a problem? Those were love taps compared to what she hit me with! I could barely move for weeks! She burned my eyebrows off!"

"You're saying she didn't take it well," said Soleta.

"That's putting it mildly. But I survived! And I joined Starfleet, and I made friends, or at least thought I did! But the suspicion, especially from you, Zak . . . investigating me . . ."

"I was right to do so," Kebron said stiffly. "There were x-factors in your past . . . the fact that we found ourselves under assault by this 'goddess' . . ."

"I had no control over that!"

"You were the cause of it."

"Zak," spoke up Soleta, "let it go."

He looked down at her. "He—"

"Zak . . . for me . . . let it go. There's nothing to be done about it now. And we need to be together on this." Soleta looked from one to the other. "Correct? Together?"

Kebron and McHenry stared at each other for a long moment.

Nothing was said, until the silence was broken by McHenry saying, "Lift, resume course."

"You two are impossible," said Soleta as the turbolift continued on its way. "Mark . . . look . . . if you really want to be of help . . . I'm still having trouble analyzing the energy emissions from this sector. They still defy analysis. I am proceeding on the assumption that your god friends are responsible, but the specific technical parameters . . . I'm still having difficulty with them. If you could ask—"

"My god friends? Soleta . . . they're not my friends. They are the bane of my existence, all right?"

"I . . . apologize."

"Never mind," he said, rolling his eyes. "I'll see what I can do."

Moments later, it had reached McHenry's destination on deck seven, and he stepped off. The last thing he saw was the suspicious way in which Kebron was watching him.

The moment McHenry was gone from sight, Soleta said with thinly veiled annoyance, "That could have gone better. Happenstance places the three of us together in a turbolift, and we wind up sending off McHenry angrier than he was before. He needed us, Zak. He needed his friends."

"He has new friends."

The turbolift slid to a halt. The doors opened and Soleta started to walk out . . . but she paused in the door, turned to Kebron, and said, "Tell me, Zak . . . if someone isn't entirely forthcoming about themselves . . . if they're something other than people think they are . . . does that automatically make them a threat to the ship? For instance . . . if I were other than I appeared to be . . . then I would be a threat?"

"But you're not," he said.

"But if I were—?"

He stared at her for a long moment. "Are you saying you are?"

"I'm not saying anything, Zak," she said evenly. "It

would be nice if I could say anything. That is, after all, what friends are able to do with one another. Perhaps you should start investigating me, just to be sure."

She stepped back and allowed the doors to close, leaving Kebron alone.

He stood there in the center of the lift as it sped down to the security work out room, where he was originally heading. As it did so, he tapped his combadge. "Kebron, requesting direct link to computer."

"Working," came the computer's voice.

"Access personal log, Lieutenant Zak Kebron."

"Accessed."

"Memo to self," he said neutrally. "Investigate Soleta."

ii.

Mark McHenry was wondering how things could possibly get any worse when he walked into his quarters . . . only to see Artemis standing there.

She had one hand on her hip, the other upraised. Her cape was hanging off one shoulder. Otherwise, she was naked. The curves of her body, her breasts, all of it was exactly as he remembered from years gone by. And his reaction was also just as he remembered from the very first time she'd appeared to him that way: barely restrained panic.

"Remember when men carved statues of me appearing this way?" she asked.

Quickly he crossed to his bed, yanked the covers off, and tossed them around her shoulders. She didn't seem to pay any attention as he did so, speaking as much to herself as to him. "They would linger over every detail," she said wistfully. "Every sinew, every line. They would treat it lovingly, attending to it as if their lives depended upon getting everything exactly right . . ."

"Yes, those were the days," he said, and then moaned as the cover slipped off her to the floor. So he got his bathrobe from the closet and drew that around her. She seemed more amused than anything else over his attempts to cover her nakedness. "Artemis, what are you doing here?"

"I am here to seduce you," she said matter-of-factly. "Am I succeeding?"

"You shouldn't be here. If there's things you want to discuss, you should be discussing them with Captain Calhoun . . ."

She made a dismissive gesture. "That one? He is so . . . dull! So pompous, so serious . . . and scheming, always scheming. I can tell. Zeus was like that sometimes."

"Was? He's not around anymore?"

She didn't bother to clarify what she'd just said. Instead she drew the robe more tightly around herself. It accentuated the lines of her body that much more. Quickly trying to keep his mind off her body, he said, "Uhm . . . Soleta . . . our science officer. She's trying to analyze this section of space and having no luck."

"I have very little interest in such matters," she said, looking utterly bored. "If you wish, I will ask Thoth to speak to her." And before he could pursue that offhand comment, she looked at him with a tinge of sadness. "I will be honest with you, Marcus. In some ways . . . you seem unhappy to see me."

"Only 'some' ways? Artemis—"

"You know . . . you were so adorable in the days when you called me 'Missy.' "

"Yes, I remember those days," he said sharply. "They were the days when you drove my father out of the house and out of my life."

She looked at him for a long moment, as if trying to decide whether she should say what was on her mind. Finally, very softly, she told him, "He would have left anyway, Marcus. Eventually. He was unhappy. He had a wandering soul . . . much like yours, truth to tell. You, however, managed to channel it into positive and useful directions."

"Have I?" he asked sourly. He leaned against the wall, hanging his head. "I've been doing some reading . . . on your brother. On the earlier known encounter with him. You seem much more powerful than he was."

"I am," she said simply. "As are the others."

"Why is that?"

She tilted her head, regarded him with an expression both curious and amused. "Why do you care?"

He took a deep breath. Lying wasn't his strong suit. He knew he was walking a fine line: trying to determine the things that the captain needed to know, without wanting to seem too labored in his inquisitiveness. "You go and tell the captain you want me to be your 'intermediary.' Your representative. Well, representatives get asked questions. Lots of them. If there's things I don't understand, then there's gonna be things that other people don't understand. And if I can't come up with reasonable answers, then people will figure that I'm either ignorant, or that I'm hiding something. Neither attitude is going to do any good."

She considered that for a long moment. As she did, he found his gaze drawn to her. Damn, she was attractive. He had always been able to perceive her, even as a young boy, even when she was invisible to others. But the full, soulaching beauty of her . . . that was something he'd only been able to appreciate when he'd gotten older. There had been a time when the merest thought of her was enough to cause him to tremble with desire right down to his very core. He had thought that time was long gone, but now he was wondering just how wrong he might have been.

"He . . . stopped believing," she said finally.

McHenry couldn't help but feel that was an odd thing to say. "Believing . . . in what?"

"In himself. In us. He isolated himself from us, Marcus. You see . . . collectively, we are able to draw energy from . . . well . . . each other," she smiled. "We have an endless capacity for doing so. As a result, we know no boundaries, have no limits in what we can accomplish. When Apollo wrapped himself in his depression, he effectively cut himself off from the rest of us. Severed himself from the energies that we provide one another, that we can uniformly generate. So he sought . . . alternative means of energy. Fashioned a sort of . . . of 'battery,' I suppose you would call it. Once that was destroyed, however, he was utterly vulnerable. Indeed, he could barely hold himself together at all at that point. He simply lacked . . . the . . ."

She stopped, looked down. And McHenry, to his astonishment, saw the slightest bit of moistening in her eyes. "Artemis . . . ?"

Artemis seemed annoyed at herself, and determinedly wiped the wetness from her eyes. "He *was* my brother, Marcus. As . . . as foolish as I sometimes considered him to be, he was my brother, and I do miss him. You'll forgive me if I choose not to dwell on this any further. It is . . . upsetting to me." She cleared her throat. "Have I satisfied your curiosity in this matter?"

"In this, yes. But there are others . . ."

"Oh!" she said in loud frustration. She wasn't so much walking around McHenry's cabin so much as she was stalking it. McHenry took a few steps back, trying to stay out of her way. He'd never felt his quarters were especially small before, but they certainly seemed cramped now. "This is absurd! Marcus, I was standing naked here, waiting for you. Men have lost their lives simply for getting a fleeting glimpse of that divine nakedness which you drank in in full measure. And all you wish to do is talk! You were more man when you were a boy!"

"When I was a boy I didn't know enough to question," McHenry replied. "Being a man means thinking with something other than your . . . impulses. Gods are supposed to be omniscient, so I'd think that you shouldn't have trouble understanding that."

"Very well," she said, draping herself over a chair. She extended one perfectly toned leg from beneath the robe. "What else do you wish to know?"

Feeling that it would probably better suit the mood— her mood, especially—McHenry went down on one knee in front of her. He did so in a casual manner, but to a "goddess" he would come across as a supplicant, and she would probably find that attitude of his quite preferable. "This whole golden age you keep talking about. What is it, exactly? You've been so vague . . ."

"Ah." She seemed to perk up, preferring this line of inquiry. "That, my dear Marcus, is indeed a very legitimate question. To be honest, it is something of an oversight on my part that I did not make that clear in our previous meeting. Perhaps the attitude of your captain distracted me. He is not what I would consider a very receptive individual."

"He's better when you get to know him . . . and when you're not trying to kill him."

She nodded in a distracted manner. "Hmm. I suppose so."

"So . . . the golden age . . ."

"Yes, yes." She brought her other leg down. The robe opened slightly and McHenry quietly rearranged it so that he would be able to keep his mind on the matter at hand. "May I assume, Marcus, that you have heard of . . . ambrosia?"

"That's . . ." He paused, remembering. "That's . . . the 'food of the gods,' right?"

"Correct," she said.

"Isn't that supposed to be the stuff that gives you immortality?"

Artemis laughed lightly. "According to myths, yes. As you know, not all myths are literally accurate . . . but on the other hand, many of them have some basis in fact. This happens to be one of the latter. We are virtually immortal by our nature, my dear Marcus. But all things tend to wear out, break down over time. Nothing is immune from entropy . . . not even the Beings. Ambrosia is a . . . a vitamin, if you will, that we have developed. There is nothing magical about it. The ingredients can be found in nature, or synthesized by your own devices. It is our desire to give ambrosia . . . to you."

"To me?"

"To humanity. To mortals. To your Federation," she said, her voice crackling with excitement, her eyes wide as if she could see a mental image of herself and her fellow "gods," moving from person to person and handing out this key to immortality. "Ambrosia will not affect you in precisely the same way it does us. Nevertheless, the impact it will have on your way of life will be nothing short of epoch-making. It will bring people to full health, slow down the aging process so that they'll practically live forever. Not only that, but it will expand their mental capabilities, make them achieve things that previously they would not have thought possible to achieve."

He stared at her, hardly able to believe what he was hearing. "You're serious about this."

"Why would I not be?"

"But . . . aren't there potential dangers? This stuff . . ."

"There will be no dangers. There will be nothing hidden." She shrugged. "We have no need to hide anything."

"Yeah, I know, I saw that when I first walked into my quarters."

Her laughter at that was soft and musical. "Very amusing, Marcus, and I suppose I had that coming." Then the laughter faded and she took on a very serious attitude. "The reason we would be hiding nothing, in terms of the composition of ambrosia, is that we would be working in tandem with your Federation and its technology to mass-produce ambrosia. So your people would be privy as to what went into it. Again, nothing would be hidden."

"I just . . . I'm having a bit of trouble believing that you're going to be that open about it all," McHenry told her. "I mean, let's face it, you folks do have this habit of moving in mysterious ways. Hiding out in Olympus, letting humans twenty-five hundred years ago believe that you were gods when you . . . well, you're more than human, but . . ."

"Less than divine?" She shook her head, looking nostalgic. "When your people were youthful, ignorant of the true nature of the universe, we could not be candid with them as to our nature for the simple reason that they never would have been able to comprehend it. I mean, after all," and once more came that musical laugh, "when we first encountered your ancestors, they were under the impression that the Earth was the center of the universe! That the sun, the stars, everything, revolved around them! A more egocentric bunch you could not possibly imagine! So how could we explain to them about life on other worlds? How could we disabuse them of the firmly held belief that everything radiated from, or related to, the little dirtball they called Earth? No, Marcus, every aspect of our interaction with them had to be simplified to the point that they could understand it.

"But now . . . now, Marcus, your species has grown up. You can better comprehend us, just as a child, grown to adulthood, can better understand the nature and thinking of his parents."

Something, however, was still not falling together for McHenry. He still felt as if there was a piece missing. "And . . . what do you get out of it? The Beings?"

"The same thing that we did in our first interaction with you," she said matter-of-factly, as if it should be the most obvious thing in the world. "The appreciation of a grateful people."

Now McHenry felt he was close to something. "Appreciation in what sense?"

"The usual sense. Appreciation. Gratitude. Regular recognition and acknowledgment . . ."

And McHenry suddenly started to laugh, very loudly and very boisterously.

Artemis' face clouded a bit. Clearly she was not thrilled with McHenry's reaction. "What is so amusing, Marcus?" she said stiffly.

He managed to stop laughing long enough to say, "You . . . you want to be worshipped! Just like your brother! I don't believe it!"

"Don't be absurd."

"You do!"

She drew her legs up, tucking her feet under herself, almost making her look as if she was withdrawing into a protective mode. "Apollo wanted to turn back the hands of time," she admitted. "He wanted to overlook a millennium of human achievement. He thought that the crew of the *Enterprise* would set aside its personal goals in exchange for a simple, bucolic life of raising sheep, playing pipes, and worshipping him. He was . . . unrealistic. We, on the other hand, are not endeavoring to suppress your goals. Instead we want to help you achieve them by making you as close to divine as can reasonably be done. In exchange, we are asking only that you revere us, bless our names, thank us daily for the incredible boon that we have given you. For Hera's sake, Marcus," she said impatiently, "we're not asking you to go out and sacrifice goats in our name. To be honest, we never wanted that, even back in the days when that was being done. It always seemed a tragic waste of a perfectly good goat. Now if you feel compelled to equate gratitude with worship, then you are of course free to do so. Tell them we wish to be worshipped, if you think they will comprehend that more readily."

"I think there's going to be serious problems no matter which way we go with this," McHenry said. "I can tell you right now that most races will not accept this offer on faith. They will need to understand what's in it for you."

"Altruism, then, is truly dead in your civilization?" she asked sadly.

"No, not at all. But you're talking about introducing something into our society that could potentially change it to its core. People will want to know how this benefits you, and they may not want to take you up on it until they have an answer that they can understand and believe. The basic answer you're giving me is that you want to be worshipped."

"You keep using that word," Artemis said with impatience. "It is a word you use, I believe, because you associate us with gods. It is understandable to a point . . . but only to a point. After that it becomes impertinent, and ungrateful, and even a bit dangerous."

McHenry suddenly felt a chill in the air, and he had the distinct feeling he knew what the source of that chill was. "Artemis . . . are you saying . . . that if we don't accept the offer of your ambrosia . . . that you're effectively going to ram it down our throats? And that if we don't let you . . . you're going to consider us a bunch of ingrates and act accordingly."

"No. I did not say that," she replied quietly. But before he could relax, she added, "And it will be up to you, Marcus, to make certain that matters do not progress to the point . . . where I do have to say that. Because the outcome will not be a pleasant one for anyone."

And with that, she swung her elegant legs down and off the chair, turned, and walked right through the bulkhead. The robe dropped off behind her.

McHenry flopped back onto his bed and stared up at the ceiling.

"This day just keeps getting better and better," he muttered.

iii.

Moke knew precisely where Xyon was the entire time.

Even as Xyon crouched behind a locker filled with maintenance equipment, Moke made a great pretense of not having the faintest idea where the younger child was. But not for a minute had he taken the chance that Xyon would actually vanish from his care. Moke was taking his shepherding duties of the youngster very,

very seriously, and had taken the precaution of asking Xyon's mother, Dr. Selar, to implant some sort of tracking device on the boy.

Selar's face remained as impassive as always, but he could see the surprise in her eyes nevertheless as she clearly wondered why in the world she hadn't thought of doing that herself in the first place. "Excellent idea, Mr. Moke" was all she said, but even that was high praise, because she had never addressed him as "Mister" before. Moke understood it to be a title of some sort, and his chest swelled with pride.

With a hiss of a hypo, she had placed what she called a "subcutaneous transponder" (two words that Moke had had to work at very hard to try and master) under Xyon's skin, and had then presented Moke with a small tracker that was keyed directly to it. So even if Xyon managed to get out from under Moke's watchful eye, it would still be a matter of minutes, even seconds, before Moke tracked him down.

Nevertheless, at this point Moke didn't need any help, because he could hear the child giggling from his hiding place. "Where's Xyon?" Moke called loudly. More giggles. Xyon wasn't talking all that much yet, but his physical development was astonishing. Within a relatively brief time he had gone from crawling to walking to running, and his agility was nothing short of phenomenal.

Moke walked all around the equipment locker, except for the place where Xyon had "hidden" himself. "Xyyyyyyon!" he called in feigned helplessness. A crewman, taking a tricorder down off the rack, smiled indulgently and went on his way. This was definitely a better place to play hide-and-seek than Moke's previous choice: the armory. That had gotten them escorted out of there inside of thirty seconds.

Then he blinked in surprise, because he saw a quick movement out of the corner of his eye, but he was reasonably sure that Xyon and he were the only ones there. He looked back where he thought he'd seen something . . . but it was gone. It . . . could have been Xyon. The child moved like lightning. "Xyyyyyyon," he called more cautiously this time, and he heard Xyon once again chuckling from the exact same hiding place he'd been in before.

And there it was again, this time at the other side of the room.

He spun quickly, looked once more, and once again it had been only the most fleeting of glimpses. But this time it lingered a moment more. It was an adult . . . a man, Moke thought, but he couldn't be sure.

"Xyon," he said, and this time there was no amusement in his voice, no sound of a young boy playing games. "Xyon, come on." Dropping the contest, he moved quickly around the equipment locker. Xyon looked up in mute, wide-eyed surprise, clearly not having expected Moke to simply walk up to him. He put out his hand and in the most no-nonsense tone he could muster, said, "I said come on. We're—"

There again.

This time Moke moved so quickly that he actually saw it straight on, and then it was gone again, but there was a visual impression burned into his eye. A man, definitely a man, shrouded in darkness, in a black cape that enveloped most of his body, and a hood pulled up over his head. He was an older man, with a beard that was dark red with streaks of white and gray in it. What little Moke could make out of the hair atop his head seemed similar in type and style. His face was wrinkled as parchment, with a broad nose and mouth, and he was squinting. Except he seemed to have only one eye, glistening dark and storm-filled in the right socket. In the left there was just darkness, with a single streak of what looked like blood, just in the corner.

He had no expression on his face at all, and that was possibly the most frightening aspect of all. Just that sheer, malevolent blankness. He had no idea how someone could be both inscrutable and threatening, all at the same time, but the hooded man had managed it.

All of that seared into Moke's brain, like a lightning bolt leaving an impression upon flashing, but when he looked right where the hooded man had been, he was gone. Moke didn't have the impression that the man was moving at supernatural speeds, or trying to get out of his field of vision. It was just that whenever Moke would try to look directly at him . . . he could not be perceived. It was as if reality was bending around him somehow, silencing him, locking him away where no one could get to him.

Moke put both his arms around Xyon and backed out of the equipment room, his head sweeping back and forth like a conning tower. He was trying to watch every square inch of the room simultaneously, while also being concerned about whatever might be behind him.

And now it felt as if the hooded man was everywhere, all at the same time.

He backed up, fast as he could, and then he was out the door and he banged into someone large, so unexpectedly that he let out a yelp of alarm.

"Is something amiss?" inquired a cultured voice. He looked up and relief sagged through him as he saw the familiar snout of Ensign Janos. "I was just passing by, and you looked a bit distres—"

"There's . . . there's someone in there!" Moke managed to stammer out. Xyon, who was now holding tightly to Moke, was not crying. He had too much quiet confidence in Moke, a childish certainty that he would be protected.

"Someone? You mean someone unauthorized?" When Moke nodded his head, Janos said firmly, "Stay here. If I am not out in thirty seconds, inform Lieutenant Kebron." Over Moke's loud protests, Janos took two quick strides forward and was in the equipment room.

"I dunno," Moke said nervously, suddenly realizing he wasn't wearing a chronometer and so was unsure of how much time had already passed.

But then, very quickly, Janos emerged from the room. Moke looked to see if the security officer looked the least bit concerned . . . or, for that matter, if his white fur had any blood on it as a result of a violent encounter with . . . with whoever that was in there.

Janos, however, simply shrugged and said, "No one is here, or there, or hereabouts or thereabouts or anywhere abouts."

Moke couldn't believe it. "Are you sure? I mean, your eyes are kind of small and pink . . . maybe—"

His immediate reaction was a low growl of annoyance, but then Janos reined himself in. "That much is true, yes. But this," and he tapped his nose, "never lies. No one could be hiding in there without this baby detecting him, her, or it. Although if you want, I can report this to the head of security . . . or, considering your personal situation, your father if you so—"

"No. No, that's okay," Moke said after a moment's thought. "I don't want to bother anyone or make anyone nervous. I was . . . probably just imagining it."

"That would not be surprising. Children are justifiably renowned for their imaginations," said Janos solicitously.

Moke knew that much to be true. But he also knew two other things: That the hooded man had indeed been in there, no matter what Janos was saying. And that for a heartbeat, Moke had thought he'd seen the hooded man standing in the corridor, single eye gleaming and watching him.

The boy did not stop watching out all around himself for the rest of the day. And anyone who encountered him thought it was some sort of bizarre game when he would be walking around, constantly turning in circles as if hoping he would be able to see in all directions at once.

DANTER

i.

SPEAKER LODEC OF THE DANTERI SENATE strode through the elaborate garden that lay in the back of his home, his arms spread wide in welcome when he saw Si Cwan waiting for him at the far end. Si Cwan couldn't help but notice that Lodec moved with a vehemence and enthusiasm that belied his aged appearance, which meant one of two things: Either Lodec was a rather old fellow with a young man's vigor . . . or else he was a younger man who had simply been through quite a lot, and the few years he had lived had weighed heavily upon him. He had a gut feeling it was the latter.

Nevertheless, he carried himself with poise, his back straight, his chin level. Si Cwan couldn't help but notice that Lodec had a very measured tread, each footfall precisely the same distance from the one before. *Soldier. Definitely soldier,* he thought. Lodec's hair and beard were neatly and precisely trimmed, and his bronze skin was glistening in the lengthy rays of the twilight sun. His clothes, various shades of blue, were loose-fitting, although his arms were bared and displayed solid muscle.

Si Cwan had to admit that the garden itself was a beautiful sight. Large topiaries, bushes trimmed into the shapes of various Danteri wildlife, dotted the terrain. There was a narrow spring trickling right through the middle of the garden that apparently fed the dazzling assortment of multicolored plant life throughout the garden. The aromas of the flowers were so pungent that for a brief time Si Cwan felt almost light-headed from them all. But it was only a minor effort of will to bring himself back to the matter at hand.

Lodec came to within two feet of Si Cwan, stopped, and bowed in greeting, hands clasped together and held tightly in front of him. "How excellent that you have come to visit me, to see my lovely garden. And I admit to being a bit surprised . . ."

"Surprised? In what way?" asked Si Cwan.

"Well, you spend so much time at the Senate, and then in committee meetings, discussions, and the like. I would think, given how much of your time is spent involved with us, that during your private time you would want to be as far removed from us as possible." Then, in a slightly forced endeavor to show that he was jesting, Lodec produced what passed for a laugh. At least Si Cwan thought it was a laugh. It might have been a strangled cough.

"I am flattered that you see me as so dedicated a worker," said Si Cwan.

"No flattery intended," Lodec assured him. "And there is much to do, much to do. Alliances to be formed, meetings to be held . . ."

"That is what I wish to discuss with you, in point of fact."

"Your work schedule?" asked Lodec with concern. "You think it too demanding . . . ?"

"No," said Si Cwan stiffly. "I am worried because I feel that I am accomplishing nothing."

"What?" Lodec once again emitted that odd sound that passed for laughter. "Ambassador, good Lord, you've been here less than a week! The Danteri Empire was not built in a day, you know, nor can the new Thallonian Empire expect a faster timetable."

"It is not the long-term timetable that concerns me," said Si Cwan. He pulled himself in, looked for the calm center, because he could feel his anger rising and he knew that losing his temper now would not serve any purpose. "It is the short-term attitude that I see being displayed by your fellow senators. Despite all the great words, the grandiose promises that were made to me in the beginning, I sense that I am being kept at arm's length from the true process of empire building."

"Whatever do you mean?" asked Lodec, wide-eyed.

Si Cwan was a good foot taller than Lodec. It gave him considerable opportunity to exert his commanding presence, and he did so at that point. Looming over Lodec, his voice dropping into a tone that had a distinct edge of warning to it, he said, "Let us cease fencing, Speaker. I walked the halls of power of Thallon. I know the difference between meetings and sessions where pretty words and sentiments are being bandied about, as opposed to meetings of true power, when genuine negotiations that will make a difference are being held."

"Si Cwan, I—"

"The primary purpose to which I have been put thus far," said Si Cwan, "is to be one who greets incoming delegates, ambassadors, representatives of other worlds. Then I am immediately shunted away to 'other' responsibilities, which turn out not to be very important at all. It is as if you are using my name, my reputation, to lure people here, and then isolating me so that you can tell these people . . . what? What are you telling them, Lodec?"

Lodec appeared thunderstruck. Si Cwan reasoned that either he was completely off the mark, or else Lodec was a formidable actor. "Si Cwan, you . . . you misunderstand!"

"Do I?"

"Yes!" He started to walk through his garden, shaking his head, seeming almost oblivious of Si Cwan, who was walking beside him. He seemed far more intent on speaking to his feet than to Cwan. "Yes, you greatly misunderstand. We are . . . we are simply trying not to waste your time!"

"Really," said Si Cwan, unconvinced.

"Yes, really! Truly! These 'power meetings' as you call them—why, they are exercises in political gamesmanship, nothing more. If you attended them, you would see. They are little more than a series of verbal feints, thrusts, and parries. People trying to feel out each other's weaknesses . . . it's fairly juvenile, in many ways. It was felt that such things were beneath you. A waste of your time. You are, after all, nobility. Why should nobility have to condescend to such . . . such relative trivialities?"

Si Cwan nodded slowly. "Your words are very flattering, Lodec."

"Thank you, noble one. I seek merely to—"

"In some ways, too flattering. As if you hope that by appealing to my ego, I will overlook certain transgressions." He snagged Lodec by the elbow and snapped him around. But Lodec instinctively pulled away, twisting his arm out of Si Cwan's grasp, and for a moment the two faced each other not as Thallonian noble and Senate speaker, but as two soldiers. For just a moment there was a different charge in the air, as if they were truly facing each other for the first time. Then Lodec, quickly and smoothly, drew a virtual curtain over himself. "I do not think that physical abuse is necessary, honored one," he said very softly.

"Really. I would wager that Mackenzie Calhoun's father thought much the same thing . . . before you beat him to death."

To a degree, Si Cwan felt annoyed with himself, because he was taking something that he knew was someone's personal tragedy, and throwing it at Lodec just to get a reaction out of him. Nevertheless, it worked. Lodec's face fell, and this time there was no quick restoring of his aplomb. "How—?"

"When you are nobility," Si Cwan said with faint sarcasm, "you're expected to know these things. Tell me,

Lodec . . . did it feel good when you did it?" He lowered his voice in an intimate manner designed to be as disconcerting as possible. "Did you enjoy exercising your power over someone who had none? Was it entertaining, depriving a young boy of his father? Did you enjoy abusing your power—"

And Lodec shot back, with an infuriated snarl, *"Power?"* He was reacting with such vehemence that Si Cwan, despite the size deferential, was taken aback for a moment. "Are you under the impression that I beat people to death because it gives me some sort of pleasure? Do you think if I had any power at all, I would have done what I did? I was power*less,* Lord Cwan. As a soldier, I had no choice. No choice."

"One always has a choice," Si Cwan said quietly. "The question is whether one chooses to take it or not."

Lodec stepped back, shaking his head. He walked in a small circle for a moment, continuing to shake his head the entire time, as if trying to dismiss the past. "If I had refused . . . my commander, Falkar, would have killed me on the spot and brought in another to take my place. Should I have sacrificed myself? For what? For what purpose?"

"Perhaps," Si Cwan suggested, "so that you would not be wondering, years later, whether you should have sacrificed yourself."

They stood there for a long time, as the shadows continued to lengthen in the garden. Then, sounding much older than he had before, Lodec said, "My humblest apologies, Lord Cwan, if you believe that you are being deliberately distanced from the rebuilding of the Thallonian Empire. I shall make certain, in the future, to do all that is possible to include you."

"That would be appreciated," said Si Cwan stiffly.

"And Lord Cwan . . ."

"Yes, Speaker?"

Lodec looked at him grimly. "If it had been you issuing the command . . . and a soldier pledged to you had refused your order . . . you would have struck him down where he stood. Do not waste both our time telling me otherwise, for we both know it to be true. And you would have given no thought to the man's conscience, or sacrifice, or principles. You would have stepped on him with no more thought than you would a bug, and dismissed him from your mind almost immediately thereafter as not worth dwelling upon. So do not lecture me on matters of principle . . . if you would be so kind."

Si Cwan's jaw twitched, but he said nothing as he turned and left . . . because he knew that Lodec was perfectly right. And worse, he knew that Lodec knew.

ii.

If there was one thing that Kalinda knew when she saw it . . . it was death.

The home that the Danteri had provided for Si Cwan and her was spacious enough, certainly. It was well designed, with copious room—and rooms—for parties, gatherings, meetings, and so on. But she felt uncomfortable when she was there by herself, and so she had promised that she would meet Si Cwan outside the Senate building and go home with him from there.

It truly was a gargantuan structure. She craned her neck to look up at the towers, silhouetted against the twin moons, and she still felt as if she was not coming remotely close to seeing the top. Thanks to optical illusion, it seemed as if the three towers that composed the senate building literally came down from the sky, rather than having been built on the ground and stretching upward.

It was a cool night and Kalinda drew her cloak more tightly around her.

Then she heard laughter, the voices of senators approaching. Apparently they had been working late. They seemed to be in exceptionally good spirits, their voices echoing through the main entranceway that led to the great front doors. And they seemed to be saying something about "Wait until you meet him" and "We knew it was right from the first moment," but she had no clue specifically as to what they were talking about.

Kalinda had trained, as had Si Cwan, in the art of being unnoticed. Had it not been nighttime, she could still have blended in with the background and easily eluded all but the trained eye, which happened to be staring right at her. But here, with night having fallen, cloaked as she was, it was almost too easy.

She simply thought of herself as not being there. There was no magic to it, no supernatural mumbo-jumbo. Long ago she had learned that people tend to be noticed because they draw attention to themselves in any one of a hundred ways. So in order not to be noticed, all one had to do was firmly believe that one was not there. Pull into oneself, as it were. Do nothing to command attention, and you would be given none. "I think not," Si Cwan had once explained, "therefore I am not."

Indistinguishable from a tree or a shadow, Kalinda melted into the background as the senators emerged. "He was supposed to be here," one of them said, and "I think you were exaggerating about him," claimed another.

Then their animated discussion suddenly faded, even became choked off, as if they'd seen something so startling that it had closed off the air in their throats. A tree blocked Kalinda's view, and she moved ever so slightly in order to make out what was happening.

That was when she saw death.

He was tall, incredibly tall . . . eight, maybe nine feet. And wide, powerfully built, muscles rippling. He was wearing what appeared to be a sort of gold-scaled kilt around his middle, and an elaborately sculpted breastplate that curved up and back around his shoulders. His skin was black, as black as night, as black as the end of days, and yet it seemed to give off a glow. But not a glow from the moonlight; it seemed generated from within.

Most terrifying was his face. It reminded Kalinda a bit of the Dogs of War, and for a moment she thought that he was one of that breed. But there was no hint of fur on him, nor were his hands clawed. But his jaws, his nose, were long and distended, like a dog's snout. The edges of his mouth were frozen in a slight upturn, like a leering death's-head grin. His eyes were glistening, red and pupilless, and to a degree they looked dead as well. The creature wore a gleaming helmet upon his head that rose in a semi-conical style, and it obscured the upper portion of his head. But she would have wagered that he had the triangular ears of a dog, or mastiff of some kind.

She perceived a dark and terrifying aura around him. He was there, right there before her, and yet in some ways it seemed that he wasn't. That made no sense to her.

The Danteri senators were paralyzed in front of him. And then, almost as one, they went to their knees, and bowed their heads before him. As they did so, the glow surrounding him became that much stronger, the aura more defined.

When he spoke, it was with a low and frightening rumble, like an avalanche about to occur, and she was afraid she would be caught up in it. "Well met," he said. "We shall talk of many things . . . we . . ."

Then he stopped.

And turned.

And death looked straight at Kalinda.

She didn't move, didn't breathe. If she could have faded through the wall at that moment, she would have done so. He was staring right at her . . . and yet she wasn't certain that he could actually see her. Rooted to the spot, she didn't move so much as a centimeter.

The Danteri were, one by one, looking up at him in curiosity. They felt something in the air, felt the tension, but didn't know to what it should be ascribed. Finally one of them ventured, "High One . . . ?"

"It is nothing," he said at last.

Kalinda's gut reaction was to let out a sigh of relief, but she caught herself a heartbeat before doing so. It would have made her presence so obvious that even the deafest of senators would have perceived her at that point.

The creature turned his back to her and walked away, the other senators following behind him like sheep. Kalinda waited a long time to make certain they were gone, and even then had trouble getting her legs to move because she'd been so paralyzed with fright.

She had no idea who or what that had been.

But she knew she had to find out.

iii.

"You saw . . . death?"

Si Cwan and Kalinda were in their posh suites, Kalinda seated on the large couch and looking very apprehensive while Si Cwan was standing, hands draped behind his back, and looking extremely grave. It was not an affected look. There were certainly big brothers who condescended to their younger siblings, but Si Cwan was not one of those. And when it came to discussing matters of death, afterdeath, ghosts, and the like, he was fully prepared to acknowledge Kalinda as possibly the most knowledgeable Thallonian alive. "What do you mean 'death' precisely? Leave nothing out, Kally."

So she omitted nothing. She told him about everything that she had witnessed: the discussions, the genuflection, all of it. And most particularly, she told him about . . . the thing. The creature that she had seen. The mere description of the thing was enough to give Si Cwan chills.

"And you are quite certain," he said after giving her comments due consideration, "that it was not one of the Dogs of War. From your description, one of those—"

"I know, Cwan, I know that. That would make the most sense." Her hands were crossed carefully on her lap, a habit drilled into her by a mother long gone. "But it wasn't. It had . . . it had a totally different aura to it. An aura of something ancient. Of something . . ."

"Evil?"

She gave it some further consideration. "Actually . . . not evil. Not necessarily. Perhaps . . . trickery . . ."

"Trickery? Why do you say that?"

"Just . . . an impression I received. Nothing I can describe precisely. Just a feeling. I think we're dealing with something much bigger, much greater than the Dogs of War. Something very ancient. Something very frightening."

"And it frightened you because . . ."

"It just did, Cwan," she said, sounding a bit exasperated. "But I think you need to do something about it."

"Yes," said Cwan thoughtfully. "Yes . . . I do." He clapped his hands together briskly. "Very well, then. Let us attend to this."

Kalinda almost felt a little taken aback. "Just like that?"

"Yes. Just like that," Cwan said. "We will talk to the right people. We will tell them the right things. We will prompt them to believe," he continued, warming to the task, "that we know more than we do . . . and they will suffer if they do not cooperate with us."

"Are you going to hurt people?"

He looked at her mildly. "Only the ones who bother me," he said.

EXCALIBUR

i.

SOLETA SAT ALONE in the officers' dining hall, having breakfast by herself, as was her custom. She tended to eat lightly most mornings, and this was no exception. She had a small bowl of *plomeek* soup in front of her, and was daintily sipping the hot broth from a spoon, when she came to the slow realization that it had suddenly gotten rather quiet. This in and of itself was unusual enough, for the dining hall was usually fairly boisterous in the morning. But when she looked up to see what could possibly have caused this unexpected drop in the decibel level, she saw that everyone was staring at her. Or, to be more precise, at a point directly behind her.

Very slowly she turned and looked over her shoulder.

A man with a bird's head was standing directly behind her, eyeing her soup.

He was dressed in what appeared to Soleta to be a

variation on Egyptian garb, except he had wings. Well . . . not exactly wings. They were more winglike ornaments that ran the length of either arm, festooned with a mixture of black and white feathers. His head . . . well, it was indeed a bird's head. The yellow eyes rotated to fix on her, the head itself was entirely white feathers, and the beak was very long and narrow, the sort of beak sported by the bird known as the ibis. Something that appeared to be a crown was perched atop his head.

Not for a moment did Soleta come even close to being disconcerted. Instead she studied him for a time. She was able to do so in relative peace, since the room was deathly quiet. Then Lieutenant Beth, who had just been finishing breakfast with Lieutenant Goodwin, reached up and tapped her com badge. "Dining hall to security," she started to say.

Immediately Soleta said, "Cancel that, Lieutenant. That won't be necessary." She slid the soup to the far side of the table, in front of the chair that was opposite her. "Have you had breakfast, Thoth?" she inquired, as if being faced with a man with a bird's head was something she had to deal with routinely every morning.

His beak clicked as he spoke. "I have not, no. But I do not need to eat in your conventional sense."

"It is new experiences that make life interesting. Can you remove that . . . device?"

For a long moment more, the yellow eyes fixed upon her. And then Thoth reached up to the base of his throat, which, until he touched it, appeared perfectly fused with his dark brown flesh. But when he touched it, it peeled away, and his bird's head retracted up and into the crown.

The face that was revealed was rather handsome at that. His complexion was as dark as the rest of his skin, but his features were almost delicate. A slender nose, a thin mouth, an angular jaw, and his eyes . . . amusingly, his eyes were as yellow as the bird's eyes in the mask that had just vanished into the crown. He had a peaceful, almost gentle look to him that Soleta couldn't help but find mildly attractive. Considering the looks that he was getting from other women in the place—and a couple of the men—she wasn't the only one who considered him in that way.

He looked down at the soup, and then held out a hand. She placed the spoon in it and, very carefully so as not to spill any, he dipped the spoon into the soup, lifted it to his lips, and took a cautious sip. He pursed his lips a moment, and then nodded. "Intriguing," he said.

"I would not have thought to describe soup as 'intriguing,' but I will accept your analysis," she told him.

He continued to eat the soup. "You do not seem surprised to see me."

"It takes a good deal to surprise me," she said, making no attempt to sound modest. "McHenry told me that Artemis said you might be coming."

"Yes. This was quite good." He seemed a bit startled when he realized that he had finished the soup.

"You are Thoth," she said. "The Egyptian moon god who oversees such disciplines as writing, astronomy, mathematics, law, magic . . ."

"Magic to the ancient Egyptians," he clarified for her. "I daresay that what you have here would certainly qualify as magic insofar as the ancients would be concerned. What is magic to some is, to others, science. But you seem to know a good deal about me, whereas I know nothing of you."

She was all too aware that every eye in the place was upon her. "I think it would be best," she said slowly, "if we were to meet with the captain. You are, after all, a newcomer to this vessel, and it would be best if that procedure were followed."

"As you wish," he said.

Soleta quickly ascertained that Calhoun was on the bridge, in the captain's ready room, in conference with McHenry. Telling Calhoun of what had just occurred, and assuring him that a security escort was not going to be necessary, she set out down the corridor toward the turbolift with Thoth at her side. She resolutely ignored the looks and double takes she got from others as they passed by.

"You still have told me nothing of yourself," he reminded her.

"My name is Soleta," she said briskly, as if it was a matter of no consequence, "I am the ship's science officer, I am a Vulcan . . ."

"And Romulan."

He spoke so automatically, so effortlessly, that it caught her completely off guard. She spun to face him, eyes wide, unable to believe what she had just heard. "How did you—?"

"So it does not take all that much to surprise you after all," Thoth observed.

She lowered her voice, suddenly extremely apprehensive about being overheard by someone passing by. Fortunately at the moment that Thoth had chosen to blurt out her dual nature, there had been no one immediately around to hear. "How did you know?"

He smiled at her indulgently. "I am a god of truth. If it is spoken, I know. If it is not, I know . . . and will also know that which is not said. Call it a talent."

"I will call it none of your business, if you do not mind," she said, walking quickly down the corridor again with Thoth following her easily. She couldn't help but notice how perfect his stride was, and how his muscles seemed to ripple so elegantly as he moved. With extreme effort, she remained focused on the subject. "You came here because of my research into this area of space?"

The turbolift was just ahead of them, and they stepped in. They turned to face one another as the doors closed. "I know that you have some curiosity about it."

"Bridge," she said, and as the turbolift moved toward its destination, continued, "I am detecting energy waves, readings in patterns for which I have been able to find no precedent. I have not been able to detect one centralized source, and the very nature of the energy escapes me."

"Do you have any speculation, Soleta of Vulcan and Romulus?"

"Will you . . ." Her voice was far louder than she would have liked, especially in the confines of the turbolift, and she lowered it as she said, "Will you . . . please . . . not make mention of that again?"

"It is a tragic thing to be ashamed of one's heritage."

"It is a tragedy I am willing to live with," she said flatly. "The consequences of my silence on this matter, however, I would prefer not to have to live with, if it is all the same to you. And by the way, you are not a god."

He smiled that megawatt smile. "Are you quite certain?"

"An advanced being, yes, but not a god."

"That is very much in the eye of the beholder, is it not? To those who worshipped me . . . you would be a god. Or . . ." He studied her ears, chuckling softly. ". . . perhaps the devil. Who can say?"

"The energy waves," she said, trying to drag the conversation kicking and screaming back to something that would be of use to her. "Are your people responsible for generating them? If so, is it a sort of spillage or overflow from your power source? Does it present a danger? Are there ways it can be harnessed? Do you—what's wrong?"

She had seen the change in his expression. Something had most definitely occurred, and she had no clue what. But it had unquestionably changed the nature of the meeting, because his expression was very clouded and his yellow eyes were deeply troubled. "Thoth," she said again, "what's—?"

"It is a pity," he interrupted her abruptly, "that you desired to know what was generating the unknown energy waves you detected. For circumstances have arisen that will enable you to find out . . . firsthand. And it will not be a pleasant experience."

Soleta most definitely did not like the sound of that. "That sounds suspiciously like a threat, Thoth. I do not think threats will be necessary." She turned as the turbolift doors opened and said, "Come. If we speak to the captain, I am quite sure that he will—"

"Who are you talking to?" asked Burgoyne, turning in hir chair to look at the entering Soleta in puzzlement.

Soleta stopped and looked over her shoulder. Only the empty car of the turbolift was behind her. Otherwise there was no sign of Thoth.

"He's gone," said an annoyed Soleta.

"He's gone?" asked Burgoyne, getting to his feet. Kebron likewise seemed most interested in the conversation. "Who's gone?"

"Thoth," she said, feeling like a fool for scrutinizing the inside of the obviously empty turbolift, as if Thoth might somehow have shrunk to minuscule size.

"A god."

"*Another* one?" Kebron said, sounding rather exasperated by the entire thing. "Why not a fleet of them while we're at it?"

Ten seconds later, Kebron would have cause to regret having said a word.

ii.

At the exact moment that Soleta was first encountering Thoth, Mackenzie Calhoun was summoning Mark McHenry into his ready room.

McHenry entered, looking rather nervous to Calhoun, like a small boy being summoned to the principal's office for talking back to the teacher or getting into fights. To some degree, Calhoun's heart went out to him. McHenry hadn't asked for any of this, and would very likely have been more than happy to go on about his life with no involvement of gods or goddesses or Cyclops or dragons or whatever the hell else opted to step out of the pages of myth and legend and insert itself into the affairs of the *Excalibur*. But, Calhoun reasoned, there was no whining about it. The situation was what it was, and the only option they had left open to them was to deal with it.

Calhoun, from behind his desk, gestured for McHenry to sit. He did so, so awkwardly that it seemed as if he'd forgotten how to get his knees to bend. Calhoun tried to adopt as avuncular a manner as possible as he folded his hands and smiled at McHenry. "So . . . interesting times we're living in, wouldn't you say, Mr. McHenry?"

"If you mean 'interesting' as in the old Chinese curse, Captain, I'd have to agree," said McHenry. He seemed a bit haggard, as if he hadn't been sleeping much lately. Given everything that had been going on, that seemed quite likely.

"Look, McHenry . . . Mark . . . I can't tell you what to do . . ."

"Actually, you can," McHenry said with what seemed a jump in hope. "You're the captain. You can do exactly that. You can tell me what to do, and I'd have to do it."

"All right, point taken, I suppose I *can* tell you what to do. I am, however, choosing not to."

"Damn," muttered McHenry, sagging back in the chair. He looked rather depressed, and yet Calhoun had to make an effort not to smile.

"I am, however, extremely curious about several matters in front of us," Calhoun said. "Kebron came to me this morning . . ."

"Oh, God," moaned McHenry, sinking further into his chair.

"Mark, he *is* still your friend . . ."

"Unh-hunh."

"He could have sought me out far earlier, Mark, and told me about his observations and suspicions. He was, in fact, belatedly chagrined over the fact that he didn't. He told me if it had been anyone else, he would have come straight to me. But because of your long relationship, he wanted to be absolutely sure, wanted to give me every chance . . ."

"To hang myself?"

Calhoun sighed and shook his head. "The personal aspects of this matter, Mark, will be something you need to take up personally with Kebron. What interests me now is what he told me."

"And . . . what did he tell you?" asked McHenry, his eyes narrowing.

"He told me that you faced down a member of the Q Continuum. Not just any member, in fact . . . but the Q who has made such a point of making Jean-Luc Picard's life so . . . interesting . . ."

"There's that word again."

He nodded, and laughed softly at the notion. But then he grew serious again. "He said that Q was physically transforming individuals . . . but was either unable or unwilling to do so with you. And he appeared somewhat surprised . . . even taken aback by you. Considering the degree of power that Q wields, that is a remarkable reaction, to say the least." He paused. McHenry didn't volunteer to say anything. "Do you want to explain it?" he prompted.

"I'm . . . afraid to."

Calhoun stared at him, uncertain what to make of that. "You mean . . . you're afraid of recriminations . . . ?"

"No. I'm just . . . afraid to think about it." He let out an unsteady breath. "Captain . . . the older I've gotten . . . the more I've felt like . . . like I'm becoming one of them."

"Them. You mean the Beings."

McHenry nodded, his face wan. "You have . . . you have no idea what it's like. I mean, when people hit puberty, there are always changes, you know? That's natural. When it happened to me, though, I felt . . . I was able to reach out, to . . . I . . ." He shook his head. "I can't explain it, really. And then Artemis and I became . . . you know . . ."

"Lovers?"

"Yes."

"But you broke it off."

"Because I was afraid," he said. "When I would be with her . . . I mean, *with* her, you know . . . ?"

"Yes, I get the picture, Mr. McHenry."

"Well . . ." And he seemed to be casting his thoughts back to that time. "I felt like . . . like she was doing more than . . . you know. I felt as if she was unlocking something, pushed a button in my head that I didn't even know was there. That's why I broke it off. Hell, maybe that's why I joined Starfleet . . . to try and run away from . . . from everything, I guess. The thing is, once she pushed that button, there was no going back, and I think it's been building over the years. And I'm becoming . . ."

"More like them, you said. But what do you mean by that, exactly?"

McHenry couldn't sit still anymore. He was out of his chair, pacing. "You see them," he said. "You see her. They're all the same. Beings who have energy at their base . . . who are able to manipulate it in a variety of ways, depending on their individual skills. Beings who . . . who . . ."

"Who what?"

He stopped pacing and lowered his voice, as if afraid of the words about to come out of his own mouth. "Who look human . . . purely because they choose to look human. And I'm thinking . . . I'm thinking the reason Q couldn't alter my appearance . . . was because my belief in what I look like, in what I am . . . held me together. Made me immune to him. But naturally that makes me start to wonder . . ."

"How solid your hold on your humanity is?"

McHenry nodded bleakly.

"You think . . . that if you stop believing in your appearance . . . in yourself . . . that you will become just like them. That you'll lose your humanity completely."

Again McHenry nodded, looking ashamed, looking frustrated, looking scared.

"That's why you've been secretive about it. That's why you've tried to repress it."

"That's just it," said McHenry, turning to face Calhoun once more, leaning with his hands on the back of the chair he'd just been sitting in. "I haven't been trying to repress it as much as I should."

"What do you mean?"

He took in a deep breath to steady himself. "Ever since Artemis and I were lovers . . . ever since she flipped that switch . . . my head's been different. It's as if I'm able to be everywhere at the same time, if I just think about it. Like there's so much information out there, more than I can handle, more than anyone can handle, that I just have to sit there and let it wash over me. I'm able to . . . how do I explain this . . . ?" His voice trailed off and Calhoun sat patiently, letting McHenry take his time, phrase it in his own way. "It's like . . . like I'm keyed into the universe at a space-time level," he said finally. "That's how I always know where I am, no matter what. At first I was afraid to do even that, but hey, it got me through the Academy, so I didn't want to question it."

"Well, that's . . . that's not such a bad thing, Mark . . . in the final analysis . . ."

"Except that's not the final analysis, Captain. It's not the final anything. You see, the more I used this . . . this 'ability' of mine . . . the more I felt like I could do other things. Things I'm afraid to do because it'd bring me closer to being one of them."

Slowly the light was beginning to dawn for Calhoun. "What . . . sort of things, Mark?"

He wanted to look down, but instead he forced himself to meet his captain's gaze. "Like . . . affecting the space-time continuum on a local level. I only did it the one time, and I wasn't even sure I could do it then. And when I did, it left me so exhausted, I could barely move for three days . . ."

Slowly Calhoun got to his feet, staring at McHenry as

if seeing him for the first time. "When the *Excalibur* blew up . . ."

"Yes . . ."

"There . . . really *wasn't* enough time to get everyone off the ship . . ."

McHenry shook his head, looking miserable. "I'm so sorry, Captain . . ."

"*Sorry?*" He couldn't believe what he was hearing.

"I wish I could have done more. If only I could have turned time backward somehow . . . prevented the entire destruction . . ."

"*Mark!* You're telling me that somehow you . . . you warped time? Took the five minutes that we had to get off the ship and just . . . just stretched it to fifteen or twenty, as if it was elastic . . . ?"

McHenry shrugged. "Well, there *is* a certain amount of subjective elasticity to time. That's why time really does fly when you're having fun, but drags on if you're involved in some boring duty. It's just an aspect of science that no one's really explored because they don't know it's there *to* be explored. I call it Chronal Infarction myself, although I'm sure smarter people than me will wind up calling it something else. Plus we use the warp engines to bend space and time around us anyway. So I was able to tap into the energy being given off by the overloading warp engines to slow things down. Make time bend to my subjective point of view. Of course, I had to convince myself that time was slowing down, which wasn't easy. But thought made it deed, and, well . . ." He shrugged, looking a bit self-conscious about the whole thing.

"Mark, you saved everyone's life! You saved mine!

That . . . that bizarre feeling," Calhoun was saying, shaking his head in disbelief, "when I was running toward the shuttle bay . . . feeling as if I was . . . was swimming through a reality that had become nearly gelatinous . . . what I was experiencing was you, bending time around me."

"Yessir. I hope you're not upset."

"Upset!" Calhoun laughed, unable to believe what he was hearing, and he came around the desk, took McHenry's hand and shook it firmly. "Didn't you hear what I said? I owe you my life. I will never forget what you did."

"Well, that's what Artemis was talking about when she said I had potential. The thing is . . . I'm not sure I want it."

"Mark, you can't deny what you are."

"Captain, with all respect," McHenry said, glancing in the direction of Calhoun's sword hanging upon the wall, "if people couldn't deny what they were, you'd still be back on Xenex running around being a barbarian warlord. The only unlimited energy source in the cosmos is the capacity for self-delusion."

"Point taken," Calhoun admitted. "We seem to have opposing views of how you handled the destruction of the previous *Excalibur,* Mr. McHenry. Whereas I would be inclined to see that you were given the Starfleet Citation for Conspicuous Gallantry, you on the other hand seem rather annoyed with yourself because you weren't capable of single-handedly preventing the entire ship from being destroyed. You never struck me as a glass-half-empty sort of fellow, Mark."

"Times change," McHenry said dourly.

"Very true. And what we have to deal with at this point is the times that are directly in front of us. Specifically . . . the Beings." He crossed his arms and scrutinized McHenry. He didn't want to overburden the already fidgety helmsman, but there was simply no point in walking gently around the situation. "Mark . . . I know we're discussing the rest of your life here. I know this is possibly the largest decision you're ever going to be faced with, and I would love to tell you to take all the time in the world. But we don't have that luxury. We're faced with a race of remarkable power with an offer on the table. We have some sort of uncharted, unknown energy emission, the origin of which we still have not determined . . . and if we're going to do so, we may have to go right into the thick of it. I will do that if necessary, but it's always better to have too much information than too little."

"What do you want from me, Captain?" He did not sound at all plaintive or whining when he said it; he simply wanted to know.

Calhoun scratched his beard thoughtfully. "You told me that Artemis came to you. That she explained this entire 'golden age' thing. This 'ambrosia.' Let's put aside for a moment the entire concept of—for lack of a better word—worshipping these individuals. What I need you to tell me . . . from here," and he tapped his solar plexus, "from your gut . . . whether or not these Beings can be trusted. You say you're becoming like them? Don't be afraid of that. Let that, instead, inform you. Let it enable you to put your mind into where their minds are. See the universe from their point of view.

The best way to *predict* your opponent is to *become* your opponent. Look into your heart of hearts and tell me: Are these Beings honorable? Can they be trusted to keep their word? Are you willing to possibly stake the direction of the Federation on their offer?"

Calhoun expected McHenry to go into deep thought. Indeed, he was fully prepared to watch McHenry stare off into space, either retreating deep into his own head or else expanding his consciousness to take in the entirety of the galaxy—or some such—before coming back with an answer.

Instead what he got was McHenry forcefully nodding his head . . . and then he said, "Absolutely not."

"What?" said Calhoun, confused. "You . . . nodded yes, but said—"

"I was nodding because I was certain, Captain. I mean . . . you know all the myths about how the gods were petty and selfish and all that? Well, as near as I can tell, it's pretty much true, and my gut—to use your word—is telling me they haven't changed. No, Captain. They can't be trusted . . . and, frankly, now that I realize it, I can't believe that I was considering, for even a moment, becoming what they wanted me to become. In fact, I—"

And that was when all hell broke loose.

iii.

Soleta, shaking her head and choosing to be tolerant of Kebron's general out-of-sorts deportment—something she'd been seeing much more frequently these days—was heading toward the science station when Kebron suddenly said, "Shields just came on!"

Burgoyne had been studying a fuel-consumption report, and almost dropped it as s/he sat forward abruptly. Tapping hir combadge, s/he called "Captain on the deck!" before turning to Morgan and snapping, "Sound red alert. Soleta, get me a reading. If we have incoming, I want to know what it is, and I want to know yesterday."

Soleta didn't need to be told. She moved straight to her science station, only a graceful sidestep preventing her from colliding with Calhoun as he emerged from the ready room, concern on his face. The red-alert klaxon was already sounding as McHenry, having emerged right behind Calhoun, vaulted the railing and slid into his post. "I can't leave for five minutes . . ." he muttered.

"Captain, detecting massive energy spikes, of the same nature we've been monitoring . . . only more so," Soleta told him. "Readings are off the scale."

"They're always off the scale," commented McHenry. "We've just to install bigger scales."

"Not now, McHenry. Kebron, talk to me: What have we got?"

"Sensors are detecting incoming at 387 mark two."

"Conn, bring us around. Kebron, nature of the incoming."

"Appears to be incoming vessels. Nothing beyond that."

"Soleta . . . ?"

But the science officer shook her head. "The same scrambling of our sensors that we've been getting from the energy emissions is continuing to block scanners, sir. They do appear to be vessels, as Mr. Kebron reported. But size, number, configuration, all remain unknown."

"Can we get a visual on it. Give me *something*, dammit."

The screen wavered and there, on the screen, were small objects, getting closer by the second. There was silence on the bridge for a long moment, and Calhoun frowned. "What . . . *are* those? Wait, that . . . that's not what I think it is . . . ?"

They drew closer still, the details beginning to take shape.

And Kebron, normally the most stoic and reserved individual on the bridge—the one so phlegmatic that he made Soleta look like a laughing hyena in comparison—said loudly, "What the *frell* is that . . . ?"

"Soleta . . . ?" said Calhoun, but it was clear that he was looking for confirmation of what his disbelieving eyes were telling him.

Soleta couldn't believe she was saying it even as she spoke. "It's a fleet of Greek battleships, sir."

And it was. A dozen ships . . . not remotely space vessels of any kind. Instead, as if the Flying Dutchman and his brothers had decided to embark on a cruise, the ships with their proud sails billowing were gliding through space.

"Now *there's* something you don't see every day," said Morgan.

"Give me a closeup on one," Calhoun said, trying to keep the astonishment out of his voice.

Quickly the screen shifted, and they were staring at one

of the ships. "It's an Athenian vessel called a trireme," Soleta said. "It is approximately fifteen feet wide, one hundred twenty feet long, with the keel extending an additional ten feet in the front to provide a battering ram, which itself is covered with gold armor. This one has followed the not-unusual practice of painting the ram to look like the face of a fierce animal: a boar, in this instance."

"Wonderful, Soleta. Now would you mind telling me what these things are doing in the middle of space?"

"The backstroke," said McHenry.

"McHenry," an annoyed Burgoyne whirled on him, "this isn't the time for—"

"It is!" McHenry protested, pointing. "Look!"

He was right. It was at that point that a massive array of oars extended from either side of the ship. They were, in fact, moving backward, and the ship—impossibly—was responding, slowing and changing its angle.

"The trireme is readjusting its course, Captain," McHenry said after a quick glance at the instruments. "They all are. If we maintain our current heading, we will be on a direct collision course."

"The one saving grace in all this," mused Calhoun, "is that if Admiral Jellico thought my report about the Great Bird of the Galaxy was dubious, he's *really* going to hate this one. Mr. Kebron, try to open a hailing frequency. Can those ships hurt us in any way?"

"Not a clue, Captain," rumbled Kebron.

"Best guess."

"No, they can't."

"Captain, they're opening fire!" called a stunned McHenry.

Through the darkness of space they came: arrows. Dozens of them. Hundreds of them, hurtling through the vacuum, leaving streaks of power behind them, and they slammed into the *Excalibur* from a dozen different directions. The mighty starship was rocked, crewmen being slammed every which way. Relays started to overload but Morgan held them in check. Calhoun almost flipped out of his chair from the impact, and it was all everyone else could do to maintain his or her positions.

"Permission to change best guess, Captain," said Kebron.

"They're spreading out, coming in on all vectors," Soleta warned. "They're trying to surround us."

"McHenry, zero degree on the Y axis. Drop us like a rock."

"Aye, sir."

Obediently the *Excalibur* descended away from the ships, which were all approaching on a single plane as if riding the crests of unseen waters. Ludicrously, the oars were thrusting away against the nothingness of space.

Calhoun was out of his chair, leaning in toward McHenry. "Mr. McHenry," he asked, in a surprisingly calm, conversational tone, "is it possible that Artemis was somehow aware of the conversation that we had in my ready room, and what we're seeing is their response to your comment about their trustworthiness?"

"I'd say it's eminently possible, sir."

"More of them!" Soleta suddenly called out. "Directly to port. They came out of nowhere! Five seconds to collision!"

"All hands, brace for impact!" shouted Calhoun.

The Greek war galleys slammed into the *Excalibur,* and the ship shuddered under the hammering of battering rams first designed in the sixth century B.C. The starship rolled, momentarily out of control until McHenry managed to bring it back on line.

"McHenry," Calhoun called, "target phasers aft, and target photon torpedoes on the forward vessels!"

"Phasers aft, aye! Torpedoes locked and loaded, Captain!"

"Fire!"

The *Excalibur* cut loose at the triremes. They watched as the phasers made contact with the vessels, saw the ships shudder under the contact. "Damage to enemy vessels?"

"No appreciable damage, Captain," said Soleta. "We, on the other hand, have sustained forty percent loss of shields."

"This is getting out of hand," said Calhoun, "and I'm not even sure what the hell it is we're fighting about. Mr. McHenry, get us out of here, best possible speed."

"Aye, sir, best poss—*oh hell . . . !* Captain, another half dozen, coming in at 291 mark four."

"Incoming!" called Kebron.

"Hang on!"

Once again the "arrows" blazed through the darkness, slamming in from all sides. Individually they could not do much damage, but the sheer number of them caused the ship to rock furiously under the bombardment.

"Shields at fifty percent and dropping!" Morgan called out, the ops systems screeching warnings throughout the ship. "Lights out on deck three! Turbolift system out between decks five and seventeen!"

"Still no answer to hails, Captain."

"All right, that's it!" called Calhoun. "All hands! Attention all hands! Prepare for saucer sep! But this is not an evac, repeat, *not* an evac! Stardrive and saucer sections will both be used in battle! Mr. McHenry, the moment you're ready, separate the saucer from the warp section."

Kebron looked puzzled. "Sir . . . the battle bridge . . . ?"

"With the turbolift out, there's no time to get down there. Mr. Burgoyne . . . Miss Primus . . . looks like we're about to test some of those modifications."

iii.

Crewmen were at their posts on the battle bridge, but the command chair and the helm station stood empty. The officers looked around as the great rumbling sounding throughout the ship signaled that the saucer section had disengaged from the warp section.

And then, just like that, Morgan Primus and Mackenzie Calhoun appeared there.

They looked around, slightly disoriented for a moment. Then Calhoun looked at the battle bridge crew and said, "As you were."

"My God, it worked," said Morgan, appearing mildly impressed. "I know the test runs operated flawlessly, but still . . ."

"You can admire your handiwork later, Morgan." Quickly he moved to his command chair while Morgan took her place at the helm. The battle bridge had

**both conn and ops at one station, and Morgan oper-
ated it with confidence. "Bring us around, heading
221 mark eight. They want ramming? Let's give them
a ramming they'll never forget."**

"Let's give them a ramming they'll never forget," said
Calhoun on the main bridge of the *Excalibur.*

He was in his command chair, a large visor over the
upper half of his head, covering his eyes. Some feet away,
Morgan was at the ops station, wearing a similar device.

Soleta saw that Ensign Pfizer, standing near her, was
looking on in astonishment. "I . . . don't understand . . ."

"Brand-new Holotechnology . . . one step beyond the
new Starfleet Holocommunicator," Soleta explained,
keeping an eye on her sensor readings. The armada
seemed confused over the fact that there were now two
opponents as opposed to one, and had been reconfigur-
ing their attack courses in order to accommodate the
new battle scenario. "The captain and Miss Primos are
able to see everything the holos see. The computer built
into the helmets has a synaptic engram link, so their
very thoughts are able to manipulate the holobodies.
The captain can effectively be in two places at once."

"Mr. Burgoyne," called McHenry, "warp sled engaged."

And that was another perk of the new *Excalibur* that
Soleta appreciated. In the past, saucer sections had been
limited in their maneuverability owing to the fact that
the faster-than-light engines remained with the warp-
drive section of the ship during separation. But the *Excalibur* was different. It had been outfitted with an
experimental warp sled, based on the type that was standard issue on most shuttlecraft, but designed to propel

the significantly larger saucer section. The warp sled had limited range and power, and didn't go much above warp one. That, however, was more than enough for the type of emergency battle situation in which they now found themselves.

"Triremes regrouping," announced Kebron.

"Bring us around at 118 mark four," said Burgoyne.

"Bring us around at 228 mark two," said Calhoun.

Morgan guided the warp section of the ship with precision as Calhoun called to the tactical officer, "Goodwin, reroute power to forward shields! Prepare to fire aft torpedoes! Primos, full speed ahead. Take us right through them!"

"If they don't scatter . . . ?"

"They'll scatter," Calhoun said confidently. Goodwin, when they do, fire a full complement of photon torpedoes!"

"Eight vessels, coming in fast to starboard, Burgy!" warned McHenry. "Four more to port!"

"Hard to starboard!" ordered Burgoyne. "Fire phasers!"

The starship's phasers cut loose, pounding the approaching Greek vessels. The ships rocked under the assault.

"Energy surge!" Soleta called out. "I think they're about to fire another wave of those energy arrows!"

"Port pursuers are closing fast!" warned Kebron.

Burgoyne thought quickly for a moment, and then said, "Mr. McHenry, get ready to roll the saucer section ninety degrees!"

"Burgy, the stress that will subject the hull to—"

"I know exactly what this ship can handle, Mark. Get ready . . . keep approaching . . . don't slow . . ."

A broadside of arrows, propelled by unseen godly archers making impossible shots, were suddenly unleashed from the array of vessels ahead of them.

"Now, Mark!"

Propelled by warp speed and McHenry's firm hand, the saucer pivoted ninety degrees on its axis. The arrows, however, had been aimed at a horizontal target. Although several struck home in the front section, the damage to the saucer was minimal. The vast majority of the arrows, however, sailed right past their intended target . . .

. . . and smashed into the four ships that had been in pursuit of the saucer. Although they showed considerable resistance to the weaponry of the *Excalibur,* their own energies directed at them had a much more devastating affect. The ships erupted, overloaded on their own power, and a moment later they erupted, blowing apart in all directions.

In a most un-Vulcan display of enthusiasm, Soleta cried out, *"Got them!"*

"Sir, they're not scattering," said Morgan. There was a touch of concern in her voice.

Calhoun leaned forward, watching the image on the screen. "Maintain course and speed. They'll move."

They drew closer, closer, and the galleys held firm, drawing in toward one another.

"Captain . . . twenty seconds to collision," warned Morgan. "Even with forward shields at full, I am not certain we can survive a head-on collision."

"They'll move."

"Fifteen seconds."

"They'll move."

The warp section of the *Excalibur,* in a deep-space game of chicken, hurtled toward the Greek ships.

"Ten . . . nine . . . eight . . ." Morgan was counting down.

The ships were closer, closer still, and Calhoun was certain he could actually see people moving around on the open deck, people in togas similar to Artemis', but other outfits as well, some with a Viking look to them, some Egyptian . . .

"Seven . . . six . . . Captain, *they're moving!*"

Sure enough, the vessels were suddenly moving to either side, getting out of the way.

And Calhoun, at the last moment, spotted the gods, arrows at the ready, on either side.

Just as he'd expected.

"Y axis, down angle, forty-five degrees!" shouted Calhoun. "Go! Go!"

The warp section angled away as the arrows were unleashed. At point-blank range, they could not miss.

They didn't. The ships struck each other, enveloped one another in waves of energy that ripped through every plank, every oar. The sails went up in electric flame, and the gods vanished in an eruption of energy that was nearly blinding.

A roar went up on the battle bridge, and Calhoun smiled wryly.

"Excellent maneuver, Burgoyne," he said.

"Excellent maneuver, Captain," Burgoyne replied. "McHenry, bring us around to—"

And suddenly Calhoun knew. Or rather he sensed it before he knew it for himself.

"Hard astern!" he called, and the warp section whipped around . . .

. . . as Soleta's sensors told her the situation at the same time as Kebron's tactical array.

"Something's happening to the ships!" she called out.

And there it was, up on the screen. The smashed-apart ships, glowing in the darkness, were being gathered up by the remaining vessels, and they were joining with one another, fusing, growing larger and larger as they did so.

"Mr. Kebron!" called Burgoyne. "Lock phasers on target—"

"—and fire!" Calhoun ordered.

The photon torpedoes blasted out of the warp section, tearing into the rapidly evolving construct, as the—

—saucer section's phasers blasted through it. And it did no good at all. The ships came together, and then they were as one, and behind the ships, hanging there in space, impossibly, was the face of Artemis, sneering contemptuously at them. Through the vacuum, she spoke to them, and she said . . .

"Did you think it would be as easy as all that?"

The vessels came together as one, and the damned thing, Calhoun realized, was almost as large as the saucer section. The battering ram, pointed and potentially devastating, gleamed as if lit by inner energies. There was that hideous face painted onto the ram, the eyes cold and merciless, and when the oars were raised upward—as absurd as such a sight should have been—it made the vessel look like a huge bat bearing down upon . . .

"The saucer section!" Calhoun called out. "Burgoyne—"

"—it's going for the saucer section!" Calhoun still had the headgear on that enabled him to see through the eyes of his hologram, but he was still physically on the bridge of the saucer section, reacting vocally to what he was seeing.

Burgoyne realized it about the same time as Calhoun did, and s/he ordered, "McHenry! Evasive maneuvers!" There was no point in giving McHenry specifics; there was no one better at getting the hell out of the way of something than Mark McHenry.

Except he couldn't.

Not that he didn't try. He cut the ship hard over, and the saucer was able to get out of the direct path of the now dreadnought-sized vessel coming straight at them. However, the *Excalibur* saucer was bound by the laws of physics, able to maneuver only just so fast and no faster, while the godship moved to laws all its own. The monstrous trireme adjusted with miraculous speed, and Burgoyne realized with horror that the pointed and fearsome ram was coming straight at them, and there, in the depth of the void, they were out of space.

"All hands, brace for impact!" shouted Burgoyne, and for just a moment a part of hir stepped back and commented, *We seem to be saying that a lot lately. Got to work on that whole maneuverability thing.*

The ram slammed into the underside of the saucer

section, a third of the way in from the forward rim. It punched through the remaining shields as if they weren't there, and lanced upward and through, driving a hole through from the point of entrance up through where it emerged on the other side. Several hundred feet further in, and it would have hit dead center and punched right up through the bridge.

The Calhoun hologram came to a complete halt. Like a puppet waiting for someone to pull his strings, he simply stood there, staring into nothingness, fritzing occasionally. The Morgan hologram did likewise.

"Bring us around," ordered Goodwin. Lieutenant Beth, who had taken up her emergency post on the battle bridge, walked through Morgan. She did so without hesitation and with an utter lack of squeamishness, knowing that this wasn't the actual person. "Let's nail these bastards."

Since they were somewhat distracted by the activities of the Beings, the crew on the battle bridge didn't notice when Morgan's hologram vanished.

iv.

Xyon was in a complete state of panic.

He was bolting through the corridors, faster than Moke had ever seen him move. "Maaaaa!" he was screaming. Moke had never been more sorry that he had taught him that damned word than right now. Xyon wanted his mother, that was all there was to it, and it was going to be impossible to explain to him that they were in the warp section while his mother (and father, for that matter) were over in the saucer section. Add to that the shaking that the ship had endured in the past minutes, the blaring klaxon of the red alert, the general air of emergency, and that had been more than enough for Xyon to get himself worked up into a total fit.

Xyon darted around running crewmen, continuing to screech "Maaa! Maaaa!" the entire time. He had darted out of the children's center when the trouble had started, and Moke had been chasing him all over the damned ship for the duration of the emergency. He would have asked someone for help, but he understood that this was a battle situation. Certainly Calhoun had schooled him on what that circumstance met. And given everything that was going on, it just wasn't reasonable to think that security personnel could or would drop whatever they were doing to help track down a panicked child. Which meant it was up to Moke.

At least Moke wasn't in danger of losing him altogether. The transponder beneath Xyon's skin saw to that. It meant that although Xyon could keep ahead of him, Moke would never lose track of him. So it was just a matter of time until he managed to rein in Xyon. Either that, or else until Moke collapsed from the strain of chasing the toddler all over the place.

He kept an eye on his tracking device and then, miraculously, he saw that Xyon had stopped moving. Finally, Moke had caught a break. He kept running, because he didn't want to pass up the opportunity to actually catch up with the child, and if Xyon went into motion again, the whole thing would start all over. But fortunately enough, he still wasn't moving, and then Moke suddenly blinked in confusion because—according to the tracker—he had somehow gone right past Xyon.

He turned and looked around, confused for a moment. Then he saw: a Jefferies tube. "Well, that figures," he said to no one in particular. He was more amused and relieved than anything else.

Moke stood at the bottom of the Jefferies tube and called up into its dark recesses, "Xyon? You up there?" He knew, in point of fact, that Xyon was. He hoped that perhaps if he gave the child the opportunity, the child would come down on his own initiative. Such, however, did not appear to be the case, for Xyon didn't stir.

This made Moke slightly nervous. What if Xyon had gotten himself into some sort of trouble? Something life-threatening? With no further hesitation, Moke clambered up the ladder inside the Jefferies tube, moving deftly hand over hand until he achieved the top. He craned his head and looked around, suddenly wishing that he'd brought a flashlight.

Cross-junctions and cramped work areas lined the area at the top of the tube. They were different from the ones he'd had to wiggle through to get Moke that last time, but it was still the same general design. He certainly knew what he shouldn't touch . . . namely, anything. "Xyon," he whispered. "Xyon . . ." He wasn't in the immediate area, but the tracking device told him that

Xyon was extremely nearby, practically on top of him . . .

Directly on top of him, actually.

Moke craned his neck, leaning as far back in the tube as he could while still holding on to the ladder, and he looked up.

There was Xyon, staring down at him from an incredibly narrow catwalk overhead. Xyon smiled lopsidedly.

And suddenly the Dark Man was right behind him. Despite how impossibly small the space was, despite the fact that Xyon should have reacted to him but didn't, there was the Dark Man, looming, staring down at Moke, and then he was reaching around Xyon, who still didn't seem to notice, and he was reaching for Moke . . .

The boy let out a shriek of pure terror and, in doing so, lost his grip on the ladder. He toppled backward, his feet slipping off the rungs, and he tumbled down the Jefferies tube. Moke bounced from one side of the tube to the other, cracking his skull on a rung, ripping up his back on piping and consoles, and he tried to find something he could grip on to, but there was nothing, it was all happening too quickly.

And then Moke hit a rung once more, bounced off, and crashed to the floor of the corridor. He lay there, stunned, staring up into the darkness, his body shaking, although whether it was from the impact or in fear, he couldn't tell.

Something was moving in the Jefferies tube. It was the Dark Man, coming toward him. He knew that with absolute certainty, and then the Dark Man was just going to . . . to suck his soul, that was all. Suck his soul right out, because Moke was an evil boy who had hurt people, and the Dark Man was here to punish him, punish him for eternity.

The shadows dispersed around the fast-moving form, and that was when the stunned Moke saw that it was Xyon who was descending the Jefferies tube. Moving with the speed and assurance of a chimp, Xyon was on the ground next to the unmoving Moke, touching his face, looking concerned and frightened.

Moke couldn't feel the lower half of his body. It frightened him as he lay immobile on his back, and he wanted to get up but couldn't.

He saw the Dark Man upon the stair . . . and he wasn't there.

"What do you want?!" screamed Moke. *"What do you want?!"* But he wasn't there again. For the moment, he had gone away.

And Moke, his fear growing as he started to feel colder, trembled and shook as he said to a wide-eyed, confused Xyon, and wondered, "Am . . . am I going to die?"

V.

There was smoke everywhere, and out of all the situations she'd been in in the past, Soleta had never been so convinced that she was going to die as she was at that moment.

Energy was crackling everywhere, relays hopelessly overloaded and blown out. Smoke was stinging her, causing her eyes to water. She was lying on the floor and when she tried to move, she felt a sharp stabbing pain in her chest that made her conclude she had a busted rib. Soleta choked back an angry sob as she tried to orient herself, tried to figure out just where the hell she was. She remembered being thrown across the bridge from the impact, and then there was nothing, darkness, smoke everywhere. She coughed violently, stayed low to the floor, trying to find air to breathe, because Vulcan or no, her lungs would collapse as readily as anyone else's.

She heard moans from all around her, and there was debris all around her. She realized belatedly that she'd been damned lucky; a foot to the left and she would have been crushed by a fallen lighting array. The emergency lights were on, but even some of those were out, and the entire bridge was a ghastly, spectral array.

"All . . . all hands." She heard Burgoyne's voice through the darkness, coughing. "All hands . . . report in . . . bridge crew . . ."

"Here," Soleta managed to get out, her voice sounded ragged. She put her hand to her forehead to shove her hair out of her face, and came away with green blood on her hand. She told herself, in as calm and dispassionate a manner as she could, that head wounds tended to bleed a lot and that it wasn't necessarily related to the severity of the injury itself.

"I'm here," came Kebron's voice. Several others

sounded off as well. But she didn't hear Burgoyne. Nor did she hear Morgan or McHenry.

The smoke started to clear ever so slightly, and she was able to see a figure standing in it. For one heart-stopping moment, she thought it was a Borg, and then she realized it was Calhoun, still wearing the connection helmet to the hologram.

Then she saw the viewscreen. Astoundingly, it was still functional. The picture was filled with static, but she could see it nevertheless. And what she saw on it did not give her cause for comfort.

The gigantic ship was coming around again. The ram had been withdrawn from the saucer, and she could only assume that the entire saucer hadn't been torn to shreds through explosive decompression because the fail-safe shields had snapped into existence over the rents in the hull. But it wasn't going to make much of a difference in a few moments, because they weren't moving and the ship was heading straight for them.

"Morgan! Move to intercept!" came Calhoun's voice, and she realized he was speaking through his holo avatar on the warp section. "Yes, Goodwin, I'm back on line!" He coughed fiercely, then pulled his attention back immediately. "Morgan . . . where's Morgan? Where's her holo . . . ? All right, Beth, plot a course! Goodwin, arm photon torpedoes . . . !"

There was nothing in his voice that betrayed any nervousness. He was utterly focused. But Soleta had seen how quickly the Greek vessel was moving, had calculated the distance, and been forced to the conclusion that there was simply no way that the warp section was going to get there in time, or any difference that the photon torpedoes would make.

And then the saucer lurched, and for one moment Soleta—along with everyone else on the ship— thought that they'd been hit. But quickly she realized that it couldn't be, that the sailing ship wasn't there yet. For there it was, on the screen, except the angle was shifting and the saucer was being pulled away from it, faster and faster, and suddenly the Greek trireme was being hit from overhead by a lethal combination of phaser fire and photon torpedoes. Then photon torpedoes exploded from the other direction as well, and the dreadnought trireme didn't know where to look first.

Another starship, flew through Soleta's mind, and then she realized: the *Trident.* Even as the thought went through her mind, the voice of Captain Elizabeth Shelby crackled through the bridge's com system. *"Excalibur,* this is *Trident.* We're a little early for our rendezvous, but somehow I don't think you're going to mind. We have you in our tractor beams and are pulling you out of harm's way."

"Much obliged, Captain," said Calhoun. He was bracing himself against the railing, which was partly bent in half. "Don't let down your guard! Keep firing! Don't let up for a second! And if a giant hand or face should appear, don't let it rattle you."

"I didn't copy that, Calhoun. Did you say a giant—?"

"Hand or face, yes."

"Who the hell are these people?" Shelby's voice demanded. "Greek sailing ships that can punch a hole in a starship? What's going on? You know what . . . on second thought, save it. They damaged you. We're going to kick their asses now and settle for answers later. And I know we can."

Soleta, making sure that no one else could see her, smiled slightly at the bravado.

"Mac, they're breaking off," Shelby said abruptly. "Apparently they've had enough."

And that did indeed appear to be the case. The dreadnought had veered off, and was suddenly retreating. The remaining smaller ships surrounded it. At first Soleta was concerned that it was some sort of trick, that they'd come back and take a run at both the *Trident* and the warp section of the *Excalibur* before turning and finishing off the saucer section.

But that seemed not to be the case. Instead the ships kept going. Soleta staggered over to her science station. Several of the sensory devices were down, but enough was functioning for her to be able to say, "They're definitely gone, Captain."

"Oh gods . . . no . . ."

It was Burgoyne's voice. It was weak and in pain, but it was hir, and then she heard hir call out, "Bridge to sickbay!"

"Selar here. Burgoyne, where is Xyon? Everything happened so—"

"He's on the warp section with Moke, he's fine! Selar! Get people up here . . . fast! Now! *Now!*"

And Soleta had a sick, awful feeling she knew what it was. She moved quickly, stumbled and fell over some fallen debris, and felt another jolt of pain through her torso even as she moved around to the front of the bridge.

Burgoyne was lying on the floor, and even from where she was standing Soleta could see that hir left leg was broken. But Burgoyne didn't seem to notice, or care. Instead s/he was looking in dismay at the two bodies at the front of the bridge.

McHenry was sitting there, eyes open, staring at nothing. He was slumped back in his chair, his head lolling to one side. The conn console was utterly fried, as if massive bolts of electricity ... or something else ... had come leaping out of there like contained lightning. The front of his shirt was completely blackened, as if a spear of energy had slammed through. The back of his chair was broken clear off.

Morgan was slumped across him. She wasn't moving. Her body was completely blackened, as if she had been roasted alive. Her uniform was crumbling away, her skin was puckered and blistered.

It was clear what had happened: Some sort of power, beyond comprehension, had come leaping out of the conn unit. Morgan, seeing it, had instinctively thrown herself in front of McHenry to try and protect him. As a result, she had borne the horrific brunt of it.

But she can't be dead, Soleta thought desperately. *She's ... she's immortal ... she can't die ... it's impossible ...*

Calhoun looked down at them. He closed McHenry's eyes, reached down and touched the burnt remains of Morgan's hair. He turned in her direction then, and she saw the pain in his eyes, but the hardness as well. The hardness of a man who had seen more death in his existence than Soleta could ever imagine. "Mr. Kebron," he said softly, "is your board functional?"

"Aye, sir. Barely."

"Route ops systems through it. Get me damage report and casualty count."

Soleta couldn't believe that Calhoun was managing to be so businesslike, so detached. Then she realized that if he had come apart, if he'd grieved in front of his crew, if he'd taken the luxury of showing how he must be feeling at that moment . . . well, that was the behavior she wouldn't believe.

There was the sound of movement on the emergency access ladder, and an instant later Selar was making her way through the rubble and debris. Dr. Maxwell was right behind her, carrying a bag and emergency surgical instruments. She saw Burgoyne's leg, and for a moment concern passed across her face, but then she spotted the two bodies at the front of the bridge. "Maxwell," she snapped, and he immediately came forward, opening the bag and handing her a tricorder.

"Captain," Kebron said, "getting damage-control reports. The breach has been sealed. Eight known fatalities, twenty-seven casualties, and three MIAs. We think they may have been pulled into space before shields were in place."

Calhoun simply nodded. He was watching Selar, never taking his eyes off her as she ran her tricorder over both of them. Maxwell was preparing hypos for the two of them, but then slowly Selar stood, turned to Maxwell, and shook her head. Without a word, his face carefully impersonal, he returned the hypos to the bag.

And when Calhoun next spoke, he sounded that much older, and that much more tired.

"Mr. Kebron," he said, "please raise a channel to the *Trident*. Tell Captain Shelby . . . that I need to speak to Robin Lefler. That I have . . . some bad news to tell her . . ."

DANTER

IT DIDN'T SEEM ALL THAT LONG AGO to Si Cwan that he had been to the luxurious estate of Lodec, the Senate Speaker. *How much,* mused Si Cwan, *things have changed, and yet how much they also have remained the same.* The exterior of the house looked much different in the middle of the day than it did at twilight. More inviting somehow. The air was crisp, however, signaling the advent of the cooler seasons of Danter.

This time, however, he had Kalinda by his side. This was not a move that he had made willingly, nor did he think it especially wise. Kalinda, however, would not hear anything about it.

"I'm going with you," she had told him in no uncertain terms when he had received the summons from the speaker.

They had been in Si Cwan's suite of offices at the Senate building. The offices had been specifically designed for him, and even bore a passing resemblance to the architectural style of the late, lamented Thallonian palace.

"Under no circumstance," he had said.

"Si Cwan . . . I'm not a fool. The reason he has summoned you has everything to do with the way you've been behaving in the past few days. You've been going from senator to senator, making passing references to 'death gods' and such. Yet you haven't been too specific about any of it, and that very vagueness has left all of them wondering. They look at you with suspicion and fear now when you pass through the hallways, because they all think you know more than you're telling, and they're all worried that you know more than they wanted you to know . . ."

"Yes, Kally, I'm aware of all that," Si Cwan had said reasonably. "I told you that was what I was going to do."

"But you've put yourself at tremendous risk."

Si Cwan had laughed at that. "Risk? From these mites? They pose no threat to me."

She had been less than enthused at the sound of that. "Do you have any idea how overconfident you sound?"

"Kally . . ."

"Don't 'Kally' me!" Glancing right and left, she lowered her voice. "In case you haven't noticed, we happen to be in a distinct minority here. There's exactly two Thallonians in residence on this world. Last I checked, there are something like two billion Danteri."

"Yes, but one Thallonian is worth at least one billion Danteri, so that evens the odds."

"You act as if this is a huge joke!"

"No, Kalinda, I do not think this is a huge joke. However, I don't consider it the cause for concern or near panic that you seem to. I am simply stirring things up. That is all. Helping to bring the pot to a boil."

"Yes, well," she had said doubtfully, "my concern is that you've been so busy stirring things up, that you're about to get yourself tossed in the pot. I doubt that the speaker has said he wanted to see you because he wishes to compliment you on your scintillating personality."

"That much is true," Si Cwan had admitted.

"And if I am right, and there is danger involved, then it would be best if I were along with you."

"Now how," he had asked skeptically, "do you figure that?"

"Simple. Either there is going to be some sort of brutal retaliation—read 'assassination attempt' or simply 'ambush'—by Lodec and the other senators, or there isn't. If there isn't, then obviously there's no problem. If, on the other hand, there is, my presence will have an effect on the situation. They will have to carry out their ambush in my presence. They may be reluctant to do so, which could wind up saving your life."

"Or," he had replied, "they will do so anyway, and simply kill you as well."

"In which case, they would have gotten around to having me disposed of anyway, so I am simply saving time."

He had found that impossible to argue with, and the result was that when Si Cwan presented himself at the front door, she was right there with him.

They were guided through the speaker's home by one of the servants, and Si Cwan was doing all that he could to pay attention to everything around him. He sought out the darkest corners, every possible hiding space, to determine whether someone was secreted within them, waiting to leap out. No immediate danger seemed forthcoming, however. That did not, however, prompt Si Cwan to lower his guard for even a moment. It did make him consider, though, Kalinda's earlier words, and he faintly started to regret the actions he had taken that had brought him to this present situation. If there indeed was an ambush, he would very likely have no chance. The odds were entirely on the side of his "hosts." He couldn't help but think that he should have planned better, and could only chalk the present lopsided odds up to extreme hubris on his part. He could only hope that Kalinda did not suffer as a result of his overconfidence.

They were waiting for him in the garden.

Unlike his previous meeting with the speaker, however, there were half a dozen senators there. All of them had been among the senators that Si Cwan had been confronting the past couple of days. They had smiles frozen onto their faces, and they bobbed their heads in greeting as if they were happy to see him. Si Cwan returned the gesture, but as he did so he looked very carefully into their eyes. Most of the time, the eyes were incapable of masking true intent, if one was perspicacious enough to read them correctly.

He was certain that he was, at the moment, looking into the eyes of people who had something to hide. The only thing he could not determine was what that something might be.

Only Lodec seemed genuinely happy to see him. Then again, that might well be because Lodec was anticipating that this would be the last time he would have to look at the Thallonian again. "Lord Cwan . . . and the lady as well. We are doubly blessed." He took Kalinda's hand, folding the one of her hands into two of his and bowing deeply.

"You have summoned us, and we are here," Si Cwan said stiffly.

Lodec looked stunned at Si Cwan's phrasing. " 'Summoned'? That sounds so coarse! 'Invited,' I think, is the better word. Or perhaps 'requested the honor of your presence.' Either or both of these would be more accurate than something as brutal as 'summoned.' Is that not right, gentlemen?" The other senators immediately bobbed their heads in unison.

"As you wish," said Si Cwan with a small, tolerant smile. " 'Invited,' then. So to what purpose have you invited us?"

Lodec extended a hand, gesturing for Si Cwan to walk alongside him. The other senators fell into step behind him. Si Cwan studied them more closely, trying to determine if this group itself might be the ambush. They did not appear armed, however, and they certainly did not look as if they were combat ready. It might again have been hubris, but Si Cwan was reasonably sure he could break the lot of them in half without going to any exceptional strain. So he walked, listening to Lodec speak as he did so.

"I . . . regret the tone and direction of our last meeting, Lord Cwan," Lodec said as they walked.

"Do you?"

"Yes, I do. I was far more abrupt with you than I

should have been . . . more so than you deserved, certainly. And the reason for my attitude is quite simple, really: Your complaints had basis in fact."

"Did they," Cwan said neutrally.

"Yes, they did. You felt that there were things being said behind your back. You felt that your presence here was not being properly valued. There is indeed some truth to that."

"I see. And you are now prepared to tell me why."

"Yes," said Lodec, exhaling deeply as if he were about to discharge the weight of the world that had saddled itself upon his shoulders. "Yes, I am prepared to do that very thing. You see, Lord Cwan, shortly after you took up residence here, we sent out word of the preparations for the rebuilding of the Thallonian Empire. The initial responses we got were very favorable, *very* favorable, as you know. You greeted many delegates from those initial contacts."

"Yes, I know, I was there," Si Cwan remarked dryly.

"But our initial announcements wound up bringing us . . . someone else."

There was something about the way he said that which immediately made Si Cwan cautious. He shot a glance at Kalinda, who mouthed the word *Death.* "Someone else?" he said neutrally.

"Yes. Someone who is apparently able to bring the Danteri race, and the new Thallonian Empire, to levels previously undreamed of. You see, this . . . individual . . . was able to present us with something that we could offer to any and all who were interested in joining the new Thallonian Empire. An amazing incentive. There are, after all, those who still do not trust the Thallonians."

"No!" said Si Cwan in mock horror.

The sarcasm went right past Lodec and the senators. "Tragically, it is true," he said. "We learned, in subsequent conversations with these individuals, that they are interested in their own selfish interests, first and foremost. They want to know what—if anything—is to be gained by them personally if their races agree to be a part of the new empire. Well," and he looked to the other senators for support. Their heads bobbed in unison. "Our new friend, our new ally, has been able to provide us with something very specific. Something to serve as an incentive so tempting, so enticing, that no reasonable race could conceivably turn away from it."

Kalinda spoke up, speaking with faint irony. "I have generally found in my experience, Senator, that races as a whole tend to be rather stupid. They think with a mass mind-set, and as a result can invariably be trusted to do the wrong thing. Only individuals tend to be reasonable."

"Well put, young lady, well put," Lodec said quickly, and once again the others bobbed their heads.

"So would you care to tell us," asked Si Cwan, "what this remarkable 'incentive' is?"

Lodec stopped walking. The others immediately ceased moving as well. They were in the center of the garden, a large fountain nearby with water bubbling out the top. The fountain had a statue in the middle, a Danteri warrior with an upraised sword, and the water was spurting out the top of the blade. For reasons he couldn't quite determine, Si Cwan considered the imagery slightly disturbing.

"Tell me, Lord Cwan ... have you heard of a substance called ..." He paused in anticipation, looked around at the others, smiling, and then said almost breathlessly, "ambrosia?"

Si Cwan and Kalinda looked at each other.

"No," he said with a shrug. "Should I have?"

"It is—to put it mildly—a delicacy. To put it less than delicately, it could be considered ... well ... food of the gods."

"Indeed. And what gods would those be?"

Si Cwan noticed that Kalinda was trying to catch his attention. She was tilting her head ever so slightly in a gesture that he knew all too well. He turned back to the senators before they could respond and said, "A moment, Senators, please. My sister wishes to speak with me about something."

"As you wish," said Lodec, sounding very expansive.

They resumed walking, then, as Si Cwan and Kalinda stepped around the fountain, the rushing water covering their words when they spoke softly to one another.

"I don't like this," she said softly, urgently. "We should leave."

"Why? I'm still not seeing any immediate threat."

"Cwan, *they're* the threat."

Si Cwan sniffed disdainfully. "Them? Those pampered, ill-equipped politicians? I could dispatch any or all of them within moments. You could as well."

"No. No, something's wrong. Their auras have changed."

"What?"

"I ... I don't know how to explain it, but their

auras . . . their pure bio-energies . . . they seem different somehow. I don't know how else to say it."

"And that presents a danger."

"I believe it does, yes."

He considered the entire concern to be somewhat obscure, but there was one thing that was beyond dispute: Kalinda was genuinely worried. And he had come to depend upon her instincts.

"Lord Cwan," came Lodec's voice from just behind him. Si Cwan was startled; Lodec and the senators were right there, and they should not have been able to sneak up on him. He was usually far more alert than that. "Is everything all right?"

"Kalinda. . . does not feel well," Si Cwan said smoothly. "I was thinking, gentlemen—and I regret the inconvenience—that we might wish to continue this another day. This 'ambrosia' is, I'm sure, quite interesting . . ."

"Interesting!" Lodec laughed, as did the others. And although Si Cwan could not sense auras and such, he was now starting to see for himself the growing confidence displayed by the senators. "Lord Cwan, you are master of understatement! Ambrosia is . . . it is miraculous! It makes you more energized! More perceptive! More physically commanding! Why, if the new Thallonian Empire were to become the central force for distributing ambrosia . . ."

The dime dropped for Si Cwan.

"It's a drug," he said slowly.

" 'Drug' has such negative connotations . . ."

"Nevertheless," continued Cwan, "you're speaking of something that sounds as if it will be potentially addictive. Once you dispense it to other worlds, they will continue to want it . . . and you will be the sole suppliers."

"That . . . is basically true, Lord Cwan. However—"

"There is no 'however' in this instance, Lodec!"

"Si Cwan, let's go," said Kalinda, and she was pulling at his elbow.

But he shook her off. "It will never work. Other worlds will simply find ways to synthesize it."

"That will not be possible. Anubis assures us . . ."

"Anubis? Is that the individual who is offering you this narcotic? You would build a new Thallonian Empire," and his voice was rising in anger, "on a foundation of drug dealing? What sort of vomitous notion—?"

Lodec's face darkened. "As opposed to what, Lord Cwan? Building it upon a foundation of fear and oppression, as the first one was? Why use the stick when the treat can be all the more enticing? I am surprised you do not realize that."

"And I am surprised," replied Si Cwan, "that you were under the impression that I would simply stand still for this. It is an insult! An insult, I tell you, to all that the Thallonian Empire once stood for! And tell me this: What does this 'Anubis' want in return? He must want something."

"He does . . . and it is the most minor of things, really. He simply wants something for himself and his brethren, something that will not cost us anything."

"And that is?"

"To be worshipped."

Si Cwan stared at him, disbelieving. *"Worshipped?* As what? Gods?"

"Yes."

"This is madness. My sister and I are among mad people here, and I will not suffer it to continue that way another instant. Come, Kalinda," and he started to walk briskly forward.

Lodec's hand shot out and snagged Si Cwan by the throat.

Si Cwan should have seen it coming. He should have been able to block it. But it happened so fast that the hand was clamped in place before he could do anything to stop it. And then he was up, up off his feet, dangling in the air, as the much shorter Lodec held him high and helpless. Unable to draw in air, Si Cwan could only gag. His hands clamped around Lodec's arm, trying to twist it free, but he felt corded muscle beneath Lodec's sleeve that had not been there only a few days earlier.

Kalinda let out an infuriated cry and tried to come to his aid, but the other senators intervened and held her back with no effort.

Lodec's smile was affixed upon his face, spreading wider as he drank in Si Cwan's helplessness. "In case you have not yet figured it out, Lord Cwan . . . we were willing to present ourselves as test cases for the ambrosia. And we are able to give firsthand testimony as to its effectiveness . . . as I'm sure you now can, as well. Oh . . . and here is our benefactor now."

A shadow fell upon Si Cwan as he saw a monstrous creature coming toward him. He was just as Kalinda had described him, and his eyes burned with fiery scorn as he gazed upon Si Cwan.

Si Cwan fought desperately to break loose, but the inability to breathe hampered him severely. He dangled there from Lodec's grip, helpless as a babe, and the world seemed to be growing dark around him.

"I know, I know," Lodec was saying. "This prospect of 'worship' and such . . . it seems absurd. But Anubis explained to us their specific desires, and we've discussed it, and we felt, truly: What is the harm? The problem was, we suspected that your pride would make it impossible for you to accept, which was why we had to keep you excluded from many of these meetings . . . and it turns out we were correct in our assumptions. But I say again: What is the harm of a bit of worship? We tell them what they want to hear. We have prayer meetings and such . . . and in the meantime they provide us and our allies with this remarkable substance."

Anubis moved closer in toward Si Cwan, an unobstructed path to Si Cwan's face, and his jaws opened wide, and the warm, fetid breath washed over him. And as blackness closed upon Si Cwan, the last thing he heard was Lodec's gently mocking voice inquiring, "Come now, Lord Cwan, honestly . . . would it harm us . . . to gather a few laurel leaves?"

TO BE CONTINUED

Look for STAR TREK fiction from Pocket Books

Star Trek®: The Original Series

Star Trek: Deep Space Nine®

Star Trek®: Gateways

#1 • *One Small Step* • Susan Wright
#2 • *Chainmail* • Diane Carey
#3 • *Doors Into Chaos* • Robert Greenberger
#4 • *Demons of Air and Darkness* • Keith R.A. DeCandido
#5 • *No Man's Land* • Christie Golden
#6 • *Cold Wars* • Peter David
#7 • *What Lay Beyond* • various

Star Trek®: The Badlands

#1 • Susan Wright
#2 • Susan Wright

Star Trek®: Dark Passions

#1 • Susan Wright
#2 • Susan Wright

Star Trek® Omnibus Editions

Invasion! Omnibus • various
Day of Honor Omnibus • various
The Captain's Table Omnibus • various
Star Trek: Odyssey • William Shatner with Judith and Garfield Reeves-
Stevens

Other Star Trek® Fiction

Legends of the Ferengi • Ira Steven Behr & Robert Hewitt Wolfe
Strange New Worlds, vols. I, II, III, and IV • Dean Wesley Smith, ed.
Adventures in Time and Space • Mary P. Taylor, ed.
Captain Proton: Defender of the Earth • D.W. "Prof" Smith
New Worlds, New Civilizations • Michael Jan Friedman
The Lives of Dax • Marco Palmieri, ed.
The Klingon Hamlet • Wil'yam Shex'pir
Enterprise Logs • Carol Greenburg, ed.

Ever wonder what to serve at a
Klingon Day of Ascension?

Just can't remember if you bring a gift
to a *Rumarie* celebration?

You know that Damok was on the
ocean, but you can't recall just what
that means?

Have no fear! Finally you too
can come prepared to any
celebration held anywhere in
Federation space.

Laying out many of the complex and compelling rituals
of *Star Trek*'s varied cultures, this clear and handy guide
will let you walk into any celebration with assurance.
Plus: in a special section are the celebrations that have
become part of the traditions of Starfleet.

From shipboard promotion to the Klingon coming-of-age
to the joyous exchange of marriage vows, you can be a
part of it all with

STAR TREK
Celebrations

Pocket Books
A VIACOM COMPANY

3116